"Okay, I believe you need my help, and I'm willing to hear you out," she said. "Let's go."

Jacob didn't let himself give in to the thick relief. There was genuinely no time now. He spun on his heel and led Norah back through the slightly rank parking lot. When they reached his car, though, she stopped again.

"What are we doing?" she asked as he reached for the door handle.

"I'd rather go over the details at my place. If you don't mind."

"You don't live here?" she asked, sounding confused.

"Here?" he echoed.

"I guess I just inferred..." She gave her head a small shake. "I'm guessing it's complicated? Again?"

He lifted his hat and scraped a hand over his hair. "You might say."

He gave the handle a tug, but Norah didn't move.

"Changing your mind?" he asked, his tone far lighter than his mind.

"No. But I need you to give me the keys," she said. "I want to drive. You can navigate."

"I thought you believed me."

"I believe you," she said mildly. "But that doesn't mean I come even close to trusting you."

Dear Reader,

If you've read *High-Stakes Bounty Hunter*, then you've had a sneak peek at Norah Loblaw, the title character in *The Negotiator*. She's the twin sister of the hero in that story! So you might already know that Norah is about as straitlaced as they come. She's terrible at even bending rules, and no one should dare to ask her to break them...

But her passion for saving children's lives is even stronger, and when she meets Jacob Pratt, she's forced to reconsider her rule-book ways. It was a lot of fun to write Norah's journey. A tough cookie on the outside. A heart of gold on the inside. And the perfect match for Jacob and his child.

Happy reading,

Melinda

THE NEGOTIATOR

Melinda Di Lorenzo

HARLEQUIN

ROMANTIC
SUSPENSE

HARLEQUIN®
ROMANTIC SUSPENSE™

Recycling programs
for this product may
not exist in your area.

ISBN-13: 978-1-335-62896-1

The Negotiator

Copyright © 2021 by Melinda A. Di Lorenzo

All rights reserved. No part of this book may be used or reproduced in
any manner whatsoever without written permission except in the case of
brief quotations embodied in critical articles and reviews.

This is a work of fiction. Names, characters, places and incidents
are either the product of the author's imagination or are used fictitiously.
Any resemblance to actual persons, living or dead, businesses,
companies, events or locales is entirely coincidental.

This edition published by arrangement with Harlequin Books S.A.

For questions and comments about the quality of this book,
please contact us at CustomerService@Harlequin.com.

Harlequin Enterprises ULC
22 Adelaide St. West, 40th Floor
Toronto, Ontario M5H 4E3, Canada
www.Harlequin.com

Printed in U.S.A.

Amazon bestselling author **Melinda Di Lorenzo** writes in her spare time—at soccer practices, when she should be doing laundry and in place of sleep. She lives on the beautiful west coast of British Columbia, Canada, with her handsome husband and her noisy kids. When she's not writing, she can be found curled up with someone else's good book.

Prologue

TELL NO ONE.
IF YOU CALL THE POLICE, HE'S DEAD.
GO NOWHERE.
LEAVE THE HOUSE, HE'S DEAD.
WAIT FOR OUR CALL.
MISS IT, HE'S DEAD.
THERE'S ABOUT TO BE A TEST.
FAIL IT, HE'S DEAD.

Chapter 1

As Norah Loblaw stepped out onto the street, she tried to tell herself that she was glad she'd decided to walk. Despite the city atmosphere that Vancouver exuded, the air was crisp and bright. Even the deepest inhale didn't bring in a hint of vehicle exhaust. The night before had been bathed in a torrential downpour. The ground was still wet. More than a few puddles dotted the sidewalk. But it was one of the best things about living there—that post-storm, dew-tinged scent. And right then, it suited Norah's mood, too.

She'd spent the better part of the early morning arguing with her twin brother, Noah.

"About *breakfast*," she muttered to herself.

Admittedly, Norah had accidentally started the fight by confessing that she'd changed her mind about attending the annual charity event put on by her chef friend at La Petite Orange. If she'd just kept her mouth shut, everything would've been fine. She'd still be in her pajamas on her couch instead of traipsing over fifteen blocks in a short green dress and her practical—but pretty—black flats. And she wouldn't have been forced to concede the argument with a promise that she didn't want to keep.

The next challenge that comes your way...roll with it. Face it. No, wait. Embrace it.

Those were her brother's exact words. And by that point in the conversation, she was desperate to end the phone call before Noah could pry anything else out of her. He'd been pretty wrapped up in his own life lately. He had a new wife and a new stepdaughter. He'd changed careers. And that was all good stuff, as far as Norah was concerned. It meant he didn't have time to meddle in her life the way his little-brother self—those four minutes *really* counted—normally liked to.

Yeah, piped up her subconscious. *It works for you because it means you can avoid the truth.*

Norah winced. Her feet moved a little faster, too. But she didn't try to deny it. It'd been a year since she'd temporarily closed the doors on her business, Loblaw Retrieval. Which also meant that it'd been a year since the second-most devastating moment of her life. It still felt like yesterday. And she had no intention of sharing that fact with her brother. Or with anyone. Hadn't she ended her own on-again, off-again relationship with a very nice PI, for the very fact that he wanted to talk about it?

Norah gave her head a shake and forced her mind to the present moment. She managed to smile at a girl walking a dog, and she averted her eyes politely away from a couple embracing against a tree. The enjoyable scents and sights washed over her, and after a few moments, the past found its way back to the compartment where it belonged. For a few seconds, she even felt good. But as she rounded the corner at the end of her block, a prickle of unexplained discomfort made her slow her pace. Unable to stow the feeling, she sneaked a glance over her shoulder. For a second, she could swear she saw a flash disappear between two parked cars. But it was gone so quickly that she was sure she must've imagined it.

Too much late-night TV, she told herself.

Except the reassurance didn't assuage the sensation that she was being watched. If anything, the farther along her long stride took her, the more the feeling intensified. And after another minute, she couldn't help but check again. This time, she was almost sure she spotted someone ducking out of view.

"What the heck…" She stared down the length of road, debating what the best course of action might be.

Did she double back and confront whoever it was? Wait and see if they showed themselves, or maybe call the cops?

And tell them what? she thought. *That I'm being followed in broad daylight on a pedestrian-busy street at, like, seven in the morning?*

It wasn't *entirely* unrealistic. Just a little absurd, considering the hour and the number of people milling around.

As if to emphasize the latter point, a group of teens stepped in front of her, forcing her to stop in her tracks. Right after that, three people on bikes sped by, one ringing her bell and making a jogger leap out of the way. The runner bumped against a stroller, which sprung from the grasp of the mother pushing it. It rolled along, teetering dangerously, and a man standing at a bus stop grabbed it just in time. The worried mother ran toward him, grateful words falling from her lips as she took a hold of the handle once more. It was chaos. But copacetic at the same time.

Still…

Norah looked around again anyway. Now she couldn't

see anything amiss. *Of course.* She pushed her lips together in mild consternation and decided to at least give
herself until she arrived at the restaurant before she acted.
If she still felt like someone was following her then, she'd
call a friend at the Vancouver Police Department. She
was acquainted with—and trusted—several members
of the force.

Satisfied with the choice, she squared her shoulders
and resumed her walk. But as her shoe hit the ground with
a first step, a taxi sped to a halt just three feet ahead of
her. For no discernible reason, the vehicle gave Norah a
chill. Even when a man stepped up to the worn yellow
car, the goose bumps that covered her skin didn't abate.
Maybe it was the way the taxi-goer wore a hood pulled
up over his head, even in the bright sun. Something just
didn't sit right.

Norah forced herself to keep going, but she did give
the cab and its patron a wide berth. Or she tried to. As
she stepped to the side, the hooded figure thrust a hand
toward her and dragged her in. And the only thing that
stopped her from screaming was the glimpse she caught
of the fingers that held her. They were small. Feminine.
With the blue-painted nails chewed down to a point that
was cringeworthy.

A woman.

It shouldn't have made a difference. But it did anyway.
Norah hesitated, her shriek stuck halfway up her throat.
And the pause gave her assailant long enough to speak.

"Norah Loblaw?" The voice was absolutely female,
albeit smoke-heavy. "If I flashed my badge and told you
this is a matter of life and death, would you come with
me, no questions asked?"

The odd query further delayed Norah's fight-or-flight
response.

"Doubtful," she replied. "Anyone can claim to be a cop."

"True," said the woman, not letting go, and not tossing off her hood, either. "But would anyone tell you to call Chief Lawson to confirm her identity?"

"Anyone might, if she thought that was enough to convince me on its own."

There was a pause. "I suppose you're right."

A new thread of worry slithered across Norah's shoulders. And as contradictory as it seemed, the foreboding intensified when the so-called police officer released her hold. And the increase in concern was warranted.

"Then I guess we'll just have to try a different tactic, won't we?" said the unidentified woman.

With that, something—some*one*—slammed into Norah's shoulder. The impact was just enough to send her off-balance. She stumbled back. Her wobble sent her in two directions—toward the cab and down. Trying to keep herself from smacking her face into the concrete, Norah stuck out her hands. Someone bumped her again. And she didn't hit the ground. Instead, her fingers slid over worn leather. Her feet lifted. And too late, she realized she should've screamed immediately. Now it was too late. She was being forced into the taxi while a cloth bag was shoved over her head.

Jacob Pratt refused to relax, even marginally. His white-knuckled grip on the steering wheel of the rusted-out hatchback wouldn't ease, either. He didn't let himself turn on the radio. He didn't allow his mind to wander, or his shoulders to roll. He did, however, crack the window just enough to let in a continuous blast of fresh air. The light wind bounced over his face, and it staved off the twisty, sick feeling in his gut.

The highway and surrounding scenery zipped by in a

blur of grays and greens and brown. Not quite as quickly as Jacob would've preferred, but he didn't dare go over the speed limit. A traffic stop was a sure-fire way to ensure that the last hour of escape would be wasted, and he was already risking enough. He didn't want to expose himself just as he was beginning to feel like his subterfuge had been successful.

Was it too easy?

The question rolled through his mind for the umpteenth time, and for the umpteenth time, he responded by going over the steps he'd taken to get himself to the current moment.

First came the quick call to his house manager and his head of security, letting them both know that he was unplugging for a couple of uninterrupted hours in his home gym. Next came his instructions to the nanny to take the day off, but to stick around her in-house suite, just in case. He didn't need any questions about why Desmond's care provider was taking off, and he sure as hell didn't want anyone to note the oddity. Lastly came the most complicated bit—trading places with his decoy. Even that, though, was relatively easy to accomplish.

The arrangement between them wasn't a new one. It'd become a necessity several years ago when Jacob's face had become too easily recognizable. The other man had joked a few times that he was like a stunt double without the hazardous work. This particular scenario, though, *was* different than the usual gig. Typically, Jacob used Steve to fool people out in public. The other man would let himself be spotted at a nightclub or an upscale restaurant or even a shopping market. A hint would be dropped on social media about "Jacob's" whereabouts, which then left the real Jacob to do something else, unencumbered by prying eyes.

They had a good system for trading places. Today

was no exception to the smoothness of it. After a quick meeting in Jacob's home gym—converted from the old garage, and which backed onto a thick hedge that only required a bit of manipulation to sneak through—the ruse was in place. Now Steve was pumping iron. Maybe getting ready for a soak in the hot tub. And Jacob was far from enjoying himself.

But at least you're not sitting on your hands, he thought.

Scrubbing his fingers over the fake beard—it did itch a little—he belatedly wondered if he should've warned his stunt double that maybe this time, the job *could* be hazardous. Steve hadn't asked, so Jacob hadn't told. If something happened to the other man, it would eat Jacob up inside. Guilt already niggled in. He wasn't the kind of person who believed that the lives of others could just be viewed as collateral damage.

"It won't come to that," he said under his breath.

He stole a glance at himself in the rearview mirror. He stared for a scrutinizing moment, then turned his attention back to the road. His reflection wasn't exactly unrecognizable, but it was at least disguised well enough not to attract attention. He'd done a quick fix with his face. Sponged-on eyebrow cream, professional-grade spirit gum and a dusting of crepe wool gave him the perfect illusion of two days' worth of beard growth. Sunglasses covered his eyes. For good measure, he'd jammed on a ball cap and pulled it low. As a final detail, on the off chance that someone had spied the car—which was registered to his company, and that he'd used for other incognito getaways successfully—pulling away from the road outside his estate, Jacob had put on a pair of coveralls that he'd pilfered from one of the tradesmen building his new gazebo.

And this will work, he told himself forcefully. *It has to.*

His eyes dropped to the single sheet of paper that sat on the passenger seat. His lawyer probably wouldn't appreciate that he'd "borrowed" the template. Like everything else, though, the waiver was a necessity. Or it would be. Assuming that Lockley showed up with the negotiator in tow. He didn't know what the hell he'd do if this whole thing didn't go as he hoped.

Jacob's hands tightened on the wheel even more, and he worked to loosen them. It was harder than he would've liked, and it grew harder still when the scenery outside began to change. The encroaching city was now visible. High-rises loomed ahead. Nearby, the wail of sirens blared to life. Everything screamed of concrete and congestion and it made him want to grit his teeth.

Even though Jacob's estate was only twenty-five minutes or so from Vancouver, he never felt like he lived *in* the city. Scarlett's place, on the other hand, was right in the sea of it. Or to give the location a more apt description…it was right in the thickest part of the storm. Her neighbors were—*had been*—a recovery shelter and a boarded-up church. Drug dealers and homeless people vied for space on the corners, and each time Jacob had set foot outside the building, he'd been propositioned.

The closer he got, the less he wanted to be there. The more he wondered if he should've picked somewhere else to meet with Lockley. He'd suggested it because it seemed to fit. He was pressed for time, it was a location they both knew, and also one no one would expect to see either of them there. Now he second-guessed the choice.

Would a coffee shop seriously have been so bad?

He knew a public hot spot wasn't viable, but truthfully, he'd come out to the apartment less than half a dozen times since Scarlett's death. Before that, just twice. Once, to give her some money. Second, to tell her he was cutting her off so long as she kept living the way she was living and with *whom* she was living, too.

A wave of regret lapped to the surface. He wished like crazy he could turn around and trade places with Steve. That he had nothing to do but drill out sadness and frustration under the weight of a bench press. But as quickly as the desire came, he buried it. Forcefully, he reminded himself that his wants were secondary, then flipped on his turn signal and eased the car from the highway to the exit. The congestion picked up immediately, reminding Jacob yet again why he chose to live outside the hub of the city. A throng of slow-moving vehicles in front of him crawled toward the very first light, and already a line had formed behind him. By the time he reached the intersection, he was already on the third red. Growing antsier by the second, he glanced at the flickering dashboard clock. Time was running short.

He wondered for a second if it'd be prudent to let Lockley know he was running behind. He dismissed the idea quickly. He couldn't, even if he wanted to. He'd left his regular cell phone with Steve to create a GPS trail. He'd forwarded all calls and texts to Scarlett's number. Yes, her antiquated phone was in his pocket, but it wasn't equipped with the ability to voice dial.

Doesn't matter, he assured himself. *Lockley will wait.*

"She'd better," he muttered, then laid on the horn as the light finally changed and an SUV cut in front of him. He breathed out. "Doing this for Desmond."

At the sound of the name leaving his lips, a different, more jumbled bag of emotions took over. Jacob embraced it. He was thankful that it was a familiar, old feeling instead of another, new jab of fear. It was the same contradiction that always unsettled his mind. If Scarlett had lived, Desmond would never have become his. Yet, not getting guardianship of the boy—maybe never knowing of his existence—would mean that *she* was alive. It hurt like crazy to wonder which thing would be worse, so he chose to simply accept the one that was true. Desmond was his. Scarlett was gone. His priorities were clear. And he sure as hell wasn't going to let threats from some robotic voice on the other end of a phone rip all of it away.

Chapter 2

Norah sat utterly still. The only movements she made were the ones necessary for breathing. And she hadn't just stopped flailing and hollering because it got her no-where, but because her protests had drawn her blindfold into her mouth, choking off her oxygen so badly that she'd seen stars. It'd taken longer than she would've liked to recover. Longer still to calm down enough to think. But now that she had, she knew that she desperately needed to use everything at her disposal to fight for her safety. For freedom. And without her eyes to guide her, she had to rely on alternative means of assessment.

She already had a half-formed, mental image of her immediate surroundings. She worked to fill in the gaps to create a fuller view of the space where she sat.

The last thing she'd spied before being hooded was the tinted rear windows, so she could easily picture that. And when she'd first sat up, her hands had come forward and slammed into a piece of hard plastic that divided the back of the car from the front. She paused, thinking about what it might look like. She imagined a piece of thick Plexiglas, screwed to the interior sides of the vehicle. An oddity. But maybe a safety feature? Not wanting to dwell too long, she moved on. Under her body, the seat was leather. Worn. Cracked in spots, too, based on what her fingers felt now.

What else?

A big part of her longed to reach for a door handle. To yank it hard, throw the door wide, and just plain leap out. But she assumed that her silent driver—be it the hooded woman or someone else entirely—was paying at least enough attention to notice if she made a move like that. And, of course, there was an inherent risk associated with jumping out of a moving vehicle. So Norah didn't chance it. Instead, she strained to see any further details through the fabric, but the only thing that filtered through was the slightly nauseating flicker of cotton-hazed light. Dropping her eyelids to block it out, she shifted her focus to ascertaining any helpful hints about where she was being taken.

It was far too late to measure the twists and turns of the vehicle. And she wasn't sure she could've matched them to nearby streets anyway. At the moment, the only thing she knew about where she was going was that it must've become somewhere out of public view pretty damn quick. Because no way would her initial, frantic movements have gone unnoticed. Not even with those dark-tinted windows.

Why didn't I scream bloody murder right away? Why did it take me so long to react? Why did I think a woman made me safer? And why didn't anyone see me?

Her breathing sped up, and her pulse tapped hard against her skull. It took some work to get both under control again. She gave her covered head a small shake.

She could curse her own reaction time for a millennium, and it wouldn't help.

Think about what you know, she urged herself. *Think about what you can control. You're literally an expert in this field.* It was true. Except she wasn't used to being on this side of things. And she didn't like the role reversal one bit. *Focus anyway.*

Heart rate slowing, she turned her attention away from self-criticism and back to productive thought. Just because she wasn't able to track her own movements didn't mean all hope was lost. There was still a possibility that she could pinpoint her location if she could hear something familiar, unique and useful. The rush of the Sky-Train, maybe. The roar of a plane engine. Or the chime of a church bell. Her ears sought any subtle change in the sounds around her. She heard nothing. Just the dulled hum of the vehicle and the vibration of the air against the windows. Every now and then, a tiny blast of wind ruffled the hood, indicating that a window was cracked some-where in the car. Not that that particular detail offered any relief, either. It just told her that her assailant was confident enough that exposure wouldn't do any harm. But Norah refused to despair. She refocused yet again, ordering her brain to work on finding an explanation for her capture or a solution that might help her escape.

Who would want to take her? That was the first question. If she could answer it, she might be able to get a better handle on how to free herself. But the reality was that she didn't have a readymade idea. She tried to make a mental list of possibilities, and it quickly became an elimination game instead.

Was the woman who'd accosted her actually in law enforcement? Doubtful. The police didn't habitually kid-nap people off the street. So she could rule out any prob-ability that this was in any way warranted.

Something else, then.

Despite the unavoidable dangers associated with her job, Norah had no enemies. Her life didn't exactly include a massive social calendar, but she was well-liked enough by those who knew her. And as far as work itself was concerned…she was good at what she did. Very good, actually, and not in a boastful way. She was successful. She infused her efforts with kindness and understanding, and she never took chances. Her personal experience gave her a unique understanding of how her clients felt, and that bred trust. The parents she helped kept in touch long after their cases were over. They sent Christmas cards and school photos of their children, year after year. Even the family who belonged to the one heartbreaking failure in Norah's career didn't blame her. Hell. She held herself far more responsible than they did.

So, no. Not them.

Shoving aside the painful memory of the one case where she'd felt like she'd let down the missing child, Norah briefly considered the other side of things. The perpetrators. The hostage takers. Not exactly a nice bunch. But in all honesty, they weren't a likely option, either. They got what they wanted as a result of what Norah did. Money and a lack of police interference. And she could confidently say that never once had a payoff resulted in an arrest.

So really, if she dismissed the likelihood of her kidnapping being job-related, only two sinister possibilities were left. One, that she was the target of a personal stalker. Or two, it was a random attack with some other goal in mind. Both options made her shiver. Especially considering that in either scenario, the chances of negotiating a price for release—her forte—were slim.

But not totally impossible, she reminded herself.

Norah couldn't help but recall the most disturbing

case of her career. A single mother had lost track of her only daughter. The girl was twelve, almost thirteen. It hadn't taken the mom long to figure out that her daughter had been abducted, and it had taken the woman—a well-known model who didn't want her name dragged through the mud—even less time to decide against police involvement. Initially, Norah had refused the case because it didn't meet her usual criteria. There was no note, no request for money. It just wasn't what she did. She'd even offered a referral to someone better equipped to handle it. But the teen's best friend had convinced her to reconsider.

The other girl had come forward and confessed that there were rumors of a human trafficking operation being shared around their private school. She had a tiny lead on where her friend had last been seen. Norah got to work. Searching. Tracking. Following clues in a manner way outside her comfort zone. And she'd successfully located both the groomer and the missing teen. Thank God the person who'd taken her had been willing to sell her back for a higher bid. When it was over, it was the one and only time Norah had felt a desperate need to report the crime. But she hadn't had to.

Less than forty-eight hours after retrieving the girl—and the same amount of time spent deliberating over the right thing to do—Norah had clicked on the news to find the perp's face plastered on the screen. Shot in the back of the head, the report said. His body was found beside an oversize packing crate. Four feet wide by three feet deep by six feet long. And *inside* that box were three more girls. Alive. But barely.

The sick feeling came back to Norah as fresh as it had been back then. Wishing she hadn't thought of it, she sucked in a breath before belatedly remembering that the blindfold would come, too. She spat out the fabric and tried to reason with herself. She didn't fit the so-called typical demographic of the ideal victim for human traffickers. She was too old. Visibly fit. Well-known in her community and connected with various law-related officials. Not exactly an ideal target. But she knew that didn't necessarily negate a crime of opportunity.

But this isn't *a crime of opportunity, is it? That woman knew your name.*

Mentally, she nodded her head. It was definitely orchestrated. Smooth. And deliberately public, too, despite the fact that no one had noticed. In fact, the lack of awareness only compounded the message coming from Norah's gut. Whoever had grabbed her did it because she, specifically, was their intended target. Which led her back to wondering why. And still no answer popped to mind. She was starting to think that until her captor deigned to discuss it with her, she wasn't going to get an answer.

But is that really something I should be waiting for?

As if in response to the silent, self-directed question, the vehicle slowed underneath her. It went over a bump and then slowed even more. Though it'd been quiet in the taxi before, the silence somehow now intensified. And whatever caused the change settled unpleasantly over Norah like a ratty, musty blanket.

Goose bumps stood up along her arms, and a slap of dread made her shiver as the car came to a complete halt. The front seat squeaked, the driver's door squealed open, then slammed shut. And those sounds were followed by the arrival of a second car, its tires screeching unpleasantly as it stopped somewhere right near the cab. Another door closed heavily, the bang echoing through the air.

Norah tensed, waiting to be grabbed and hauled out. It didn't happen. Instead, an anger-tinged conversation carried through whatever window was cracked open. She kept very still and pretended she wasn't listening at all.

"What the hell is this?" asked a male voice, confusion and worry clear in the question.

"This…is Loblaw." The reply was definitely spoken by the same woman who'd stopped Norah in the street—there was no mistaking the thick, smoke-heavy timbre.

"Loblaw?" the newcomer echoed.

Norah fought a shiver at hearing her name repeated by both parties.

"As requested," the woman confirmed.

"Why does she look like she's been *kidnapped*?"

"Think of it as me doing my best to firmly convince her that it's in everyone's best interests for her to talk to you."

"Like *this*?"

"She wasn't going to come with me," said the woman.

"You can't know that for sure," replied the man.

"I asked her outright."

"You walked up and said what? Pretty please?" His sarcasm was clear.

"Not exactly,'" she admitted. "But I did ask, and even if I hadn't, my research skills work just fine. Norah Loblaw hasn't taken a case for thirteen months, her website is shut down, and the number she used for her business is out of service."

Norah's eyes closed. The more she heard, the worse she felt. They knew far too much about her. And if the woman's question about coming with her if she'd flashed a badge amounted to asking nicely, then Norah was afraid to find out what being asked *not* nicely looked like.

Not good, that's for sure, she thought, another roil of fear making her sweat. *How am I going to get out of this without getting killed?*

She breathed in again, listening for something—anything—that might help her.

"And that equates to kidnapping?" the man was saying.

"It could've equated to not bringing her at all," responded the woman, her voice softening marginally. "But since this was *you*… I took the only alternative I could come up with."

"You could've at least warned me that—" He stopped short.

"That what?" The woman paused. "Oh. I see. That Loblaw was a *girl*?"

"I don't care about gender," the man muttered.

"Then what's the issue here?"

"I came to you for help! If all you were going to do was send in a girl in a party dress, then you should've just said no."

"You didn't specify whether you wanted a man in a suit or a woman in a dress or a clown in oversize shoes. If you had a special need, you should've mentioned it."

"Just—" He stopped abruptly again. "I needed this favor."

He sounded truly desperate, and for a second Norah actually felt a stab of sympathy before common sense reminded her just how unreasonable that was.

"You said any means necessary," the woman replied. "So here she is. Unless the fact that she *is* a she changes things. In which case we have a new problem." There was a small pop and hiss, and the pungent smell of cigarette smoke filled the air.

"But the sack over her head…" the man said. "Was that really necessary?"

"I honestly don't know." The woman's statement was full of poorly veiled impatience. "Maybe if you told me a little more, I'd be able to answer that properly."

She doesn't know what this is all about, Norah thought, quickly filing away that particular tidbit for possible later use.

The man grumbled something unintelligible, then

cleared his throat and spoke a little louder once again. "I would if I could. You have to know that."

"Fine. Do what you want. Let her out. Take off the blindfold. Buy her dinner, too, for all I care. But do it after I leave," suggested the woman. "She doesn't need to see my face, too."

"Right. So if she gets away and goes to the police, it'll be me who winds up in the sketchbook," replied the man.

A renewed chill ran up Norah's spine, distracting her from her analysis of the situation. *If she got away.* The words were ominous. Both because of the "if" and because of the implication that the police—the real ones—were, in fact, needed.

You already knew it was true, she reminded herself. *You need to concentrate on figuring out a way to turn that "if" into a definite thing.*

She needed to shift her brain from mere thoughts of self-preservation to analyzing the dynamic outside the cab and deciding how she could use it to her advantage. A viable plan. That was what she needed. But she didn't get a chance to come up with one. The door nearest to her shoulder whooshed open without warning, and a rush of damp, fuel-tinged air washed over her. She didn't get even a moment to process that before a hand took a hold of her elbow and yanked her unceremoniously out of the taxi.

The second her feet hit the ground, adrenaline surged up, and her safety mechanisms tried to wrestle control.

Fight! they urged. *Get away while you still can!*

She beat back the need to listen to the frantic command. Getting shot or punched—or worse—as a result of a desperate attempt to flee was the last thing she needed. She blew out a small breath, waiting. For a long second, there was nothing but weighted silence. Then the man spoke up again, and now his voice was roughened by something that sounded close to regret.

"Take off the hood," he said gruffly.

"She'll see us both," the woman pointed out.

"I'm aware. But she doesn't do me any good like this."

Norah fought a desire to simply take away the decision by making a break for it.

You want to come out of this alive, she firmly reminded herself. *Running off, sightless and directionless, isn't going to help you.*

There was some kind of shuffle—like the sound of fabric being moved around—and the man spoke up again, now sounding deeply concerned. "What are you doing?"

"Protecting us."

"With *that*?"

"I'm not going to shoot her."

The blood drained from Norah's head. Her fingers tingled, and she truly believed for a moment that she was going to collapse. But she didn't dare put out a hand to try and steady herself. She forced in another shallow breath and ordered herself to stay on her feet.

The man's voice dropped lower. Maybe it would've been a whisper if not for the slightly echoey quality of his words.

"So put away the damn gun," he said.

"Just…" The woman trailed off like she really couldn't believe the suggestion. "Are you sure about this?"

"No. I'm not sure. But you kind of tied my hands, didn't you?"

"Your message sounded desperate."

"It was." The man's two-word response couldn't have been grimmer.

"Maybe there's another way I can help you. If you trusted me—"

"I do trust you. With this." His firm tone said he meant both the first bit and the second. "You know I do. I trust you not to spread this around. And I trust you to believe it when I say I'd tell you more if I thought it would benefit me. But I can't."

"Then I guess you'll understand why I can't stay."

The change in the conversation made Norah abruptly curious. And instead of thinking about herself and her escape, she found herself considering the content of the back-and-forth itself. What was the man keeping from the woman? What was the history between them? And how did they get to this moment here?

She was so distracted by the jumble of questions that she didn't realize what was happening until a car engine chugged to life. And she barely had time to register that before heavy boots hit the concrete right beside her and the bag was pulled from her head.

Norah immediately sucked in a breath, and almost choked again. Only this time, it was rank, gasoline-tinted air. Coughing at the taste and blinking at the sudden change in her vision, she swung her gaze around, trying to take in everything in case they decided to blindfold her once more. Even though her eyes were still adjusting, she could see that they were in an underground parking lot of some kind. A very beat-up brown hatchback was parked across two very faded stalls. From what she could see, there was nothing remarkable about the vehicle or the space it occupied. Zilch that would differentiate it from a hundred other generic apartment garages. In fact, the poor lighting meant little could be seen more than ten or so feet away. After another heartbeat of trying, Norah realized she wasn't going to gain anything useful from her environment, so she didn't waste any more time trying. She swept her attention around, and she spied the cab that had been her mobile prison.

It was the source of the engine noise. It was also on the move, pulling a multipoint turn a hundred feet away. As the car finished its maneuver and paused with its grill pointed in her direction, Norah could see for sure that the woman behind the wheel was the same one who'd stopped her in the street. She recognized the gray hoodie, which was now pushed to the woman's shoulders, revealing a head of platinum blond hair. A grossly yellow overhead light shone down on the windshield, showcasing the woman's features. She was surprisingly young, with a well made-up visage. She also held a cigarette clamped between her lips, and she appeared to have zero interest in Norah. Her eyes stayed fixed forward as the engine revved. A moment later, the vehicle jumped forward, then sped past.

Automatically, Norah stepped back from the fast-moving car. Her back hit something solid, and it took her brain a good, long second to catch up.

The man. I bumped into the man.

And even once the fully realized thought slid to the front of her mind, Norah's reaction still wasn't what it should've been. She spun. *Toward* him. And then froze. Her eyes inventoried him when her feet should've been moving instead.

He was a rough-around-the-edges type, clad in paint-spattered coveralls and a faded ball cap. In spite of the relative dimness of the musty space, a pair of dark-tinted sunglasses covered his eyes. He was tall. Maybe six foot three or even six foot four. And not overly wide-shouldered or particularly hulking, but definitely built in a way that suggested some hours spent at the gym. What she could see of his face was covered by a smattering of a day-old beard, medium brown in color. But none of those specific characteristics stood out. What held Norah's attention was his haggard expression and the visible, all-over tension in his body. Like every muscle was coiled to the point of pain. And in spite of everything else—and as counterintuitive as it might've been—she was curious once again. She wondered what was causing him to hold himself that way. She very nearly opened her mouth to ask. But then his hand came up as though he was about to touch her, and sense finally kicked back in. Like slap of icy water. And with it, Norah realized she couldn't stick around to wait and see what he wanted. She had to act now, before she had no chance at all to save herself. Praying for luck to go her way, she kicked a foot forward, straight into his shin, then took off at a very belated run.

Chapter 3

Pain shot up Jacob's leg. His eyes watered as he watched the pretty woman disappear into the depths of the underground lot. He knew he ought to be giving chase. The longer he waited, the harder it would be to find her. When he took a step, though, the stab intensified so badly that he almost doubled over with the teeth-gritting sting. The slightly pointed end of Norah Loblaw's shoe had caught him right below his knee, jarring every nerve. He had to pause to draw a breath.

His hands came to his hips, and one of them brushed the keys in the pocket of his coveralls. He debated dragging them out. Technically, he could just climb back into the hunk of junk and take his chances.

He turned and eyed the car. He took a step. Then he growled. Walking away wasn't really an option. Even if he'd been the kind of guy who'd abandon the blonde woman to Lockley's questionable mercy—which he wasn't—he needed to stick around. His issues hadn't magically disappeared. He still required help. Desperately. Norah Loblaw was his best hope, even if there was a 99.9 percent chance that she was going to tell him to stuff it.

He limped forward and peered around for a better hint as to which way the blonde had headed. His old friend's unexpected means of introducing the negotiator had startled Jacob all on its own. The discussion that followed had unsettled him, too. He'd spent the last few minutes of his journey distracting himself from the seediness of the neighborhood—and the fact that Scarlett had spent her last days living in it—by building up an idea in his head of what the negotiator might look like. Cop-like. No-nonsense. Maybe a hint of swagger, hopefully born of repeated success. In no part of his imagination did he consider that Loblaw the negotiator might turn out to be equipped with long legs, a green dress and a mess of dark blond curls that flowed just past her shoulders in a shimmery cascade. He *really* hadn't been anticipating having his breath taken away by her looks. Hell. He couldn't even believe he'd noticed her looks at all. Or recall the last time he'd even noticed a woman, for that matter.

What about her running away? prodded the part of his mind that was actually keeping pace with current events. *Or the blindfold? Were you expecting any of that?*

He gave his injured leg a shake and moved again, scratching his fake beard. Obviously, he hadn't planned that things would start this way. If he'd had even a hint of it, he would've asked Lockley to back off.

Really? Would you have turned her away...*or just turned a blind eye?* His jaw tightened, and he started to shake his head in denial of the self-directed accusation, then stopped before he could make himself into a liar. *For Desmond.*

Taking Norah Loblaw hostage in order to get what he

needed might not have been his first thought. Or a part of *any* of his thoughts. It was definitely ironic, too. He just honestly wasn't sure what desperation would drive him to do.

And speaking of Desmond and desperation...

Jacob's stomach dropped, and he ordered himself to shove aside the sick feeling. He needed to stow it in the same place as the stab of the incoming headache that threatened to punch through his temple. He didn't have time to dwell. Or to waste. Especially not searching for a negotiator who clearly had no interest in negotiating.

"Where is she?" he murmured.

The garage wasn't big. One and half floors. It wasn't very full, either. Mostly owing to the fact that the majority of the apartment building's inhabitants couldn't afford to own and insure cars. Even if that weren't the case, Norah Loblaw couldn't go very far, anyway. To exit the garage, someone either needed to swipe one of the custom-made key-cards over the sensor, or they needed to type in a code on the digital pad. The security feature was far more than was possessed by any other residence in the neighborhood. Jacob knew all about it, because he was the one who'd personally paid for its installation. He was the one who doled out the key-cards. He was the also the one who'd given Lockley a working code—a long time ago now. He somehow doubted that the PIN had been passed along to Norah Loblaw.

His hand slid to his pocket, reached in and tightened on his keys. The edges of the small plastic card that opened the garage immediately dug into his palm. As he squeezed a little harder, he realized something else.

Quickly, he released his hold on the keys and lifted his eyes toward the curved ramp that would lead to the exit. No, Norah Loblaw couldn't escape out the front. The only possibility was to hide and wait for someone else to open the gate, which was a bit of crapshoot.

But there's one other option.

Jacob swiveled his head toward the lower end of the ramp. Just around the corner was the only door in the entire garage that didn't require a key-card or a code. He remembered arguing about it with the installer. He'd lost the fight. The local fire and building codes required a safe escape route, and the man with the tools and the paperwork wouldn't budge. So the door was left as it was, leading straight from the cement structure to an exterior stairwell. From there, it was eight steps to the road. It was also alarmed with a siren that would alert every person in a five-block radius that something was wrong. The thought made Jacob's palms sweat.

And if Norah Loblaw is half as smart as Lockley thinks she is…

She'd undoubtedly find the door, and Jacob suspected she wouldn't give a damn about attracting attention. In fact, she'd probably welcome it.

He considered firing a text to Lockley in case he needed backup, then quickly rejected the idea. He'd do better on his own. Especially if he wanted to stand even the smallest chance of convincing Norah that she should help him. With that sliver of hope in mind, he slid his keys back into his pocket and loped on silent feet toward the ramp. He paused at the top, pressed his back to the cold wall, then inched around. A quick look was all it took to spot her. She was crouched low, her knees bent up almost to her chin. She had her back against a dark-colored minivan and her eyes on the armed door. On the escape. Jacob's own attention hung on her. For too long, probably, while his mind noted things it really had no business noting.

Her current stance somehow emphasized her height.

Maybe because of the way the green dress had made its way up to the very top of her well-muscled thighs, showcasing just how distractingly long her legs were. If he had to guess, Jacob would say she was over five foot nine, for sure. She had knockout, double-take curves, too. It was hard to say if those dips and swells contradicted her obvious strength, or if they were simply enhanced by it. Either way, Jacob couldn't quite stop himself from taking another head-to-toe look.

Norah Loblaw wasn't just a pretty blonde; she was stunning. No doubt about it. She was a classic beauty. High cheekbones. Full lips. Arched brows. She would've caught his attention in a crowd. She was one of the most beautiful women he'd ever seen.

Totally, completely, utterly irrelevant, he told himself.

In spite of the thought, he couldn't quite stop his mind from taking an odd moment to wonder how her frame would fit with his. Would she be short enough that he'd be able to rest his chin on top of that mess of curls? The mental picture caught him so off guard that he nearly bit his own tongue while trying to hold in an unexpectedly sharp breath.

Seriously, Pratt? You're not an animal. You think she's gonna wanna cuddle *after being blindfolded and chased?*

He wasn't even sure how her looks were managing to slide in under everything that marked his morning.

Reminding himself that he was there for a damn specific reason, he issued a stern, self-directed order to concentrate on doing what he was supposed to be doing—stopping her from getting to the door. Stealthily he moved forward, closing the gap between them as quickly as he dared, cautioning himself the whole way.

Slow.

Five more steps.

Steady.

Another three feet.

Easy.

Norah didn't move. Her gaze stayed fixed where it was, and her body remained visibly tense. Fists clenched. Jaw set.

Slower.

Steadier.

Easier.

Jacob held his breath. He was almost on her—practically within touching distance—when she finally eased away from the van behind her. Except instead of moving toward the door, she turned and leaped in his direction. As her fist came for his head, he clued in. She hadn't just been waiting for the right moment to run for the door. She was listening for Jacob. And she'd found him. Obviously.

With just enough time to spare, he leaned back enough to put himself out of reach. Air zipped between her hand and his face as her blow missed him by a hair's breadth. She didn't let that faze her. She immediately wound up for another shot.

"Stop!" Jacob said, jumping back.

"Don't think so," she breathed, lunging again.

He danced out of reach. "I can explain."

"You wouldn't believe how often I hear that statement in my line of work."

"This wasn't a part of my plan."

"That's a pretty common claim, too." She bounced back and forth like a boxer, her raised fists adding to the impression. It might've been comical if Jacob hadn't believed she could follow through on the promise held by the stance. "It never ends well for anyone who says it."

"Ms. Loblaw…one minute. That's all I'm asking."

She ignored the plea. "It won't end well for you, either."

"It's not me I'm worried about."

As soon as the words left his mouth, he realized they had an ominous undertone. Norah's perfect eyebrows lifted just a fraction of an inch, and he knew that she'd heard the accidental threat, too. Her response, though, didn't hint at any concern.

"Whatever—or whoever—you're worried about doesn't really matter," she said. "Because either way, nothing good can come from taking someone against their will."

Mentally cursing Lockley once again, Jacob responded with a frustrated grunt. "You think?"

"Sarcasm isn't going to much help, either."

"Let me explain," he repeated.

"No."

"Please."

"Very polite. But still a big fat no."

She came at him again. Only this time, her move was a feint. She drove her right arm forward, palm up, as though to strike his chin. The moment he tried to dodge it, she ducked and jammed a foot toward his shins. If Jacob hadn't been thrown slightly off-balance by his attempt to avoid a broken jaw, Norah's maneuver would've worked. As it was, her heel just barely grazed his leg. She'd clearly been counting on success, too, because her momentum was too great to stop. Her non-kicking leg slid over the pavement in a way that made Jacob cringe. She let out a whimper.

Concern flooding in, he stepped toward her. "Are you all—"

Her foot shot out a second time, cutting him off. This second ruse worked out better than the first. Her toes slammed into his thigh and sent him stumbling backward. Before he could recover, she was on her feet, diving in again. Her balled-up hand caught him just under the ribs, and her knee came up toward his crotch. He threw himself out of reach with barely a heartbeat to spare. The reprieve was brief; Norah clearly wasn't ready to give up yet.

An impressive string of curses dropped from her mouth, and she threw herself at him with full force. Her body was as solid as a perfume-scented battering ram. Jacob's back hit the cement wall. The impact knocked the wind out of him, and he had to work hard to grab another breath. Strangely, though, his lack of oxygen took a momentary back seat to an ill-timed, inappropriate realization.

No, he thought. *She's definitely too tall for me to put my chin on top of her head. Not comfortably, anyway. Which means she's gotta be at least five foot ten, rather than five foot nine. And she smells good, too.*

Her elbow jabbed hard into his side, and the sharp pain yanked him forcefully back to the more important parts of the current moment. Like regaining a modicum of control.

He fired out a hand and took a hold of Norah's wrist. "Could you just—"

Her free arm swung out, forcing Jacob to slide sideways to avoid being hit. Again. He didn't let her go as he moved, though, and the sudden jerk made her lose her footing. Her wobble set off a chain reaction.

She tilted to the left. He held on.

Her tilt became a tip. He held her *up.*

She flailed her loose arm. He couldn't maintain his grip.

Her feet slid out. So did his.

And just like that, Jacob had her pinned to the ground in what should've been an advantage. Except as he stared down into her half-defiant, half-scared, hazel gaze, he knew that he'd never be able to press it.

A million frightened butterflies smashed against Norah's rib cage. They beat so furiously that they cut away her breath and stilled her voice, stopping her from what she should've done from the start—screamed for help. They also seemed to have swept away years of self-defense training and all of her calm self-confidence with the beat of their imaginary wings. But what the butterflies didn't do was drown out the frantic rush of her thoughts. Especially not when both the man's palms closed over her forearms, and she noted that his hands were big enough that they could both hold her down and press her to the floor at the same time.

Dear God. Why is this happening?

Don't hurt me. Please.

Are you giving up? Fight!

The last one jarred her to life. She tensed herself to do what needed to be done to survive. To headbutt and bite and spit if she had to. But then something unexpected happened. She caught sight of the look in her assailant's eyes. And though he held her down, his large body covering hers completely, there was nothing but worry in his gaze. It was enough to give Norah pause. And maybe it wasn't smart. Or reasonable. Or even close to safe. But something about the look in his eyes—which were a shade of deep forest green—made her stop struggling.

And stranger still, the moment she ceased her resistance, a half dozen other details about him came into focus. And every single one of them made her more curious than scared. Like the deep circles under those green eyes. What caused the defeated, exhausted look? And the sag around the corners of his mouth that looked at odds with the few laugh lines creasing his face. What caused the contradiction? Where did the obvious pain come from? She felt weirdly compelled to know, and she continued to study him for a moment. His dusting of a beard was unkempt and looked oddly unnatural on his cheeks and chin. Under that, though, he was ridiculously good-looking. That was truly the only way to describe him. He was the kind of man who made grown women sigh simply by walking into the room.

What about when he's got those grown women pinned to the ground after a fistfight? demanded the reasonable part of her mind. *Does he still make them swoon then?*

Her face warmed, but before she could react to the sardonic, self-directed questions—either by renewing her attempt to get free or by telling her subconscious to leave her alone—the sigh-inducing man in question spoke up, his voice laced with sadness and honesty.

"Ms. Loblaw…" he said. "I could really use your help."

Though his tone fit with his expression, the statement wasn't one Norah had expected to hear. A warning or a threat? Sure. A plea for assistance? No way.

It threw her off even more, and she stared up at him, uncharacteristically puzzled. And to make matters worse, her brother's voice chose that moment to pop up in her head, stopping her from telling this strange man that he had to be completely insane if he thought this was the right way to ask for help.

*The next challenge that comes your way…*she heard Noah say in her mind. *Roll with it. Face it. No, wait. Embrace it.*

And hadn't she agreed?

Yeah, sure, she silently told her faraway twin. *But don't we draw the line at being kidnapped?*

Norah opened her mouth to tell the guy—who was still poised over her, his body still draped across hers—what he could do with his request. But he beat her to it again.

"I'm at a loss," he said, his enviably long lashes practically brushing his skin as he blinked down at her. "If you say no, I'm not sure what other option I have."

Fighting curiosity and sympathy, she made herself answer evenly. "Look. I'm not sure what you think I do, or how you think I do it, but—"

"You're a hostage negotiator. The best, according to Lockley."

"Should the name Lockley mean something to me?" she asked.

"Lockley is the detective who brought you here," he clarified.

"The detective?" Norah drew in a breath as she clued in to who he was referring to. "You mean the woman with the gun and the cigarette?"

"You saw the gun?"

"I heard you argue about it. So her story about being a cop was real?"

"Yeah. 'Fraid it is."

She had no idea why she was having a discussion with him instead of giving him a black eye and running for her life. But she didn't seem to be able to stop herself from engaging.

"What kind of detective kidnaps someone?" she said.

"The kind who spent a few too many years undercover and never really got over it," he replied, then winced a little. "I shouldn't have said that. I know she's not exactly a great example of what it means to be in law enforcement, but Lockley's…complicated. And she owed me a favor."

The vague explanation sounded like an excuse, and it was enough to knock a bit of sense back into Norah. It'd been only minutes since she'd been stuck in the back of the cab against her will. She bet if she looked around for a second, she'd see the blindfold lying somewhere nearby. The offending item had somehow gotten hooked to the bracelet on her left arm, and she'd only noticed—and dropped it feverishly—a few moments before realizing that the green-eyed man had found her.

Fear and disgust roiled up at the recent memory, and

she channeled some of that into strengthening her tone as she replied. "I'm sure her backstory is fascinating, but let's be honest. Saying she 'brought' me here is glossing things over with more efficiency than your average euphemism."

Her words made his features pinch. "It wasn't a part of my plan."

"That's good to hear, actually. Because kidnapping isn't the preferred way of obtaining professional services."

"I swear to you, Ms. Loblaw…" he added. "Lockley was my best hope of getting to you quickly. And if it weren't for—" He cleared his throat. "None of this was a part of my plan."

"You've said that twice now."

"Right," he muttered. "What can I do to convince you that I'm sincere?"

Now his face wasn't just pinched. It was deeply pained. And as much as she willed herself not to, Norah couldn't help but study his expression. His green gaze held no hint of subterfuge. But that didn't mean he was telling the full truth. Norah had interacted with her share of master manipulators over the years. People who could look someone else right in the eye, tell a complete lie and sound utterly convincing.

So why do I want to believe him?

And not only that…but why did she want to believe him so *badly*? It made zero sense. Just like all her other little tickles of curiosity. They had no place in the current moment. And yet here she was, answering him in a totally reasonable voice.

"You could start by letting me up," she stated. "I'm far more amenable to conversations when I can breathe."

After she said it, Norah swore that a bit of burnished red crept up under his stubble. Like he'd just realized that their current position was something less than normal. But she didn't get much of a chance to figure out if the blush was real, because he quickly cleared his throat, then rolled off her. He landed on his back and stayed there, staring up at the damp, pipe-lined ceiling in momentary silence.

It was a chance. Norah could practically feel her imminent escape. She could bound to her feet, dart across the small distance between their current spot and the door and burst out into the open. Likely before the green-eyed man even realized what was happening. But she didn't move. And after another few seconds—like he could read the turn of her thoughts—he cleared his throat again.

"If you want to go, I won't stop you," he said. "Just let me open the gate for you so that you don't set off the alarm."

He could be lying, Norah told herself right away. *Lulling you into complacency.*

But he made no move to hold her. He didn't even budge when she pushed to her feet and took a couple of steps away from him. Or when she actually turned toward the door. Which made her stop and look his way again. She frowned. He'd closed his eyes, and his face sagged with defeat. Any sense of danger he might've imbued a minute earlier had dissolved.

How about you run now, then? Seriously. Because it seems like it would be a good time to send a kick between his legs, then tear through that door over there and never look back.

Except Norah's feet stayed planted. The only part of her that showed any interest in moving was her hands. And all *they* did was smooth down her dress and give the hem a sharp tug as she noticed for the first time that the struggle had resulted in a practically indecent amount of exposure. And her attacker—if she could still call him that—maintained his position. It was Norah who ended up breaking the silence, her words contradicting her brain's repeated suggestions on making a run for it.

"And if I don't leave?" she asked.

I must be insane, she thought as soon as the words were out.

The man's eyes flew open. He pushed up a little—just to his elbows—and looked at her with as much surprise as she felt. And under that was guarded hope. "You don't want to go?"

"I do want to, actually. Staying here—and having this conversation, too—goes against every instinct I have," she admitted. "Most people send an email when they want to talk to me. Not a questionable cop with a blindfold."

"I guess an 'I'm sorry' won't cut it at this point."

"I don't know if there's a satisfactory set of words to cover for coercion and kidnapping."

"But?" He looked like he was holding his breath in anticipation of a positive outcome.

Norah bit her lip. She really did have to be going crazy. This was probably her last chance to get away easily. Maybe at all. And yet there she stood. No clue what she might be signing on to do. For all she knew, she was about to listen to this man's plot for world domination. And instead of worrying about that—or any truly dire consequences—she was thinking about what he might look like without the beard.

She took a breath and gave herself a mental headshake, then said, "*But.* Since you went to that kind of trouble and you're not planning on killing me or hurting me in any way, I feel like I have to know a little more. So I'm giving you thirty seconds to convince me. If I'm not sold, then I'm going to run through that door and alert every non-corrupt cop I know about what's going on. And for the sake of fair warning, there are a lot of them."

It was almost a reasonable compromise. Sort of. If

there was such a thing. The green-eyed man seemed satisfied by the offer, anyway.

"I'll take what I can get," he replied quickly.

When he slid to his knees, adjusting his body to make the transition to his feet, Norah took an automatic step forward and held out her hand. And he took it. His warm, strong fingers wrapped around her own, and with a tug, she helped him stand.

He smiled the smallest smile. Seeing it flooded Norah with a sudden desire to make it amplified into a true expression of happiness. She had a feeling it would change his whole face. Make him even more handsome than he already was.

Maybe so. But making him smile isn't even close *to the aim at the moment.*

In spite of the reasonable reminder, she didn't pull away. In fact, for an oddly long moment after he became fully upright, their palms stayed locked together. And Norah didn't even feel a need to let go. Instead, she actually enjoyed the way heat transferred from his hand to hers. She hadn't even realized she was cold until right that second. But when the trickle of warmth slid up her wrist, then spread across her forearm and traversed up to her elbow, the air around her pressed in with a damp chill. She shivered. Pleasantly.

Norah might've stopped to question the curious sensation—or, if she was being sensible, tell herself to stop feeling it altogether—but she didn't get a chance. As he finally dropped her hand, he also reached into his back pocket. And somehow, she knew it was going to be a picture before he even finished dragging the item free. But her breath still burned sharply when he held it out. Because she hadn't realized until that second that she wanted it to be a mistake. A misunderstanding of who she was and what she did. Something that would save her from having to face her own failure.

But when her eyes dropped to the photo, she knew that there'd been no error.

A baby with caramel skin and wide green eyes smiled up at her. If Norah had to guess, she would say that the infant was about four months old in the shot, and the blue blanket made her fairly sure it was a little boy. She stared down at him for several seconds before lifting her gaze back to the man's face. And when their eyes locked, any questions about whether or not he had the right person slipped away. She could see it all in his face. The baby wasn't just a son to the stranger who stood in front of her—the little guy was his everything. And the child—the everything—had been taken from him.

Norah had seen that look in many parents' eyes. She knew it well. And for a moment, it swept aside all else. The fear that he wasn't being forthcoming about everything else. The frightening ordeal that had led to this moment. Even the self-doubt and overwhelming sadness that had been hovering over her mind and heart for the last year took a temporary back seat.

Norah opened her mouth, unsure what she was going to say. And she didn't get a chance to find out, either. The shuddering crash of a closing door carried up from somewhere else in the parking lot. It cut her off before she could even start, and the sound of muffled voices announced the imminent arrival of someone else.

Chapter 4

Jacob's attention swung in the direction of the slow clatter of feet on pavement for a tenth of a second, then came back to the negotiator. He was sure his face showed every bit of emotion—worry at being spotted and recognized, hope that Norah was about to say yes, and a whole lot more little things he didn't have time to pinpoint or analyze. His lips clamped together in a grimace. If the former happened, the latter wouldn't even matter.

"I can't stay here," he said, his feelings transferring clearly into his words.

Norah's eyes flicked a look over his shoulder. "Is it someone you know?"

"Doubtful," he replied.

He could see the puzzlement in her frown, and he might've tried to offer the world's briefest explanation, but the booming echo of a man's laugh followed by a feminine titter stopped him. The unwelcome company was getting closer, even if the footsteps were unhurried and punctuated by pauses. How much longer did they have? A minute? Less?

"If you're not going to help me, then fine," he said quickly. "Just tell me, and I can drop you off wherever you need to be. But I've got to go."

"Do you have a weapon?" she replied.

The question caught Jacob off guard. "A weapon?"

"A gun in the glovebox," she elaborated. "A knife under the seat. Anything like that."

His shook his head. "No. Nothing."

"And if I ask to frisk you?"

A vision of her hands on his body made him momentarily forget that they were about to be inadvertently ambushed, and he had to shake off the unexpected heat before answering.

He cleared his throat. "I'd ask you to hurry."

"Because if I *don't* hurry...those people who are coming...who you don't know...will do what?"

"See us, and if they recognize me and somehow word gets back to whoever has Desmond..." He trailed off, unable to quite voice any possible what-if, and he cleared his throat again. "Please. I can't take the chance."

She sucked in her lower lip. Her eyes darted over his shoulder again.

"Put your hands on your head," she ordered.

"What?"

"Do you want to ask questions, or do you want me to hurry?"

The voices lifted again, and Jacob obediently brought up his hands and placed them on his head, then took a wide stance, closed his eyes and waited for her to do her thing. It wasn't the most dignified position but sacrificing a bit of pride would be more than worth it if she could retrieve Desmond.

Desmond.

For a moment, thinking of his son made him lose the ability to focus on the current moment. The little guy's sweet face filled his mind. The gap-toothed smile and the distinct, left-cheek dimple. The memory of baby-smell and baby giggles. It made Jacob's heart compress painfully. He hoped like crazy that whoever had Desmond had enough heart to hold him if he cried.

No, he thought abruptly. *I hope they hold him* before *he cries.*

Jacob was so lost in the crushing worry that he didn't realize Norah had moved closer until her hands came in contact with his shoulders. When her touch landed on him, it gave him a start. He had to force himself not to jump, and he let out a slightly ragged breath.

"Sorry," Norah murmured, her voice low. "Didn't mean to startle you."

"It's fine," he replied.

As her fingers began their ultra-quick search, his brain let immediate thoughts of Desmond go. At least for the moment. Maybe because Norah's touch was gentler than he expected. Not that he'd had a lot of experience with pat-downs, but if he'd been thinking about it at all—even subconsciously—he would've assumed it to be a rougher experience. Unpleasant for both parties, perhaps. Except it wasn't the case right then. At all. As Norah's hands slid rapidly down over his biceps, then to his forearms, he could feel their warmth through his long-sleeved coveralls and the T-shirt he wore beneath them. The sensation was almost welcome. The human contact felt good. Comforting. *Needed.*

Jacob's eyes sank shut as Norah's search continued. Her palms skirted over his shoulders, then down his back. They tapped lightly along his hips, down his outer thighs and calves. They moved inward and patted the length of his pants again, this time along the inner seem. When that was done, she slipped her hands around him and chased the lines of his chest, stomach and hips. He was sure she was almost done—and the whole thing probably took fifteen seconds or so—but he more than half wished she wasn't.

Relax, Pratt, he told himself firmly. *No need to be a creep. She's not here to help you feel better. She's making sure you don't have a knife in your pocket. And speaking of pockets...*

Norah's hands had stilled overtop of one right then, and Jacob stiffened as he recalled what it was that he'd stuffed in there just over an hour earlier.

Norah tapped the denim-covered device. "Cell phone?"

"Yes," Jacob replied.

She slid her fingers in anyway, then yanked out the slim black device. She stared at it for a second, probably confused as to why he was carrying around such an obviously antiquated device. Then she shrugged and held it out. As he dropped his hands to take it from her, she met his eyes, her unusual hazel gaze unwavering. Probing. Measuring. Yet under that...there was an intelligence and understanding that drew Jacob in and held him.

The voices had paused again, and he knew they should take advantage of what little moments they had to get back to the hatchback. Yet he found himself speaking instead.

"I meant it when I said I wasn't trying to hurt you," he told her.

"No," she replied. "But you're happy enough to accept the collateral fallout." There was no venom in her words, and her expression didn't show any more anger than her tone. "Is he yours?" she asked softly.

Her question wasn't one Jacob anticipated, and it startled him more than the one about the weapon. In fact, it smoked him in the gut more thoroughly than a punch.

Yes, he thought. *Mine. More than mine. The only thing that's mine and matters.*

It was true. Desmond was legally—and emotionally—his son. His lawyer had made sure there were no loopholes, and anyone who cared to delve into it would find nothing amiss. Yet something held Jacob back from just blurting out an affirmative. Maybe his hesitation had partly to do with the fact that Norah hadn't yet completely agreed to helping him. Maybe it was also because he hadn't even brought up the nondisclosure yet. Except he had a strange feeling it was more to do with Norah herself. With the way she was looking at him. He thought she deserved the full truth.

And I can't give it to her here and now.

"It's a complicated situation," he stated, hearing the lameness in the sentence even as he said it.

"Like Lockley?" Norah replied.

"She's a different animal completely."

The voices started up again, and Norah at last relented.

"Okay, I believe you need my help, and I'm willing to hear you out," she said. "Let's go."

Jacob didn't let himself give in to the thick relief. There was genuinely no time now. He spun on his heel and led Norah back through the slightly rank parking lot. When they reached his car, though, she stopped again.

"What are we doing?" she asked as he reached for the door handle.

"I'd rather go over the details at my place. If you don't mind."

"You don't live here?" she asked, sounding confused.

"Here?" he echoed.

"I guess I just inferred..." She gave her head a small shake. "I'm guessing it's complicated? Again?"

He lifted his hat and scraped a hand over his hair. "You might say."

He gave the handle a tug, but Norah didn't move.

"Changing your mind?" he asked, his tone far lighter than his mind.

"No. But I need you to give me the keys," she said. "I want to drive. You can navigate."

"I thought you believed me."

"I believe you," she said mildly. "But that doesn't mean I come even close to trusting you."

Jacob nodded again, then held out the keys. As she took them, though, and he moved around to the passenger side, he realized that her words dug at him in a surprisingly forceful way. It wasn't that he didn't understand. He wouldn't have trusted himself, either, if the roles were reversed. Hell. It'd be a foolish move. It made perfect sense. But that didn't mean Jacob had to like it.

Norah stuck the key into the ignition and pressed her seat belt into place. She had questions. A lot of them. Starting with where they were headed and how far away they were going. Followed closely by whether he really expected her to take some kind of road trip with him after everything that had just happened. But she could see that the queries—and the others that went along with them— would have to wait until they were out of the parking lot. Maybe even farther away than that. She didn't know what it was about the approaching people that'd spooked the green-eyed man, or why he thought they might recognize him. But what she *did* know was that his tension was too high to discuss it right that second.

She saw his reaction as she guided the car past the people in question. They were a young couple fully immersed in each other—locked at the lips and pressed to a concrete beam, to be specific—to care about Norah and her passenger. Yet he still adjusted his hat and jammed his sunglasses back on his face. His shoulders scrunched up, he kept his mouth shut, and his head stayed tucked low, even when they'd gone past the amorous pair.

She thought about trying to draw something out of him as he told her in a low, troubled voice how to open the slow-moving gate, then thought better of it. She opted for nothing more than a quick nod when he said she should aim for the freeway. And then she let silence reign, waiting patiently for the man to speak up. She was sure he would. Not only because he obviously had to, if he wanted her help, but also because she could see that his tension needed an outlet.

Norah gave the steering wheel a squeeze, flicked on her signal and eased carefully onto the next road without looking his way.

She was experienced at reading people. It was a professional necessity, really. Some of those she encountered over the course of her career tried their hardest to show very little. They kept their motivations close to their chests until forced to do otherwise. They wanted to appear strong. Or they needed to project that outward strength in order to keep from collapsing completely on the inside. But after almost a decade of doing what she did, she'd learned how to see through it all. She spied subtle ticks that gave away true feelings. A raised eyebrow here, a touch of the glasses there. Like interpreting the tells at a poker game. Of course, there were many times when she had no need to use her skills at all.

A high number of the people she met while on a case were already so on edge that their emotions bubbled to the surface and stayed there. After all, her experience lent itself to working closely with folks at the worst times of their lives. She'd seen more than her share of scared parents through the years. And her need to understand people didn't stop with her clients, either.

Oftentimes, her chosen profession brought her shoulder to shoulder with the most awful parts of humanity. She'd also worked with a great variety of people on the *right* side of the justice system. Police at multiple levels. Psychologists and doctors. Specialists in forensics and even a handwriting analyst. Norah prided herself on understanding them all. Not boastfully. Just as a matter of necessity to do her job well.

It was the same with her ability to filter out personal feelings. She supposed it was a kind of compartmentalization, even though she hated the term. She shared in her clients' pain, but she didn't make it her own. It was all about professionalism mixed with sincerity.

She couldn't afford to treat this case—if that was really what it was about to become—any differently, not matter how it started out.

Right, she said to herself. *Which means that if you're really thinking about taking this case, you need to get the process underway.*

But her tongue stayed stuck to the roof of her mouth as she brought the vehicle down to the end of the next seedy block, then turned up another. And she had to admit that it wasn't just about waiting for the man next to her to speak up. Her own self-doubt was holding Norah back, too. Because the silence wasn't just letting it creep back in; it was letting it sweep through her like a storm. And the lack of confidence couldn't even pretend to be subtle. It simply asked the most direct question it could.

What if she failed again?

Norah wasn't sure what would happen if it played out that way. She was afraid to consider the consequences.

Trying to distract herself from positing an answer, she focused on the drive. The people and streets flashed by in what felt like slow motion. Traffic and construction held them up, and two minutes stretched into three, and three became five. The bad neighborhood transitioned into a better one, then a good one. From there, they took an exit and headed out to the highway, and Norah began to wonder if she'd made a mistake. If she *hadn't* read him right. Maybe he was actually just a serial killer with a very elaborate plan.

Only if the elaborate plan in question is filled with flaws, she thought. *Because he's given me a half a dozen chances to get away, and I could literally drive anywhere I please right now.*

She stole a quick glance in his direction, trying to decide if she'd missed some sign. But aside from the obvious insanity of going along with him simply because he'd shown her a photograph and said please, Norah didn't pick up on any dangerous vibes. Just the opposite. His shoulders had gone from being tense to being slumped. The grim line of his mouth had sagged. Norah couldn't stop herself from thinking of his brief smile those few minutes earlier. Of how she'd wanted to see more of it. And, if she was being honest, she still *did* want to.

She was well aware that her emotional reaction might have something to do with the ordeal she'd been put through to get to this point. Understandably, it had created a bit of a raw nerve. But she was sure that it hadn't completely clouded her ability to interpret things. There was something about the other woman that left her unsettled in a way she wasn't accustomed to experiencing.

She couldn't quite stop herself from looking at the green-eyed man—she *really* needed to ask him his name—again. His good looks were even more undeniable in the small space. His jaw, even set as it was, was perfectly chiseled. His cheekbones were strong but not overly prominent. Now that she could see him properly in daylight, she realized that the bits of hair sticking out from under his ball cap were a fairer shade than she'd thought. More of dirty blond than a light brown. A perfect, sun-kissed shade. But the color looked natural. The stubble, on the other hand, still stood out. The hair was darker, and strangely shaded against his skin. But a casual observer probably wouldn't have noticed it at all.

And why does any of that matter?

It didn't. She knew it didn't. It was irrelevant to anything that had to do with the missing baby. Whom they still hadn't discussed. But as her eyes hung on him, she itched to reach up and touch his face. So strongly that her hand started to move without her permission.

Embarrassed by the unexpectedly visceral urge, Norah jerked her attention back out the front windshield once more, and she squeezed her fingers to the wheel to keep them from disobeying her. But her gaze no sooner found the horizon than he finally spoke, jolting her attention his way again.

"Are you good at it?" he asked.

His voice was notably strained, and his sunglasses-covered eyes appeared to be fixed out the front windshield.

Norah frowned at the tone and the puzzling question. "Good at what?"

"Your job."

Her heart dipped down more than she would've liked, but she managed to answer in a steady enough voice. "I like to think I am."

"Lockley told me you stopped taking cases," he said.

She didn't tell him she'd overhead the conversation, and instead replied, "Should I ask why Lockley knows that?"

His shoulders moved up and down in a minute shrug. "Hazard of being a former detective. She makes a good stalker."

Norah bit her lip to keep from asking more questions about the other woman—her status was about as relevant as the man's good looks—and chose to answer honestly, if taciturnly. "Her sources are correct. I've been on a bit of a personal hiatus."

"Why?"

Now her heart didn't just dip; it sank to her knees and stayed there. "What's your name?"

He paused for so long a moment that Norah started to think that he might not answer at all. But after another prolonged second, he took off his sunglasses, and she could feel the way he'd fixed his attention steadily on her.

"Jake," he said. "Jake Pratt."

He sounded so stilted and resentful that Norah actually thought maybe she'd misunderstood. Or that he was lying.

"Sorry?" she replied.

"My name." He cleared his throat. "Jake Pratt."

"No, I heard that part, I just…"

"What?"

She glanced his way yet again. His face was tense, and his emerald eyes were zeroed in on her with near-ferocious expectation. He didn't look like he was covering something up. If anything, Norah would say that his expression was more along the lines of being concerned at her reaction to the truth. But why? Should his name mean something to her? His expression said maybe it ought to. But he didn't elaborate. And she decided not to ask. For now, anyway.

"Should a call you Jake?" she asked instead. "Some of my clients prefer to keep things formal. The detachment helps them through it. If you'd prefer to be called Mr. Pratt…"

He shook his head right away. "No. Jake is fine. I think tackling you in a parking lot kind of forgoes the need for any formality."

Norah couldn't muster up a smile. "Okay. Jake it is. Here's what I'll tell you. I'm all for transparency while working a case. It's necessary, really. I'm acting on your behalf, and I'm directly responsible for your child's well-being." She tried not to wince as she said it, and she hoped he didn't notice the extra breath she needed to take before going on. "So there has to be an element of trust. More than an element, really. But there're boundaries, too. I don't share much about my personal life."

Norah waited for him to ask for more of an explanation in spite of her words. And truthfully, she *did* feel a little like she was lying to him. Or maybe more than a little. Not the part about not sharing her personal life. That part was very real. Although most of the lack of disclosure was just about logistics. Either way, when she was working, there wasn't a lot of time to discuss her upbringing or her favorite movies or her penicillin allergy. When a child's life was on the line, those details were inconsequential. Sure, she occasionally found it relevant to insert an anecdote—maybe to soothe, or lighten, or help build a connection. Sharing this, though, would be something else. And not only that…but it was most definitely tied to work. Did the pain she'd buried behind the last thirteen months of avoidance need to become a part of her résumé?

But thankfully, Jake didn't push her any more than she'd pushed him.

"Does it go both ways?" he wanted to know.

Norah let out a soft, relieved breath, but then frowned again. "The idea of boundaries?"

"Yes."

"If you're asking if you should keep things from me, the answer is no. Not if I ask you directly. That's actually one of the first things I tell my clients. If I want to know what your Great Aunt Josie had for breakfast last Tuesday, then it's probably important."

His thumb tapped against his thigh, and then he nodded decisively. "Okay. This is probably a good segue, then." He reached down between his seat and the console and pulled out a sheet of paper. "Before everything went, uh…south… I had this made up."

Norah eyes flicked toward the paper. "What is it?"

"A waiver. A nondisclosure, really."

"For me?"

"Yes." He paused. "Well, not you specifically. It's the one I use for everyone I employ."

Norah did her best not to send a startled look his way. But she couldn't quite stop herself from eyeing his stained coveralls. She wondered who he employed. Was he a contractor of some kind? The owner of a construction business? And if so, why did he need a nondisclosure?

"It's simple, really," he told her.

"Tell me what it says."

He shifted in the seat, squeezed the waiver, then started to read aloud.

Chapter 5

The more he said, the more Norah felt her eyebrows go up. He was right: the wording was short and simple. But the content—and the implications of it—bordered on shocking.

"That's, um, one hell of a nondisclosure," was all she could manage to say in response.

"I know. And I guess it's probably moot now, with everything that happened. I'm just hoping you'll consider what it says anyway." He scratched at his beard. "It's the next exit."

"What?"

"The turnoff just up there. And you'll want to go west. Then left at the bend, and straight for another five kilometers or so."

Norah blinked, just barely managing to collect herself in time to turn on the signal and follow his instructions. The exit led to a street lined deeply with evergreens. In between the trees, glimpses of houses peeked out.

But Norah barely noticed. She was too engrossed in the sweeping nature of Jake's waiver.

"It literally says that I can't tell anyone who you are, where we're going, or what we're doing for all eternity? In those exact words? And the same goes for your son, Desmond."

"That's right," he replied.

"And you want me to sign this?"

"I did. Before Lockley took my request and turned it into some kind of federal crime."

"Jake…even if you'd contacted me about this in a normal way, I wouldn't have been comfortable agreeing to the terms. I don't know how anyone would."

"I pay well," he stated, not sounding the least bit facetious.

Her eyes slipped from Jake to the sheet of paper. It wasn't the request for a complete gag order that made her balk. It was the closing words that he'd read aloud. They were more or less an acknowledgement that if she *did* disclose any of the information, and something happened to Desmond as a result, she was legally culpable. Not criminally. But responsible all the same. What was the price tag on something like that? And why did he need the nondisclosure in the first place?

Norah opened her mouth to ask, but her voice was stilled when Jake reached across the console and pressed his palm to the back of her right hand. And Norah was too surprised—and a little distracted by the contact, as well—to pull away. His touch was warm, his palms just shy of rough. It felt oddly good to have her own fingers engulfed by his, and she had to work to keep from dropping her gaze down to see if there was a physical reason for the electrically pleasant sensation. She was sure it should've made her want to pull away, at least a little. Instead, she tightened her own fingers around his.

"It's to protect him," he told her, his voice heavy with emotion. "And I want to explain it to you. But first..."

"You want me to sign that paper," she filled in.

"Yes." He let her hand go.

Norah heard the guarded fear in his voice. She could see it in the intensity of his eyes. And she knew it was real, even if it didn't make sense to her.

But would you really think about signing that, just to find out where it's coming from?

It was something she couldn't even consider. So why was she looking back over at Jake now, thinking there had to be some loophole? Why was she seeing the desperate plea written all over his face and feeling it roll off his body and wishing she could just scrawl her name over the bottom of the document?

"Please," he said, the single word infused with a hundred pounds of hurt.

Norah swallowed against the thickening in her throat and stared out the front windshield. "Listen to me. No one knows better than I do what it's like to experience this kind of loss. No one knows better than me what it feels like to need some kind of assurance that someone will be held responsible for however things go." She inhaled, wondering if he could tell that she meant the words on a personal level as much as a professional one, then quickly went on. "But you *have* to know I'm not going to sign my life away like that."

He didn't respond to the statement right away. Instead, he gestured out the window.

"You can take the next right turn, and head up the hill," he said. "You'll pass some houses. Then it'll look like you're heading into nowhere-land, but once you hit the top, you'll see where we're headed."

Norah nodded her understanding. But her mind was still on the waiver. She couldn't seem to think of the appropriate thing to say about it. And not having the right words was a rarity. Normally, she was good at filling in the quiet gaps as needed. She could tell when she needed to drive things forward with questions pertaining to a case at hand, or when it was better to talk about the missing child's first words or cute pajamas. She had a process that worked. A means of garnering the correct information and putting it into play. Quickly. Which was good because—of course—in every case, time was an essential factor. But words seemed to be failing her. The nondisclosure just seemed to be the weird filling inside an already weird sandwich of circumstances.

Three times she opened her mouth. And three times she closed it when she realized that the thing that felt the most right was an apology for not wanting to sign the paper. She didn't owe him one. It was entirely unreasonable to think that any part of the current situation would lead to her saying sorry. If anything, she was putting sanity on hold and taking a crazy risk. So her lips stayed pressed together, and it was Jake who broke the silence as they started up the hill he'd mentioned.

"I don't know what else to do, Norah."

The way he said her name just then—like it was its own kind of punctuation mark—tugged at her heart even more. Which was probably why her mouth decided to speak without her brain's permission.

"If you want a promise from me, I'll give you one," she told him. "Unless it's for the sake of Desmond's life, I won't do any of the things outlined here. I won't tell anyone I'm working for you, now, during or after the negotiations. I'll do everything in my power to help you, and I'll do it with the utmost discretion. But I won't sign this. And I guess that means you're going to have to trust me a little bit."

He heaved a heavy sigh. "You don't know how hard of a thing that is. I—stop the car!"

"What?"

His hand thrust out to grab a hold of the steering wheel. The vehicle swerved, and panic reared up. Norah just barely managed to keep from letting out a shriek. Heart thundering, she hit the brakes and flung a half-angry, half-frightened glare his way as the vehicle came to a jerky halt.

"What was that?" she demanded. "I swear if this is the moment you turn out to be a deranged—"

She snapped her jaw shut. There was no point in continuing. Jake had already hopped out. He was striding the last few feet to the crest of the hill. Norah watched, puzzled into motionlessness, as he stepped into the cover of one of the trees there. He stood still, hand to his brow, peering at something out of Norah's line of sight. What was he looking for? Or at?

Forgetting her frustration and surge of fear, she followed his gaze. She couldn't see anything that would seem to warrant Jake's reaction. She wondered if she should get out, but after a brief consideration, decided to stay put for another few moments. She glanced around, trying to gauge their surroundings. They were almost on top of the hill, and the only things in immediate view were a couple of large, gated properties on either side of them.

Speaking of which...

That was yet another question. Why *had* he brought them into this obviously wealthy neighborhood? His car stuck out. *He* stuck out. Even if he hadn't been standing on the side of the road seemingly staring at nothing, his presence would've looked odd. From his faded ball cap to his scruffy face to his work-stained coveralls, he was the very picture of blue collar. And though Norah hadn't stopped to think about it before—probably because she'd been too caught up in the other, dizzying confusion of events—it struck her now that Jake Pratt's appearance didn't fit at all with her usual client profile. The neighborhood, on the other hand, lined up perfectly. It spoke of wealth, influence and something to lose by going to the police. Certainly the people who occupied the estates down the road had more than enough pennies to cover a hefty ransom. Where did Jake and his son fit in?

More puzzled than ever, Norah watched him pace back and forth for a second before deciding that she shouldn't be sitting and waiting for an explanation to magically appear. He wanted her help. Needed it. And if she was going to push past her mental block and offer her expertise, then she needed to know more, not less. She reached for the door handle. But before she could even fully extend her hand, Jake changed from pacing on the spot to stepping toward her side of the car. He'd shoved his sunglasses on again. Under those—plus his hat and beard, to boot—his face was still noticeably drained of color.

"What's going on?" Norah asked as he flung open her door.

"You said a little trust, right?" he replied and held out his hand.

"Yes, but I didn't mean—"

"We should hurry. Before they notice us."

"Before *who* notices us?"

"Come on," he said, reaching down to close his fingers around hers.

Once more, Norah felt like she should protest a little harder. But his urgency trumped her arguments. She let him pull her from the car, expecting a little more of an explanation. But she no sooner got to her feet than Jake released her again.

"Stand back a sec," he said.

"What?"

When she didn't move, he put his hands on her shoulders and gently forced her back a few feet.

Worry flickered through Norah. And with good reason. Because as she watched, Jake opened the door and leaned inside the vehicle. He made a couple of quick movements that she couldn't see, then pulled back into the open again. And the car started to roll.

Norah stared in stunned silence as it coasted down the hill, picking up speed with each second. She was sure that her jaw had actually dropped open. But she didn't get a chance to see its final target. Jake took her hand again, and this time he tugged her into a run.

Letting the car coast down the hill was a risk, but it was a calculated one. Jacob was very familiar with the curve of his own street, and he was also hyperaware of the large bulge just over the edge of the hill. A tree root had taken hold under the ground, punching up through the concrete. Jacob had come at it a little too fast one day the previous week, and if he hadn't been on the ball, he would've sent himself sailing. He'd called the city, frustrated with their negligence. Now, though, he was happy that they hadn't yet done anything about it. He'd taken that into account, turned the steering wheel on the rusted-out beater to just the correct angle so the tires would have no choice but to hit at least a part of the bump.

And just a few seconds after he started to pull Norah along—from the edge of the road to the other side, then over the ditch that separated the asphalt from the line of trees and finally into the cover of the wooded area itself—the plan came to fruition. The unmistakable sound of metal on metal screeched through the air. It was a jarring, cringe-worthy noise, but that was a good thing. It meant the car had hit its intended target.

Jacob couldn't help but picture the destruction. The front end of the car would've lost its battle with the wrought iron fence. The structure was an unwieldy beast, three-quarters of the way down the slope. The black gates stood ten feet tall, and they'd once led down a meandering, white-pebble road into the estate. One of the first things Jacob had done when he bought the place was to build a new entrance at the bottom of the hill. A thoroughly more modern setup, complete with video cameras and a two-way speaker system. Though the old driveway was no longer in use, it was really more of a novelty than an eyesore or an inconvenience, so Jacob had left it as it was.

And thank God for that, he thought now.

He exhaled and kept moving, his and Norah's palms still pressed together. He was relieved that the hastily made plan had worked, but the whole point of creating the chaos was to use it. Stopping to enjoy his own cleverness wasn't an option.

The van at the bottom of the hill would've spelled a definite end to his current subterfuge. He knew too well that the people who owned it weren't there for his help. The married couple worked as a team. The wife shouted out personal questions. The husband filmed Jacob's inevitably angry responses. The two were his not-so-favorite paparazzi stalkers. Jacob had no idea why they were there right that second, and he didn't have time to dwell on it.

The moment he'd spied the familiar, globe-themed bauble sticking up from the van's antenna, he'd known he needed to make an adjustment. He usually stored the run-down car inside a well-hidden, oversize shed. The building was on his property but tucked some distance into the woods. So far, it had never drawn the public eye. Unfortunately, the structure was a little too far down the hill to go unnoticed by someone sitting in front of Jacob's gated driveway.

Doesn't matter anymore anyway, he told himself. *Those two will be perfectly happy to photograph a car crash on my property as an alternative to shots of me in compromising positions.*

He pushed on. When they reached the midway point on the hill, he slowed the pace just a little. Not because he wanted to survey the damage and its effect—he would've been just as happy not to see—but because the trees grew sparser. It was necessary to move more carefully.

Tightening his grip on Norah's hand, he stopped against a particularly wide tree, then pulled her close. Lifting his free index finger to his lips, he indicated that they should keep quiet, and when she wordlessly nodded her agreement, Jacob peered carefully around the large trunk. Sure enough, the photo hounds had abandoned their van and moved up the hill to the crash site. The woman was talking in an animated way, while her husband snapped photos in quick succession. Both of them had their backs to Jacob and Norah.

With a silent prayer of thanks, Jacob brought his attention back to Norah. He didn't dare speak. Instead, he pointed to a thicket of salmonberry bushes about three feet away. When she nodded again, he began a silent countdown with his fingers.

Three...

Two...

One...

The moment he lifted the final digit, they darted toward the bush. Their feet hit the ground with enough force that Jacob half expected to hear an outcry from his unwanted guests. But when he and Norah reached the patch of thicker foliage—where they both had to crouch down to maintain coverage—the only sound was his own heart thundering in his chest. His pulse raced. Not due to exertion, but rather fueled by the fear of being caught. Jacob could only imagine what Norah was feeling. Or what was going through her head. Kidnapped. Begged for help in the most unceremonious way possible. Dragged off and driven away to an undisclosed location. Now this. Accessory to destruction of property. With a side of reckless endangerment, too. Without any further explanation. Which he really did more than owe her. He turned her way to offer her an apologetic look—the best he could do under the current circumstances—but the idea of saying sorry evaporated as a new sound carried to his ears. It was a shout. Masculine. Familiar.

Kyle.

His head of security. Who'd clearly heard the calamity and come to investigate.

Chapter 6

So much for a calculated risk.

The spontaneity of his decision to send the car rolling had made Jacob lose sight of the other potential side effects. The last thing he needed was for someone on his staff to call in the police.

Cursing himself for not thinking things through, he pulled his hand out of Norah's so he could drag Scarlett's phone from his pocket. He eyed the battery indicator. Unsurprisingly, it was near dead. He hadn't charged it long, and it was old to start out with. Did he take a chance and use it now?

From out in the street, the commotion increased. Kyle was hollering something indecipherable, but Jacob didn't have to guess to be sure that the other man was unimpressed. His head of security hated the paparazzi as much as Jacob himself did. More, maybe.

"Jake?" Norah whispered, prompting him to lift his gaze.

Her expression was understandably worried. She might not yet know exactly what was going on, or what the stakes were, but it was obvious that things weren't ideal.

"Screw it," he muttered, ducking his attention back to the phone to send off a quick text—he was taking another risk, either way, so he might as well go with the assurance of help.

Hey, Steve, he typed. It's me. Have I ever told you that you're my favorite stunt double? Some stuff is going on out front. Can you use my phone to fire a message to Kyle and ask him what's going on? When he explains— he won't call if you text first—tell him to threaten the reporters with a restraining order, then let him know you'll deal with the rest yourself.

There was a two-second pause, and then the phone buzzed. In typical fashion, Steve agreed without question.

You got it, bro, the message read.

Jacob took another look at the battery indicator, noted gratefully that it hadn't budged from its near-dead status, then stuffed the phone away again. He gave Norah a short nod before repositioning himself so he could steal a look at the ongoing argument coming from the street. The photographer was still clicking. His female counterpart was now gesturing emphatically between Kyle—whose arms were crossed over his chest—and the car. No one was paying the slightest bit of attention to anything outside of the small sphere of the orchestrated crash.

Jacob held out his hand to Norah once more and whispered, "Ready?"

"I suspect not," she whispered back, but she closed her fingers on his anyway.

With Jacob taking the lead, they ducked out from behind the salmonberry bushes and hurried to the next bit of cover—a short row of manicured hedges that had a matching set across the road. They stopped there for a few rapid heartbeats. Then Jacob gave Norah another lit-tle pull, and they set off again. The run was farther this time, but they were covered from view, and their pace was quick. In about thirty seconds, their speed brought them to a gravel cutout just up from the house.

For a moment, they were fully exposed. A single glance their way would've drawn every bit of attention that Jacob was trying to avoid. He didn't pause to check if anyone had spied them. Instead, he wished for luck and pushed the pace even harder.

They could've slowed a bit once they were out of view. Silently, Jacob acknowledged that it might even have been a good opportunity to let Norah in on the specifics of what had happened. He already wasn't sure why he was holding back, except for maybe a fear that there was really nothing more to tell her. Another two minutes wouldn't change that. Besides which, the urgency to get back into a secure space was amplifying. Jacob didn't want to take the chance that someone on his staff would feel a need to speak to him in person, then head down to his workout studio and find Steve in his place. On top of that, he just plain didn't want to be out in the open anymore. So he kept silent, and he kept them moving, too.

He guided Norah along the muddy edge of the low shrubs. The path widened and narrowed, then widened again. It felt like they were getting farther away from the house. Jacob knew better. The path wound back on itself, bringing them closer with each step. When they reached the run-down shed where he usually stored the now-shattered car, he barely glanced at it despite the fact that he could feel the curiosity rolling off Norah.

Past that point, the going became a little rougher. The ground underneath them was uneven and littered with forest debris. Broken branches, pine cones and rocks of varying size jutted out from everywhere, but Jacob stayed sure-footed. He'd traveled this way numerous times before. They were both breathing heavily by the time they finally neared Jacob's goal destination.

Just a few feet ahead, a thick wall of green rose up from the manicured lawn. White decorative rocks—the same type that lined the old driveway—peppered the ground below the seemingly impenetrable hedges.

Jacob's eyes automatically sought the rear corner. Just a few dozen feet more, and they'd be at the hidden entrance. *Almost there.* Relief released a smidgeon of the tension coursing through him. When he moved toward the ten-foot-high greenery, though, the temporary reprieve slid away, because Norah finally put up some resistance. As he stepped forward, she pulled back hard enough that their hands parted. For a good second, the separation felt so unnatural that Jacob looked down. He stared at his palm for a moment, puzzled by the sensation that it was missing something. Unable to shake the feeling, he brought his eyes back up to Norah. He was surprised to see that she'd taken a step back. Her arms were crossed over her chest, and she had a stubborn look in her eyes.

"What's going on?" he asked right away.

"For real?" she replied. "You expect me to follow you in *there*?"

Jacob's attention flicked to the piece of roof that jutted out above the hedges. "That's an issue?"

Her arms dropped down, and she sighed, then lifted up a hand to smooth back a piece of hair from her face. "I don't want to downplay your need of help, and I truly believe your son is in danger. Because of that, I've tolerated an awful lot over the past hour, Jake. But breaking and entering without a damn good reason is where I'm drawing the line."

He almost smiled. He couldn't help but notice that she hadn't said she was opposed to a B and E on principle.

She needed a reason to justify it. Except there wasn't much that was funny about the situation. His mouth tipped back down before it could fully curve up, and he let out his own sigh, then dragged off his sunglasses and stuck them into the coveralls' front pocket.

"You really don't know who I am, do you?" he asked, feeling embarrassed by the pretentious edge to the question.

Her pretty features knotted into a frown. "I don't even know why I *should.* Are you an actor?"

Now his lips *did* turn up. "Not in the strictest sense of the word. But I might've been on TV a time or two."

She studied him as though she could will herself into recognizing him, then gave her head a slightly rueful shake. "Sorry."

"Normally, I'd be both mildly insulted and mildly pleased by the anonymity. But right now, all I want to do is to get inside *my* house."

Norah's eyes moved from him to the property, then back again. The look she gave him wasn't exactly disbelief. Not quite.

"I promise you," he said, "I could walk around to the gate, punch in the correct passkey, then go in through the front doors." His smile faded. "I *would* do it, if it weren't for the fact that whoever has my son assured me that they were watching every move I make."

"Those people back there?" she replied.

"No. They're a pain in the butt. In *my* butt, specifically. But they're not criminals. Just sensationalist reporters."

Her expression cleared marginally, and her gaze ran over him, head to toe. Her attention hung on his chin and cheeks, and her forehead creased.

"The beard…" she said, understanding filling her face. "You're wearing a disguise."

"I am," he admitted.

She scrutinized his appearance again, more slowly this time, and Jacob quite abruptly found himself wishing he *wasn't* wearing a disguise. Not that there was anything particularly terrible about his current look. Just that if he was going to get that much attention from a beautiful woman, he'd have preferred it to be while he wore clean pants, a fresh shirt and absolutely zero phony facial hair.

What did she see? He watched her eyes, trying to discern her thoughts. Her lips were pursed a little, and her stare was more curious and analytical than interested, but it warmed him anyway. For some reason, it also made him want to squirm and hold utterly still at the same time. He ordered himself do the latter. He wanted to give her a chance to find something that would convince her that he was being honest about his ownership of the house behind them.

Truth be told, Jacob was used to prefabricated opinions. Not so long ago, there'd been plenty to choose from. On his looks. On his life. On every move he made. He had fans, and haters, and a long line of people who didn't care, too. He tried not to dwell on any of them, or at the very least, not to let their thoughts on him run his life. For once, though, an opinion—*hers*—did matter. He hoped that Norah Loblaw didn't find him lacking, and though there was logical reason for that, he also felt the need for approval on a personal level. Even if he couldn't pinpoint why.

He let himself shift from foot to foot. "Is it that bad?"

She didn't answer right away. Instead, she stepped forward. Her hand came up. Slowly, but not hesitantly. It met with his face and ran over his fake stubble. Not once. Not twice. Three entire passes over his cheek and jaw. Her touch was warm, and Jacob's body heated even more.

"It's not bad at all," Norah said at last, her voice soft

and a little husky. "Except for the beard. It's a bit too pirate-esque for my taste."

She was so close that Jacob could smell her light perfume. He couldn't stop himself from drawing in a small breath. Immediately, a very recent memory washed over him—the feel of her body pressed to his in the moments after their struggle back at the underground lot. Her curves. The perfect blend of softness and strength. He wanted to feel it again, and when she took a step back, he wished forcefully that she hadn't. He flexed his hands to keep from reaching out to pull her close, and he expelled a breath.

Get a hold of yourself, he ordered silently, while aloud he said, "Well?"

She shook her head. "I'm sorry. I still don't think I'd recognize you without the disguise."

A chuckle escaped before he could stop it. "I think my ego can handle that, so long as you believe that I'm someone important enough to afford this house."

She stepped back again, her gaze slipping up over the hedges again. "I'll take your word for it until you pull out a lockpick. But I should warn you that I'm very fast."

He frowned. "Why does that matter?"

"Because if this *isn't* your house, and the real owners have dogs... I'm going to let them go ahead and eat you."

He started to laugh again before remembering that there really wasn't anything to be amused about at the moment. Insidious fear wriggled in again, and he rolled his shoulders, trying to force it away.

"All right, then," he said gruffly. "Let's go."

He started to turn away, but he paused when Norah's hand slid out to clasp his. Surprised—and thankful—he gave her fingers a squeeze, then guided her toward the hedges.

* * *

A not-so-small, very reasonable voice in Norah's head told her she should let Jake's hand go. Or that she shouldn't have reached for him in the first place. Clinging to him on the mad run from the shattered car was one thing. A heat-of-the-moment impulse. And guidance through the unknown woods was needed. But now she had neither excuse. They were moving slowly and carefully. Their destination was known, and she couldn't very well say that she'd get lost if she released him.

But it's normal to offer a client comfort of some kind, she pointed out to herself as Jake guided her along the row of high hedges.

And the idea of comfort did fit. She'd caught the look in his eyes when she'd reached for him. Gratitude had flooded his features. The contact between them was anchoring him, no doubt about it.

It was also completely true that a light, well-timed touch had a place in her business. A hand on the shoulder. A gentle and reassuring hug. Once she'd even had a distraught mother fall asleep with her head resting on her knee.

Have you decided that you're helping him for sure? A slither of panic tried to crawl through her chest. *Can you help him properly even if that's what you choose to do?*

Forcefully, Norah steered her mind away from that particular direction. It was actually easier to question herself about the hand-holding than it was to fight against her own shortcomings.

Was it all right for their fingers to remain intertwined, with the soft, tender spaces between them meshed together? Even if it was as innocent as standard comfort, did that make it okay?

Norah considered it as they inched their way toward the end of the bushes. And she had to acknowledge that she already knew the simple answer to her own ponderings. *No*. It wasn't the same solace she always offered. *No*. It probably wasn't okay.

For one thing, she didn't have enough information about Jake's situation to even offer him specific support. She hadn't even laid out the same queries as she did for every other potential client. And she could try to blame that on the fact that she'd been dragged off the street by his friend, she'd kicked him in the shin, then somehow wound up riding willingly alongside him. But in reality, that should've bred more questions. Not fewer. And she actually felt like the more time that ticked by, the less she knew. Until just a minute or two earlier, she'd thought he was an average guy who'd gotten himself in over his head. She'd figured he'd give her the rest of the story the moment he felt able. But realistically, whatever she might've speculated that tale would become, she wouldn't have guessed it would lead to hiding behind a mansion that belonged to Jake.

Jake Pratt.

She rolled his name over in her mind, wondering if it really should've sparked some kind of recognition. It wasn't like she was completely out of touch. She watched TV, even if it was mostly the news. Sports weren't her thing, but she thought she caught most of the major players' names. And Jake definitely wasn't a politician—that, she was sure of. In fact, the only thing that seemed really familiar about him was the way his hand felt in hers. And that made no sense.

Norah inhaled. Their mutual grip held fast as they paused at the green-hued corner. Even when the tall, well-built man leaned forward to glance past their covered position. It was a good time to subtly—and without any pretended excuse—separate. But neither of them took advantage. They just let their arms stretch out as he took his perusal.

Norah used the extra moment to stare down at the way their hands looked, molded together. Her skin was a little fairer, a little smoother. She wouldn't say that the visible strength in his fingers and knuckles made hers look weaker. But she *would* say that it was a nice contrast. A yin and a yang. She liked it. But it definitely crossed a professional boundary. And really, no matter how she tried to play it off, hand-holding with a client wasn't exactly a regular occurrence.

In fact, hand-holding in general wasn't something she did. Norah couldn't actually remember the last time her fingers had been so intimately attached to someone else's. Her brain hung on that, trying to recall it. Her relationship with the PI hadn't been the kind that involved sweet nothings and walking along the beach at sunset. It had been practical. But surely, they must have held hands? Except if they had, Norah had no specific memory of it.

"We're good." Jake's voice startled her.

It was right in her ear—a thought-disrupting rumble that managed to seem even more intimate than their enmeshed hands. It almost made her want to blush. Which was even more unusual than the hand-holding.

So just go ahead and let go.

But she didn't. And truthfully, she didn't particularly want to. Jake's grip was warm and sure. It felt good to have her palm pressed to his. The last hour and a bit— *was it really only that long?*—had been harrowing. Norah was used to being in control. Not just of herself but of the chaos around her. Whatever storm raged within the families she helped, she was the one providing a guiding light. Being the storm's target instead…it was unnerving.

And you're sure that it's Jake *who's looking for comfort and support?*

His voice cut in again, worried this time. "Norah? Are you all right?"

Now her face *did* heat. And she realized that she *had* to let go. While her professionalism still stood a chance of remaining intact.

"I'm fine," she whispered. "Are we ready to go?"

The concern didn't quite clear from his green eyes, but Jake nodded. "I was just a little worried that the gardener might've made his way back here. He likes to sneak in a cigarette now and then, and this is his favorite spot. But I don't see him, and I don't smell any residual smoke, either. He's probably gone for the day."

Norah didn't blink at the revelation that he had a staff. The house alone gave away the need for one. What did give her pause was the realization that when he'd earlier referenced the people he employed, he must've meant the ones who worked *here*. Which in turn implied that they had signed that same, sweeping nondisclosure. She couldn't quite wrap her head around it.

How many people have sworn not to tell anyone that they work for Jake Pratt?

She didn't have time to process the thought before the man in question made his next, strange move. Still tugging Norah along with him, he took a step around the corner of the hedges, then reached out and *lifted* a section of the thick greenery to reveal a man-sized hole in the shrubs. It had been utterly unnoticeable a moment earlier. Seeing it now was startling enough that Norah didn't move forward immediately. Instead, she peered into the expansive yard.

The spot where they stood didn't allow a terribly wide view, and there was some kind of structure just on the other side of the hedges that limited what she could see. But she could still make out the basics. The outline of an in-ground pool. A cedar building that was probably an outdoor sauna. A yard that carried far past her sight line, and a glimpse of the house itself, which hinted at some evidence of ongoing renovation—the steep roof had a piece of scaffolding all the way up to the shingles.

It all made Norah curious. She wanted to ask a whole whack of new questions. How long ago did he buy the place? What made him choose an older home? Why not buy something newer instead of sinking extra money into modernizing this one?

She wasn't sure what it was that made her need to know. She encountered all sorts of well-off people in her line of work. It kind of went with the territory. Ransom demands meant having the funds to pay them. What those wealthy people did with their money rarely piqued Norah's interest. She'd grown up in a big house with all the accoutrements herself, so she wasn't even a stranger to wealth in a personal sense. But for no real reason at all, she really wanted to know what motivated this particular man's tastes. She took a small step forward, and her intrigue must've been obvious on her face, because Jake cleared his throat.

"It's a bit over-the-top, I know," he said apologetically. "The previous owners liked to show off. I've been slowly scaling back to something that suits us better." He paused, his Adam's apple bouncing as he swallowed, then spoke again in a thicker voice. "I want to put in a playhouse and swing set, too. When Desmond's a bit older."

The last part of his statements filled Norah with a need to comfort him. Maybe to pull him into a hug, run her fingers over his back, and tell him everything would be okay because she'd make sure of it.

As if holding his hand isn't enough?

Except as she stared up into his eyes—made an even darker green by the surrounding foliage—the impropriety of it all slid away. Since when did professionalism outweigh human connection, anyway?

Without further thought on her concerns, Norah lifted her free hand and placed it on Jake's chest. His eyes darted toward the contact. But if he was particularly startled, or if the touch was unwanted, there was no sign of it. And suddenly, Norah was engulfed. Jake's arms surrounded her. So did his light, masculine scent. His chin pressed to the side of her head, and she felt the slow, unsteady breath he drew in. He was all but shaking. Probably not crying, but pretty damn close. Or trying not to. And Norah couldn't blame him. She tightened her grip on him, not realizing until then that her own arms were wrapped around him like they belonged there. Like it was totally normal to have her body flush against his, and like the trickle of warmth that swirled in her stomach was an everyday occurrence.

It's just a hug, Norah thought.

But it was hard to hear herself over the increased tempo of her pulse.

Just a hug.

With a man who was about as near to a stranger as someone could be. Not only that, but he was also an almost stranger who was there because he needed her expertise, and whose corded back muscles she shouldn't be thinking about let alone touching. It wasn't just unprofessional; it was unreasonable. And embarrassing.

Norah tried to take a steadying breath, but the inhale brought in more of the pleasant aroma that seemed to exude from Jake's pores. She had to pull away. It was the only solution. Because she seemed to have no control over her body, which was tingling all over and was clearly uninterested in behaving sensibly.

She eased back, an excuse on her lips. But as soon as she'd put a minuscule amount of space between them, she caught sight of Jake's expression, and she knew that she wasn't alone in her ill-timed desire. His pupils had dilated, and his breathing had quickened in a different way. The warmth under Norah's skin intensified and bloomed outward.

Still just a hug? her conscience piped up.

But the question barely registered, because Jake's attention had dropped to her mouth. The way his eyes hung there left no doubt as to where his mind was going. And where the moment was leading. Neither thing fit properly into the circumstances. Yet Norah still tipped up her face and inched closer, heady anticipation momentarily overriding all else. But just when she was certain that his lips were about to meet hers, a cough and a clatter from out in the yard interrupted. She jerked back, her eyes flying open.

Chapter 7

The noise should've brought reality back like a slap. The craziness of what had almost happened should've reared up. Instead, Jake's tight hold stayed for another few seconds. So did his gaze. And his stare was intense with a longing that had no place in the current situation. But Norah felt it, too. Even as she told herself to let it go, she still couldn't more fully disentangle herself. It wasn't until a second, nearby cough sounded—this time followed by the light splash of something hitting water—that the spell finally broke.

Jake dropped his hands and lifted his gaze over her shoulder. "Probably just the pool guy. He'll be done any second, too. He and the gardener both work early morning. But that's probably our cue to get inside before anyone sees us."

Norah exhaled and nodded. But as much as she should've been relieved to not have made a huge mistake like kissing a client, all she felt was a pinch of disappointment. Which was probably why she didn't resist when Jake took her hand again as they renewed their trek.

How many times in an hour can I tell myself not to do something before it becomes ridiculous? she wondered as she let him lead her through the somewhat narrow space between the hedges and the structure in front of them. *You need to keep your mind on the case. Or at least on whether it's going to* become *a case.*

But the moment Jake swung open a door on the side of the building in question, Norah forgot about her resolve. She didn't know what she'd been expecting to see inside—maybe some kind of workshop, or even a custom garage. What she got instead was a view of a state-of-the-art gym.

Her gaze swept over it, automatically taking an inventory. It was better equipped than the workout room at Norah's apartment building. It stunk far less, too. There were machines and free weights. An enormous flat-screen TV hung on the wall in front of a treadmill. The barest scent of chlorine and just a tiny hint of steam in the air made Norah think there was probably a hot tub tucked away somewhere, too. But none of that was what made her still and tongue-tied. It was the ridiculous picture that had formed in her mind as they stepped in that did it. Because when she spied all of the equipment, the very first thing that popped up was the seconds-old memory of Jake's back under her hands. Of his solid, sculpted chest pressed against her own torso. In turn, those memories made her imagine him in this space. *Using* this space. Sweat glistening. Muscles bulging. Like some fantasy-man showcased on a teenage girl's poster hanging over her bed.

God, Norah, she thought with an inward groan. *What is* wrong *with you? There're more important things to be thinking about. Like a missing kid.*

But she was afraid to even glance at Jake, let alone ask why they were here or press for more information about Desmond. She was sure a single look would give her away. He'd see something in her face that gave away the fact that her usually analytic, hardworking brain was busy elsewhere. Maybe he wouldn't know that her mind was full of images of him pumping iron, but she suspected the heat in her cheeks would at least hint at something licentious. Her embarrassment distracted her enough that when the clang of weights reached her ears, it made her jump. They weren't alone. Which—if she was being honest—was a disappointment as well as a worry. But the latter feeling was assuaged a bit when Jake issued a calm, light-toned salutation.

"Steve," he said. "Don't stop on our account. We'd hate to mess up your reps and have your left side become disproportionately large."

A booming laugh—the kind that seemed like it ought to belong to a game show host—bounced off the walls, and a moment later, the man attached to the deep chuckle swung up from one of the benches on the far side of the room. The sight of him made Norah do a bit of a double take. And not just because his size and general presence should've been noticed right away. He—unlike Jake— looked familiar. Which made her frown. She was 100 percent sure that she'd never seen him before in her life. So why did she feel like she knew him? She studied him as he strode over to pull Jake in for a bro-style hug and a solid clap on the back.

"Hey, man," he greeted. "I was starting to actually worry about you." His stepped back, his eyes flicked to Norah, and he issued a smirk that was more entertained than obnoxious. "But now I see why you were being so secretive this time. Well done, man." He stuck out a hand in Norah's direction. "Steve Harris." The smirk morphed into a grin. "Stunt double."

His last two words clued Norah in. The reason Steve seemed familiar was because he looked an awful lot like Jake. His size. His haircut. Even the shape of his face. And she suspected that once Jake had taken off his disguise, the resemblance would be even stronger. But there was one big difference—when Norah reached out and took Steve's proffered handshake, there was no electric zap of attraction. That might've piqued yet another bout of self-questioning if not for the fact that this was the first real glimpse into Jake's life, and she really felt like she ought to pay attention to the interaction between the two men.

"So there were no other problems?" Jake asked.

Steve shook his head. "Nah, man. Your security dude was pleased as punch to *not* have to lay down any smack. No one else even knocked."

As they continued their conversation, which was mostly small talk, Norah paid more attention to what they didn't say rather than what did say. Her mind automatically switched to work mode. She noted that neither man mentioned the fact that Desmond was missing. In fact, the boy's name didn't come up at all. Not even when Jake recounted an anecdote about some mishap with a snack that he'd tried to prepare the previous evening. Nor when Steve said that his older sister had successfully finished her nursing program earlier that month. It was clear that the two of them knew each other more than casually, and it struck Norah as odd that the little boy didn't get a passing mention.

Steve could just be the kind of guy who's not focused on kids, she reasoned. *And it makes sense that Jake wouldn't want to talk about Desmond right this second. But still...*

Now that her head was in the game instead of on the

hand-holding, her instincts were telling her the omission was a small piece in the bigger puzzle.

Murmuring a noncommittal answer to something Steve said, Norah studied Jake a little more closely, this time with a concentrated effort to notice everything but his good looks and her reaction to them. His face was relaxed. His voice was unconcerned. Almost jovial, really. The smile Norah had been looking for earlier…it was there now. He had straight, even teeth, and the left side of his mouth tilted higher than the right. It really *did* bring his attractiveness up to yet another level. But Norah couldn't enjoy it. Because she wasn't sure it was genuine. She could see that Jake's all-over-body tension was definitely still there. It was visible in the set of his shoulders. In the way his hands flexed every couple of seconds. And obviously, that was understandable. Nothing had changed. His son was still missing, he'd still sought her out for her expertise. But he also clearly knew this man well enough to be comfortable with him. So why didn't Desmond come up?

And what did Steve mean when he called himself a stunt double?

He'd sounded like he was being facetious when he said it, but based on his looks and stature, it could very well be true. Which of course begged the question of why Jake needed a stunt double in the first place.

Norah's fingers strummed lightly against the skirt of her dress. She suddenly felt antsy with a need to be alone with Jake to ask him all the questions that had been building up. The fear of failure had gone by the wayside, at least momentarily. She watched impatiently as Steve finally signaled that he was leaving. He handed over a cell phone—a far newer, higher tech one than what Norah had found in Jake's pocket—then gave Jake another solid clap on the back before turning her way.

"Make sure you take good care of my boy. He's a cranky son of a you-know-what, but I'm pretty sure there's a heart in there somewhere," he said, offering her another cheeky grin. "Good meeting you, Laura. I'm sure you must be something special if you're putting up with Pratt."

Thinking he must've misunderstood something Jake had said about her name, Norah started to correct him. But then she caught the warning look on her green-eyed companion's face, and she stopped and smiled instead.

"Likewise, Mr. Harris," she said easily.

He snorted. "Mr. Harris. Probably the first time in my life anyone's ever called me that without sounding like they're about to send me to detention or give me a speeding ticket." He issued a wink. "See you soon, Jakey P."

Jakey P.

The nickname struck a chord of recognition somewhere in the back of Norah's mind, but she couldn't quite put a mental finger on it as she watched Steve slip out. She slid her gaze back to Jake, whose own eyes moved from her to the closed door, then back again.

"Sorry about that," he said. "I figured the less he knew about you the better." He brought his hand to the back of his neck and gave it a sheepish rub. "I didn't correct him about the, uh, nature of our relationship, either."

"No, I..." She trailed off and started again. "I mean, yes. That makes sense. But it wasn't what I was thinking about. I'm guessing that he doesn't know what's going on with Desmond?"

"No, he doesn't, but—" Jake's brow creased. "Oh. You think he's a suspect?"

"Everyone you know is a suspect, more or less," she told him, then shook her head, refocusing her brain once more. "But that doesn't matter much for what I do."

"What do you mean?" As soon as he'd said it, he shook

his head. "Wait. Don't tell me yet. I feel like the longer we stay here, the more likely it is that someone's going to come looking for me for something. Let's go into the house."

Norah bit a guilty lip. She had more than a sneaking suspicion that Jake had grossly misread what she was capable of doing. And she was sure she needed to clear things up quickly. But she could see that his worry about being stuck in the gym was genuine, and if being in his house instead was going to make him feel better, then she'd go with him.

She nodded. "Lead the way."

Glad to be moving back into safer space, Jacob guided Norah across the gym to the door that led out into the main part of the yard. He knew it was risky to be out in the open, but there was no real way to get back to the house without at least some exposure. He just made sure their pace was quick, with no pauses. They stepped swiftly past the outdoor sauna and walked past the pool, which—with Desmond's safety in mind—he'd segregated from the rest of the yard with an eight-foot fence. They skirted around the partially built gazebo, and the two spots he'd had cleared for the eventual addition of the swing set and playhouse.

Everything reminded him of his son, and his chest ached with a resurgence of worry as he led Norah up the rear patio steps. He suddenly couldn't get inside fast enough. He'd already wasted so much time.

With urgent hands he pushed open the sliding glass doors and gestured for Norah to step inside. When she did, she stopped quite abruptly. And Jacob couldn't blame her. The kitchen was his own, personal sanctuary. It was a chef's paradise. The cabinets were original—real wood, heavy doors, and old-fashioned knobs—but they were in pristine condition. Granite countertops sparkled. Two ranges and two built-in ovens took up a wall. An enormous fridge stood beside a walk-in pantry, and an impressive collection of expensive-looking pots and pans sat atop a set of open-front shelves.

"Do you cook?" Norah blurted.

At the question, a real smile worked its way onto his face. "You might say it's a hobby of mine."

Her gaze swung around again. "I'd hate to see what it would look like if you were a stamp collector."

He felt his smile widen even more, and he held out his hand. "Normally, I'd take time to brag about everything. But right now…"

Norah nodded, then took his hand and let him pull her from the room. Jacob could feel her curiosity mounting with each step, and he truly wished he could give her a more formal tour. He loved his house, and—in a strange and forceful way—he wanted her to love it, too. His guests were few, his interest in sharing his personal space all but nonexistent. Yet right then, he found himself making a mental note to show it all to Norah at a later date. He hoped the small glimpse she got into it was enough to make her want to. Once they had Desmond back where he belonged.

Jacob's throat tightened, and he moved a little faster, taking Norah through the formal dining room and out into the wide hall. Their feet tapped lightly on the polished hardwood as they went past his personal library—complete with rows of hardbacked, leather-bound books and an antique-appearing chair—and then into the expansive foyer, where a chandelier hung overhead. From there they made their way up toward the spiral staircase, and at the top, they stepped onto the new, plush carpet. He tried to keep going past Desmond's closed door—which was marked with a bright blue *D*—but Norah stopped so hard that he had no choice but to do the same.

Jacob exhaled. He had a feeling that she wanted to see inside. Rightly so. Probably to take a careful look for anything significant that he might've missed. Clues that might give her a leg up in the negotiation process. But Jacob couldn't do it. He didn't want to relive that moment of realization and loss. Not again. Not yet.

"This is the nursery?" Norah asked gently.

"Yes. So. I don't know. If you want to…" He trailed off, cleared his throat, then gave up and just gestured ahead with his free hand.

She shook her head. "It's fine for now, Jake. We need to talk more than I need to see the room."

His relief was physical. "Okay. Let's go."

She followed him a little farther up the hall, and he swung open the next door and stepped back to let her go in first. Norah took a quick peek before moving forward, and a moment of unexpected self-consciousness took Jacob over as he closed the door behind them.

He let his eyes roam over the bedroom, wondering what she might perceive about him as a result of what she saw.

It was a fully modernized, fully functional master suite done up in what Jacob suspected might be stereotypical bachelor style. Gray walls, dark blinds, black furniture. That wasn't to say it was entirely uninteresting. For one thing, the room wasn't four-walled. Instead, it was almost divided into compartments.

One section housed a long dresser with a mirror bove it, an open-concept walk-in closet, a king-size bed and two nightstands. The dark-colored ensemble was made less utilitarian by the presence of one of Desmond's duck-patterned baby blankets, hanging from the headboard.

A second section held a full-size desk and a leather-backed chair. There was a tabletop shelving unit piled tidily with papers, and the wall behind it had been hung with three photos of Desmond by himself, and a fourth shot of the two of them. There was a spot for a laptop, though the cord sat empty. A moment of paranoia about the safety of his firewall had prompted Jacob to stash the computer elsewhere.

The final part of the room was a reading nook. Two, overstuffed chairs sat on either end of a window seat, which was currently stacked up with children's board books. A low table punctuated the setup, and several novels with broken spines rested on top of it.

But what does Norah see?

Then a question slipped out before he could stop it. "What do you think?"

"If this is where you're most comfortable setting up, it works for me," Norah replied.

"Okay. But what about the room itself?"

"The room?" Her forehead creased, then cleared as she swept the room with her eyes once more. "Well. You value tidiness, but not to the point of letting it overrule your life. You like things classic and tasteful, but don't want to be boring. You designed this before you had Desmond, but you've made room for him without minding."

"Accurate and impressive. But I really just meant do you like it?"

"Oh. It's nice. But it could use a woman's touch." Pink crept up her cheeks as she said it, and she looked almost like she wanted to clap a hand over her mouth.

Despite everything going on, Jacob chuckled. "Fair enough. For both the analysis and the opinion. But just so you know, you're the only woman who has ever been in here. Besides my housekeeper, that is."

Curiosity immediately played over her pretty features, and Jacob realized he was straying into areas that were far too personal. Norah was an attractive woman. That was undeniable. She was stirring up parts of him that he deliberately kept cordoned off. But it was one thing to acknowledge that, and a whole other to act on it.

Jacob cleared his throat and did his best to move the conversation back to where it belonged. "Anyway. It's the only room in the house where I'm pretty sure no one is listening. I gave it a full sweep before I left the house."

Her brow furrowed again. "I understand not wanting anyone to see me coming here. I'm used to being discreet. But do you actually think someone bugged your house?"

"They said they were watching and listening. And I believe it."

"Okay. Now might be a good time to tell me exactly what happened."

He sank down onto the window seat, closed his eyes, and explained in quick, short sentences what he'd witnessed that morning.

Chapter 8

Even though it only took a couple of minutes to recount the story, Norah could tell that it left Jacob bereft. She could feel his pain as he told her how he'd heard Desmond crying on the baby monitor, and how he went into the nursery and found the digital recording device in his son's place. His remembered panic was palpable, his fear for his son a living, breathing thing.

"The cries weren't even real," he said softly, opening his eyes and staring down at his hands. "They were just bait. And there was a note."

Hope stirred. Notes were something Norah was used to dealing with. Oftentimes they even gave insight in how to deal with the kidnappers.

"Do you have it?" she asked.

"I didn't touch anything," Jacob replied. "I was worried about fingerprints. But I took a picture."

"Let me see."

He shifted on the window seat, lifted up one of the paperbacks and extracted a digital camera from underneath, then clicked the device twice and held it out. "Here."

Norah's gaze flicked over the foreboding words on the little screen. The second to last line stood out immediately.

"What does this mean about a test?" she asked.

"That's the part that makes me sure they're watching. About ten seconds after I found everything, my nanny, Beverly, turned up in Desmond's room. She heard him crying, too." He squeezed his hands into fists. "Well. Not *him* crying. But you get it."

"And you didn't say anything to her about this?"

"How could I chance it?" He shook his head. "They called me a minute later. They said I'd passed the test. They showed me a video for proof of life, and told me that they'd call back in three hours to make sure I was following their instructions on keeping quiet."

"Three hours…" she murmured.

"That was a little over two hours ago now, I think."

"And that's it?"

"Isn't that enough?"

"Jake…" There was a hundred pounds of worry behind her voice, and she couldn't rein it in. She had a very bad feeling about how he was going to answer to her next line of questioning, and it made her words tumble out quickly. "How much did they ask for? Do you have ready access to the amount? If you're short in liquid funds, we can try to get an insured bond. Or find something to use for a collateral loan. I don't mind getting creative if need be."

"They didn't give an amount," he told her.

Even though she'd tensed to hear something negative, the response still caught her off guard. "What?"

"They didn't ask me for any money at all," he stated.

She blinked at him, swallowed nervously, then spoke

in a very careful voice. "What, exactly, did your detective friend tell you I do for a living?"

"To be honest, she didn't say anything that specific. She once mentioned to me that she knew of a hostage negotiator, and I guess I made my own leap as to what that would entail. Is there a problem?"

"Jake…" His name on her lips was even heavier than before, and she knew that the words that followed would be a punch in the gut. "My job…it's *all* about retrieval. I do that by getting the hostage-taker to trust me enough to arrange a drop and an exchange. If I think it's possible, I'll try to negotiate a lower ransom, too. But ultimately… my clients are paying what the kidnapper has asked for."

"And if there *is* no ransom demand?" he replied.

"Sometimes, it's a crime of opportunity, but since this happened here in your house, I think we can rule that out. Which means it's probably about something personal."

"Personal how?" His fear for Desmond was clearly funneling into frustration. "I don't have some cartoon nemesis lurking around some corner waiting to club me with a mallet."

Norah didn't let his tone bother her. "Almost everyone knows someone with an ax to grind against them. An annoyed neighbor. A business rival. Maybe a parental rights issue, or—"

"No." He blew out the word forcefully, then lifted his eyes to meet hers again, his gaze unwavering. "Nothing like that. Custody isn't in dispute. But it doesn't even matter, does it? Because you're saying you can't help me, aren't you?"

Norah reached for his hand before she could think to stop herself. It was an appropriate moment for comfort. She didn't need an excuse. The touch would've been one she offered to any other client in need. Except the moment her palm landed on the top of his hand, it became more.

And not just because he twisted his wrist so that their fingers twined together, which would've been enough on its own, but because the second the sensitive skin met…the so-called hug came rushing back. Norah fought against it, but she didn't let him go.

She just squeezed his hand tighter, then spoke gently. "Listen," she said, "Can you give me the benefit of the doubt about something?"

"Do I have a choice?"

"I guess not. But it's better if you agree."

He let out a breath. "I'm listening."

"This is going to sound counterintuitive, but you have to trust that I'm telling you the truth. You should take a few minutes to get yourself out of the disguise. Doing something as mundane as putting on a fresh shirt and washing up will clear your head." She pointed toward the slightly ajar door across the room. "I'm guessing that's your en suite bathroom?"

"Yeah. It is."

"So go use it. I'll guard the door."

He let her hand go, lifted his fingertips to his chin, then scratched. "I'm dying to get this stuff off my face. But you're wrong. It doesn't just sound counterintuitive. It sounds completely selfish."

"It's not," Norah assured him. "You'll be more useful to Desmond if your brain is working. Have you eaten anything today?"

"No," replied Jake. "I don't even know if I could."

"But you need to. You need to sustain yourself. All you're doing right now is waiting for them to call, right? Dedicating five minutes to yourself won't make that wait any shorter."

"No, I guess it won't."

"Clean up. Then we can grab a PB and J and a coffee."

"Peanut butter sandwiches? That's your professional advice?" he asked.

She shrugged. "It's been my favorite comfort food since I was about five." She nudged his knee with her own. "But in all seriousness, you *do* need to eat. And if you really feel like you can't use a little separation from the situation, then you can make a mental list of people who might harbor some negative feelings toward you while you scrub your face. And when you're done with that, you can concentrate on coming up with a valid, unsuspicious reason for inviting me into your house."

"Okay," he said. "A list and an excuse. I can do that." He pushed to his feet. "It's just five minutes, right?"

"Yes. And you'll thank me," Norah told him.

He moved across the room, snagged some clothes from the dresser, then headed for the en suite door. Before he went in, though, he stopped to turn a scrutinizing look in her direction.

"What?" she said with a smile. "Do you want me to pinky swear that I'll be here when you get out?"

"No, but it just occurred to me that you might've been *handling* me these last few minutes."

She lifted an eyebrow. "You wanted to know if I was any good at my job, and I just tricked a grown man into getting into the shower, so if that's any indication…"

"So long as you admit it." Surprisingly, he felt his mouth tip up the briefest second, but it dropped again almost immediately. "Norah…what if they *don't* ask for money?"

She bit her lip. She didn't want to tell him that if someone else had come to her with this particular situation, she would've referred them elsewhere. She knew exactly what she should say. In her head, she could even hear herself speaking the words aloud.

My specialty is finding a way to pay a reasonable

ransom while ensuring no one gets hurt. That's what I'm best at. Anything other than that is outside my area of expertise.

She was sure she should also mention the black mark on her résumé. Jake deserved to know.

But all of the statements and confessions stayed inside her head. Because after all the bizarre trouble he'd gone to in order to get her there, she wasn't sure what would happen if she had to let him down. Would he accept a referral to a stranger? Would he go back to Detective Lockley for her advice? Truthfully... Norah didn't *want* to pass him off to someone else. The idea of doing it made her feel strangely uncomfortable. So instead of saying what she knew she really ought to, she found herself making a promise.

"If that happens," she said, "I'll do everything I can to help you figure out who has Desmond so we can get him back."

He stared at her for a moment, his green eyes both piercing straight into her and pinning her to the spot at the same time. Then his shoulders dropped, and his face filled with so much relief and appreciation that Norah felt it hit her like a touch. And she could've sworn that he was about to stride across the room, sweep her into his arms and kiss her breathless. When he didn't—when he instead issued a short nod, then spun back toward the bathroom—she wasn't just surprised. She was disappointed. Unequivocally.

Jacob needed a minute. He had to breathe. To pull back and gain a tiny bit of perspective. Insane as it was, it had nothing to do with Desmond, either.

He closed the bathroom door and leaned against the white-painted wood.

There'd been a moment out there, when his fear had

spiked with a vengeance, and he'd thought he might lose it. Hope had slid away. Jacob had known that a humiliating—albeit warranted—collapse was imminent. He didn't care. He would have begged for Norah's help. What father wouldn't, under these circumstances?

None of that, though, was what made him click the lock shut to stop himself from striding back out to the bedroom. What held him were the heartbeats that came after. The look in those hazel eyes when she'd sworn that she *would* help him. Her assurance had swept the dread away. For a moment, it had almost swept *him* away along with it. There'd been something in her expression—a fierceness that made it seem like she needed to make the promise to help Jacob as much as he needed to hear it—had made his heart lurch. In a good way. In the best way, maybe.

It didn't make sense. He'd known the woman for all of what might as well have been a heartbeat. A blip in the thirty years of his life. Three quarters of that minuscule amount of time had been spent trying to convince her not to kick him or punch him any more than she already had. Yet he'd been close—so, *so* close—to kissing her once already, and beyond compelled to make their lips meet just two minutes ago, too.

Jacob didn't do relationships. He didn't do trysts. He knew too well how precarious it was to put it all on the line, then have it yanked away. Hadn't Scarlett taught him that? Wasn't the current situation with Desmond a solid reminder of just how easily a heart could be ripped out?

But isn't it worth it? said a voice in his head. *The love you feel for him...would you trade that in to feel nothing?*

"It's not the same thing," Jacob muttered. "Love for my kid and wanting to kiss a beautiful woman aren't comparable."

That didn't mean he could shake it. When he tried to

push down an image of her lips, her eyes took their place. When he attempted to dismiss her eyes, he recalled the soft swell of her curves pressed up against his chest.

With the mental war still waging, he pushed his body off the door and glanced down at the phone he'd unconsciously pulled from his pocket and which he now held clutched in his hand. He'd already used up at least half of the supposed five minutes. Sighing, he grabbed the charger from the drawer where he'd stored it. Once the device was plugged in, he moved to the shower faucet, twisted it to a deliberately cool setting, then quickly stripped down and jumped into the stream. He welcomed the goose bumps that rose along his skin. They were a better alternative to the surging heat that had started to course through him as his mind tried to slide back to Norah. Again. Except he still couldn't stop thinking about her. Hair, lips, eyes. They refused to leave.

With more aggression than necessary, Jacob yanked the bottle of liquid bodywash from its holder and squeezed a thick dollop into his hand, then slapped it to his chest.

Part of his brain wanted to pass it off as some kind of extension of the rest of the raw emotion he was currently experiencing. He knew nothing about psychology, but he was sure there was something in some textbook somewhere that would justify his lack of control of his libido. Feelings could bleed into each other, couldn't they? He was scared for Desmond. Angry at the people who'd taken him. Undeniably on edge. Surely that negative intensity could be seeking some more positive outlet.

Except Jacob knew it wasn't true. Not for him, anyway.

In denial much, Pratt?

He shook his head at the self-directed accusation and tried unsuccessfully to get the bodywash to lather up properly. Years of battling Scarlett's demons had taught him to compartmentalize quite well. On top of that, his son was everything to him. No way would he be unable to draw a line between the little boy's cherubic face and a woman he barely knew. Wherever the undeniable, unexpected attraction was coming from, Jacob was certain it had nothing to do with the bundle of frayed nerves that danced unpleasantly through him. If anything, thoughts of Norah—those waves of silky blond locks, the pink flush of exertion in her cheeks—soothed those raw edges. It made him want to drag her in. Bury his face in her hair. And yes, dammit. Kiss her. A lot more than was reasonable.

The need to do it all—which was far too specific to be dismissed as a random extension of other emotions—leaped up again. Fighting a groan, Jacob turned the tap from cool to cold. The change in temperature just about made him yelp. Worse than that, though, was the fact that the icy water didn't dampen the desire in any noticeable way. Images of Norah Loblaw insisted on staying at the forefront of his mind.

No matter how cheesy it sounded, there was something about the woman that spoke to him. That made him want to ask questions about her. About her life. About why she'd chosen the career she'd chosen. All stuff that was irrelevant to the search for Desmond. It was almost embarrassing. But he wondered also, if she felt the same pull. Hell. Maybe it would be more accurate to say he *hoped* she did.

Giving up on the punishment of the pounding chill as a distraction, he turned the faucet back to a decent temperature. The suds finally bubbled properly over his chest, then slid down the drain. He ordered his mind back where it belonged, grabbed another palmful of bodywash and scrubbed it over his face. That, at least, was an honest bit of relief. He'd been telling the truth when he'd said he wanted to get out of the fake beard and coveralls and back into his own things, and it actually did make him feel a little better. The hot water washed away a few physical aches, as well. It also—finally—cleared his head, and with that clarity came the realization that he hadn't been thinking straight since the first moment he'd discovered that Desmond wasn't in his crib. Sure, his mind had been working a little. His trick with Scarlett's phone had been clever. It'd required a modicum of brain power. And it'd served its purpose, bringing him the negotiator. Bringing him Norah.

"But your head wasn't on right enough to ask Lockley any useful questions before your raced out of the house, huh?" he muttered into the stream of warm water.

His plan had been fueled by fear for Desmond's life. He hadn't stopped to weigh in on what would come after. He hadn't considered the idea that Loblaw the negotiator might not be in the victim retrieval business, let alone wondered if she—though, of course he'd thought it would be a *he*—might refuse to take his case.

Probably should've been worried about all of that before leaving the house. He scrubbed his hand over his chin another few times, ridding himself of the final bits of fake beard, then soaped up his jaw and neck once more, just for good measure. *And maybe you should've taken a minute to look up the definition of "negotiator," too.*

He grunted an acknowledgement. Logically, he understood that the job was all about coming to an agreement about surrender. Except he'd only been thinking about the "surrender" bit, not everything that led up to the part where that actually happened. Not figuring out who had Desmond and why. Not worrying about the lack of a ransom demand.

He turned around, letting the water cascade across his shoulders, then tipped his head back so it could wash away the residual soap along his hairline.

When Norah had explained what her job actually entailed, it'd been like being knocked over. It was the same heart-stopping worry he'd experienced when he'd first walked into his son's empty room. He'd been rendered helpless again. Only this time, it was almost worse, because he'd thought he had a plan in place. Hearing that Norah might not be able to do what he'd been counting on had yanked out the rug yet again.

Okay, but are you saying that if you'd known that she wasn't in the business of going after the kidnappers directly, you wouldn't have followed the same impulsive path to get her? The question popped up abruptly, surprising him. He paused with his hand on the back of his neck. He had to admit to himself that it was a hard question to answer objectively now. "But not what I'm supposed to be focused on."

One thing he knew for sure was that if he continued with his impetuous decisions and inability to be patient—even though he'd been given explicit instruction to do so by the kidnappers—it would bring an end to things in the worst way possible. He needed to rein in his need to think of Norah as anything but the negotiator. If he couldn't do that, he'd not only lose his son, but also the only person who he was sure might be able to help him.

There was plenty more to be done, and he wouldn't—couldn't—stop until his son was back where he belonged.

After that, though...he let the thought trail off, then blinked at the fact that an "after" was on his mind.

Of course, once it was there, it took root. As he spun to face the showerhead again and closed his eyes, his brain conjured up a picture of himself and Norah seated at a candlelit table. Wine. Roses. Soft music. It was all there, in typical perfect-date form. He almost laughed at his own lack of creativity when he realized that in the fantasy, she was still wearing the same green dress. The chuckle died, though, before it ever made its way out, because the imaginary view of the dinner scene widened to reveal a third guest at the table. Desmond in his high chair. Jacob inhaled, then sputtered, choking as he dragged in a mouthful of water with the startled breath.

"Clearly…" he said aloud to himself between coughs. "I'm going insane."

He lifted his face to the water for a final rinse, then twisted off the tap. As he climbed out and reached for a towel, he belatedly remembered the mental list that Norah had suggested he make. She was right about doing it. Maybe it should've been the *first* thing he'd done. Methodically going through every person in his life who might hold a grudge just made sense. It wasn't as though it would take long. Jacob could narrow it down by first only including those who knew of Desmond's existence. There were few. He'd made sure of that. The last thing he needed or wanted was for the press to get a hold of his situation so they could turn his son into a media spectacle. It wasn't a subterfuge that would be maintainable long-term, and Jacob knew that. For now, though, it was what he wanted.

Toweling off his shoulders and back, then his torso, he seriously considered the short list. There was his lawyer, who knew more about Desmond than anyone else. Except so far as Jacob was aware, their business relationship was as pristine as cold, hard cash could buy. He couldn't imagine a scenario where the tightfisted man would trade in that paycheck for a different one. Not even for a pay raise. The guy might be creative when it came to drafting affidavits, but he'd commented a few times that he'd never let money outweigh ethics. He *liked* being a pencil-pushing, paperwork lawyer. He enjoyed being able to afford the best of everything—cognac, Italian leather shoes…even toilet paper—and he wasn't huge on risk.

"So not *you*, my business-minded buddy," Jacob murmured.

He tossed aside the towel, grabbed his boxers and slid into them.

Out of necessity, Desmond had a pediatrician. She was a sixty-something woman who had the Hippocratic oath framed and hung up in three spots in her office. She was an incredible doctor, and Jacob had screened her carefully. She also had two aging office assistants who sat behind the desk and peered myopically at him every time he came in. Somewhere over the course of his son's first appointment, one of them had mistakenly entered his name into their system in reverse—Pratt Jacob—and he'd never corrected them. He couldn't picture the two older women conspiring to rip away his world anyway, but it was made even more unlikely by the fact they couldn't even keep who he was straight.

As he yanked on his jeans and did up the fly, he realized that he was even more efficient at secret-keeping than he'd thought. Aside from that small circle of people, the only others who had the details of Jacob's living arrangements were those who were employed in a close enough way that it was necessary. Three of them actually lived in residence.

There was Beverly, the retired nurse-turned-nanny who cared for Desmond. She was a widow, with one daughter who lived in Europe.

There was Kyle, his head of security. He was three times divorced, had no children, and often grimaced as he told Jacob how glad he was that all of his exes had remarried.

The final person in the group of live-in staff was his housekeeper, Judy. She'd fled an abusive situation a decade earlier and abhorred violence in any form—even video games.

Jacob had vetted every one of them, including Judy's former husband, who had done a bit of jail time, reformed himself and married into a very pious family.

Jacob yanked his shirt over his head, then grabbed his brush and ran it through his hair, still mulling it over. There were more off-site staff than on-site, but only three were aware of Desmond. The two men who worked under Kyle were named Philip and Pardeep, and both were single men in their early twenties who aspired to start their own security firm one day. And there was Ha-yoon, the woman who managed his accounts. She'd moved from Korea to Canada in her teens, and she was about as by-the-book as one person could be.

All three had signed the waiver.

He set the brush down and gave the counter a quick wipe.

Jacob hadn't mentioned Desmond to his gardener, or to the pool guys. He hadn't discussed his son with the construction workers, or the woman who delivered his groceries. He supposed that someone could've figured it out. They could've spied Desmond and come to their own conclusions. Or someone who knew could've leaked it.

He balled up his dirty things, tossed them into the laundry bin, then reached for the recharged phone. He paused just short of pulling it from the cord. His brain had made a leap. If someone who didn't belong there had come onto the property, one of his security officers should've seen something. It was their whole job. If they *hadn't* seen someone, then that pushed more suspicion on the people who worked for Jacob.

Satisfied that he had at least a little something to share with Norah, he finished yanking the phone free. A tentative plan even formed. He could introduce her to the rest of the staff as a new hire. A tech specialist of some kind, maybe. He was sure she'd be able to find a subtle way of garnering information from the rest of them.

Like she said…she tricked me into getting into the shower.

He put a hand on the doorknob and gave it a twist. Then stopped. Because Scarlett's cell buzzed to life.

Chapter 9

Nervous sweat beaded up along Jacob's upper lip. The phone vibrated again.

With his pulse tapping so hard that he could feel it in his throat, he tapped the answer key.

"You're early," he said.

"We are," replied the robotic voice. "Mostly because we noticed that you have a visitor. She's very pretty. Nice green dress, too."

Damn. Damn, damn, damn.

Did they know who she was, too? The sweat increased, and the last vestiges of Jacob's clarity and relief dissipated.

Stall, he ordered silently. *You can do that.*

"Look," he said, his words taking on an echoey quality that made him close his eyes. "I didn't have a choice. It would've looked suspicious if I'd turned her away."

"I'm sure you could've given her a good enough reason to go."

"She wouldn't have left. Trust me on that."

"And why is that, Mr. Pratt? Who *is* she to you? Someone special?"

The word special dragged him back to Steve's assumption, and whatever Jacob had been about to say morphed into a new, far more unreasonable lie—one that burst out. "My fiancée."

There was a long pause, and he thought for sure that the person on the other end was going to call him out for the falsehood. He tried to think of a reasonable way to backpedal. He wasn't sure there was one. Except in the end, he didn't have to.

"Your fiancée?" replied the caller after another moment. "That's an interesting turn of events. And not very convenient."

Jacob infused his voice with a blend of sarcasm and disdain. "And what? You think it's completely convenient for me? Since this was exactly how I was planning on telling people about my marriage plans?"

"I'm surprised you managed to keep it a secret this long."

"Well, then. I guess it's safe to say that you haven't been watching me quite as closely as you'd like to think."

"I suspect it's not so much a lack of close watching as it is a matter of what I've been watching *for*."

His skin crawled, and he breathed in, trying not to let it bother him. "Where's my—" He stopped, remembering what the caller had said to him before about his son's true parentage. "Where's Desmond?"

"He's here, Mr. Pratt. Not to worry. Would you like another video?"

He started to answer with a furious and resounding yes, but cut himself off just in time as he remembered that he was still using the forwarding to Scarlett's phone. The older device was unlikely to take kindly to receiving the transmission. Jacob didn't even want to think about what would happen on the other end if the kidnappers suspected something was amiss.

He adopted a clipped tone. "What I want is to have my boy back where he belongs."

A robotic chuckle carried through the line. "There's some irony there, Mr. Pratt, though you may not realize it yet."

A slice of searing cold permeated Jacob's heart. Where did the person on the other end think his son belonged? He was afraid to ask. Afraid to conclude that it meant no ransom demand would be forthcoming. Maintaining a calm voice took more effort than he wanted to admit.

"Have I proven myself to you yet?" he asked, hating the way the question sounded so acquiescent. "Are you ready to tell me what *you* want?"

"I have to be honest," the kidnapper replied, "I wasn't expecting you to obey the rules."

"Desmond means more to me than you can possibly know."

"Oh, I have an inkling. But I'm surprised that you didn't at least reach out to your old pal. What's her name?"

"I don't know what you're talking about."

"The detective," said the robotic voice. "Lockley, is it?"

Was it a trap? If it was, Jacob wasn't going to fall for it.

"Detective Lockley hasn't been a part of my life for quite some time," he said evenly. "The fact that you're bringing her up now makes me *really* wonder just how closely you've been paying attention."

There was a crackle that could've been a sigh. "Actually, Mr. Pratt. That *is* something I was aware of. But I also thought this situation might make you desperate."

He *was* desperate. Of course he was. Did they want

to hear it? He inhaled. Exhaled. And decided on a middle road.

"My desperation doesn't outweigh Desmond's life," he said carefully.

"All right," the kidnapper replied. "I believe you've been well-behaved enough. So far. But now that your *fiancée* is there, I'm going to need a little more time to assess."

"No!" It was more of a gasp than a protest.

"You want to argue with me, Mr. Pratt? Because that seems like a gamble."

"No," Jacob repeated, his voice lower. "I don't want an argument. I just want Desmond."

"I think we've established that. What we *haven't* established is trust."

"What do you want?" The question came out just shy of a growl.

"Tell me what she knows."

"She doesn't know anything."

"You're keeping this big a secret from the woman you love, Mr. Pratt?"

He did his best not to snap. "Yes."

"Tsk, tsk." The distorted sound clicked unpleasantly over the line, but its disdainful message was clear.

"Would you prefer that I *had* told her?" he countered.

"We both know the answer to that. But I can't help but think that a lie is a very bad way to start a marriage." The robotic voice paused, then said, "But I'll give you the benefit of the doubt and assume it's the latter. Go back to doing your thing. When I'm convinced that you haven't—and aren't going to—tell your fiancée anything, I'll call again. Let's go with another three hours?"

They're going to hang up! Don't let them do it!

Jacob opened his mouth, but he was too late. The line went dead.

Damn again.

Slowly, he opened his eyes. Until that moment, he hadn't even really realized he still had them squeezed shut. He found his own reflection in the mirror. He pressed his hands to the counter and scrutinized his appearance. Whatever bit of confidence he'd had in regard to pushing forward had been visibly wiped away. His wet hair was a wild mess. His eyes were bloodshot, his freshly washed face all but ashen. He looked like hell. To make matters worse, as his gaze found a spot above his own mirrored shoulder, he clued in to something else. When he'd twisted the handle before the phone rang, he'd inadvertently opened the door. And Norah stood in the frame.

Jacob met her eyes, and the word *fiancée* came rushing to the forefront of his mind.

"How much of that did you hear?" he blurted.

"All of your side," she replied. "I wasn't eavesdropping, I promise. I just wanted to make sure you didn't say anything you shouldn't."

"Was it bad?"

"No, not at all. It was perfect. You were confident without being condescending, and you were calm without sounding indifferent."

"They didn't ask for any ransom," he said.

"I figured not." Her voice was even, her face unreadable—two things Jacob was sure weren't a great sign.

He swallowed against the sudden thickness in his throat, then dropped his gaze so he didn't have to look her in the eye. "Sorry about the fiancée comment. I don't know why the hell I said that. I was thinking about what you'd said about making a list of people I know who might be suspects, and I'd literally just decided that it was someone I knew, it would have to be a staff member. So I got this idea that the best excuse for having you here was as a new employee, but—"

He stopped abruptly as he felt her fingers land on his lower back. He jerked his eyes up again, fixing them on her reflection. Her hand left his body, but she didn't step away.

"No," she said. "The fake fiancée trick works."

"Yeah?"

"Maybe even better than the employee story. If I were working for you... I'd have to find a way to look like I *was* working. As your fiancée, I have a good excuse to talk to everyone, and a perfectly valid reason for doing nothing all day other than letting you feed me peeled grapes." She smiled, then paused. "So long as your staff finds it believable."

"I guess we'll just have to convince them."

"You think it will that easy?"

"You think it won't?"

"I didn't say that."

He met her eyes, and heat zapped through him as a dozen ways to do the convincing sprung to mind. It took most of his willpower not to suggest a practice round, right then and there. Forcefully, he reminded himself that he'd already resolved not to let his unusual feelings about Norah interfere with finding his son. He pushed off the counter and turned to face her, schooling his voice into a congenially professional tone.

"They'll believe it so long as we sell it well," he said. "But I think I should give you the syncopated version of mine and Desmond's life before we do anything else."

After a nearly indiscernible glance at his lips, she nodded. "All right. I'm ready to listen, if you're ready to talk."

Jacob's heart jerked more nervously than he would've liked, and when Norah stepped from the bathroom back into his bedroom, he couldn't make himself join her on the window seat. Instead, he paced a little as he spoke. He started out woodenly, trying to keep his emotions in check, but as he got going with the story, the words came out in a rush that matched the light thump of his bare feet on the floor.

He told her how until three months ago, he hadn't known Desmond existed. He stressed that it wasn't because he was some kind of deadbeat, but rather that he'd cut Scarlett out of his life. Repeatedly. Though he didn't go into terrible detail, he talked about the addiction issues. The alcohol dependency. The seedy route she'd taken to support her habits.

"It was too much," he said. "Just over and over. I'd think, 'Here's rock bottom,' and then she'd fall even lower."

"I'm sure you did what you could, when you could."

"I did." He said it more harshly than he meant to, and he tried to rein it in as he went on. "I paid for rehab. I bought that apartment building just so she could live in it, rent free." He ran a hand over his head, paused for a second in his pacing, then started up again. "It sounds crazy, but when you love someone…there's just not much you won't do."

Jacob took a deep breath, then went on. As difficult as everything else was to say, the next part was even harder. He told Norah anyway. He explained how Scarlett had met a man named Milo Knight How Milo had taken away whatever good was left.

"I didn't realize what kind of hope I was holding onto until I truly realized it was futile." He stopped in front of Norah but fixed his gaze on the blind slats behind her and shook his head. "Telling her I was really and truly done was the most painful thing in my life up until that point." He swallowed. Next came the part he didn't want to admit to. He knew he needed to say it anyway. "The last time she reached out to me, I refused to take her call.

It'd been almost three years since we talked. I was sure she just wanted more cash."

"Jake, you don't have to—"

"I do." He finally sank down beside her, and the moment his knee brushed up against hers, he felt stronger. "I found out after that she'd left Milo. That she'd actually met someone who was good for her. A guy named Parker. He was able to help her in a way that I just couldn't, I guess. But it didn't matter in the end. Milo stalked them both. He killed them both."

Jacob had to stop again. He closed his eyes, doing his best to steady the painful thrum of his heart. It wasn't until Norah's hand came out and found his, though, that he was able to continue.

"The investigation was short, because the cops already had an undercover officer investigating Milo for a myriad of other things," he said. "Gang affiliation. Drugs. Pimping."

"The officer was Lockley," Norah filled in.

He opened his eyes and issued a short nod. "Yes. I'd met her. She seemed just as scummy as the rest of the lowlifes, as far as I could tell. But she was good friends with Scarlett. Or that's what I thought. Except Lockley's job was to watch Milo, so when he and Scarlett split... so did Lockley. Which made sense from a work stance."

"But it didn't feel like it made sense from a personal one."

"Exactly. And it wasn't—*isn't*—just me who thinks so. Lockley knows it, too. She told me herself that she thought she could've stopped it somehow." His voice was hoarse now. "She was *there* when Milo did it. She was with him when he tracked down Scarlett and Parker. She was *in his truck* with him when he drove them off the road."

"Oh, Jake. I'm so sorry."

It was funny. He'd heard those words from a lot of people in the months following Scarlett's death. They were the *only* thing he could remember being told at her funeral. Even the judge at Milo's trial had uttered them more than once. Yet hearing them said by Norah Loblaw made him feel entirely different. It wasn't even that Jake thought the others who said the phrase didn't mean it; there was just something in Norah's hazel eyes that said she felt his pain on an equal level. He wished he knew why, and he wished he had time to ask her.

But you don't, he reminded himself. *Desmond needs you.*

He slid his thumb along hers. "Lockley's testimony helped put Milo away. After he was behind bars...that's when I found out about Desmond."

He told her about getting the call from his lawyer. About agreeing to meet with the other man at a motel. He'd walked into that room, having no clue what he was going to find. But he'd been at a low point. Throwing money away, subsisting on a mix of whiskey and potato chips while knowing he couldn't continue drowning in his own sorrows. Then the lawyer showed him the baby, fast asleep in the playpen.

"I just knew. I knew he was hers, even if I couldn't quite believe it," Jacob told Norah, an unexpected chuckle escaping his lips as he remembered the next bit. "My lawyer handed me a stack of papers. Formal guardianship. A bunch of legal stuff. Some terms about how I would raise him, and an agreement to keep tight-lipped about it all. And a big damn bill."

"A bill?"

"Yep. For lawyerly services rendered, and for the family who agreed to confidentially foster Desmond until the trial was over and done with. Scarlett somehow managed to put *my* apartment building up for collateral. Probably *still* laughing at me from heaven." His smile only lasted for another moment. "She was so damn smart. Smart enough to know how to plan in the event of her own murder. I'd be proud of her if it weren't so damn heart-breaking."

"That's a lot of damns in there," Norah replied softly.

"Trust me. There've been a lot of worse things in my head."

"I can't imagine how all of that must've left you feeling."

"Shattered," he admitted, his voice layered with the emotion to prove it. "I'm just glad that the one and only silver lining was Desmond. He was only five days old when Scarlett died. She and Parker had left him with a neighbor so they could grab some diapers. Five days." He swallowed. "I know it's unfair on my part to say he's my whole world…but it's true."

"That's not unfair," she said. "That's parenting. I think it's in section one of the handbook."

"I guess."

His doubt-riddled comment made her pull her hand free, and for a second, he felt a little empty. Then the tips of her fingers found his cheek in a touch that was undeniably intimate. Jacob couldn't help but lean into it a little as he met her eyes once more.

"Hey," she said. "There aren't very many people who know like I do what it looks like to parent during hell on earth. This part of your story… I understand. You feel guilty because you think you've let Desmond down. You wonder—again and again—if there was something you should've done differently. You're almost sure that letting him be your world somehow made this happen, and maybe a bit like it puts pressure on him to prop you up, even though he's a baby. But I promise you, Jake, you aren't doing this wrong."

Norah's words washed over him, lapping at the sensation that he was to blame, then pulling it a little farther away. Making it tolerable. Her hand didn't drop away from his face, either. Instead, it shifted. Her palm found his freshly-washed jaw and gently cupped it. Her eyes held him. Jacob couldn't help but inch forward. He watched her eyelashes flutter, then drop. He felt the catch of her breath. He leaned in even more, his body vibrating with a need to make their lips meet. And for a moment, they did. It was the barest brush. The slightest touch. It was also an explosion. Heat slammed into Jacob, making him want to drag Norah in and explore every inch of her mouth his own.

Except he no sooner started to reach for her than it was already over. Norah jerked away, her face flushed, and her eyes wide. Want was clear on her face, but so was surprise. When her lips parted, Jacob expected an exclamation of some sort. An unnecessary apology, maybe? Or perhaps a vehement *I can't do this*. Except those must've just been his own thoughts, because when she spoke, what she said actually wasn't even close.

"Your wife should've found a way to tell you about the baby before all of that happened," she stated.

Jacob pulled back. "My...what?"

"Your wife. Wait. Ex-wife? No?" The color in her cheeks changed from light pink to dark. "Sorry. I shouldn't assume you were married."

He blinked. "Hold up a sec. Who's my wife?"

"Scarlett."

"Scarlett wasn't my wife. She was my sister."

A strange expression passed over Norah's face, and for the life of him, Jacob couldn't have said exactly what it was. If he'd had to pick a single word to describe it, he would've chosen *recognition*. Though he had no idea why that particular look would apply to what he'd just said. He frowned, but then Norah gave her head a tiny shake, and the odd expression disappeared.

"Okay," she said, sounding so matter-of-fact that it was as though sparking attraction between them and the odd conversation had never happened. "If we move forward with this plan, I want you to know that *I* know it's going to be hard not to worry about Desmond during every second. But you have to remember that everything we're doing is just another step closer to him. And I think if it's going to work, we should get things rolling right away."

She was right about all of it, so Jacob nodded. He was also well aware that he'd broken the promise he'd made to himself about keeping this professional almost as fast as he'd made it. But right then, it didn't seem to matter. As Norah launched into an explanation of how she thought they should proceed, he was distracted. His mind was stuck on the previous two minutes. On the light brushing of their lips. Could it even be called a kiss? What about that bit of recognition? Was the current discussion nothing more than a change of subject? If so, what did it mean?

It wasn't until she jumped up and moved to his closet that he was able to properly refocus. If the term focus could even be applied to a situation where Norah Loblaw was telling him that wearing his shirt—and not much else—would add some authenticity to their story.

"This will work," she called out as she slipped behind his bathroom door.

She sounded so sure that Jacob let more than a sliver of hope crawl in. It *would* work. She'd meet the staff, they'd figure out which direction to go, and they'd bring Desmond home.

When she came back out, though, Jacob realized it

wasn't just going to be hard to keep his attraction to Norah from undermining his resolve to keep things professional. It was going to be damn near impossible.

Chapter 10

As she poured a tablespoon of milk into the pancake batter, Norah stole a glance at Jake, who was digging through the oversize fridge in search of some fresh strawberries that he swore were hidden in there somewhere. She knew the ruse was unorthodox. Maybe it was even ridiculous. But so far, it had gone off without a hitch.

Her eyes moved without her permission, seeking the big red rock on her ring finger. It was a single ruby set in a twisting, white gold band. It was real. She knew it without being told. It was also, coincidentally, her very own birthstone. Not to mention the fact that it was one of the most beautiful rings she'd ever seen. Jacob had dragged it out of a shoebox marked with the name *Scarlett*, then insisted that she put it on. The fact that it fit perfectly was almost too serendipitous.

And she hadn't been able to argue about it, either. Because just a moment later, his housekeeper knocked on the door, announcing that she was there to clean the bathroom. Jake had swept Norah close to his side, then called for the woman—Judy, he'd said her name was—to come in. And of course, Judy did.

The sixty-something woman, her plump body clad in khaki pants and a plain black blouse, had slipped into the bedroom, where she paused to accept Jake's introduction. The older woman seemed nothing but delighted that "Laura" was his new fiancée. She'd fawned over the ring, laughed over their story about meeting in a parking garage, and teased Jake about being really good at keeping secrets. Then she disappeared with her plastic tray of cleaning supplies to do her job. That was it. No disbelief. No startled arguments. Just an acceptance that actually made Norah feel a little guilty for lying to her. And now… the ring already felt natural. Just like that barest kiss had.

God, that kiss…

Just remembering it made Norah want to shiver. And it made her wonder what a full-blown meshing of their lips would be like, too. Something she'd been deliberately *not* going over. Because she'd almost gone over the edge. The fire where their mouths had met had been a matchstick to flint. A combustion. It was a minor miracle that it wasn't the *only* thing on her mind, really.

Unconsciously, she lifted her free hand and touched her own lips. She could still practically feel his mouth on hers.

Maybe it was the revelation about his sister that had intensified the reaction. Because Norah knew the pain of losing one. She understood how it felt to be convinced of the responsibility for a sibling's death. Because she'd been there herself. Hearing Jake echo her own experience—albeit in very different circumstances—had made Norah's heart do a strange flip in her chest. It was one part empathy. Another part tangible connection. And a third part that made her want to tell him all about her own past. If she hadn't redirected the conversation right then, she had no problem imagining that she would've poured it all out. And who knew what would've followed from that. Things that made Norah want to know if Jake's king-size bed was as soft as it looked.

She told herself to be stop being so unreasonable. To stop thinking about kissing a client. To stop letting her head run away with a fantasy that involved a whole lot more than kissing. Or at least to feel guilty about it. It wasn't right. Her mind should be on Desmond. But part of her brain insisted that being attracted to a man didn't make her want to help him less. If anything, it made her even more invested.

Exactly, said her conscience. *It's not right.*

But Norah's eyes still hung on the taut lines of his T-shirt–covered shoulders for another few seconds before he let out a triumphant, "Aha!" that forced her to quickly redirect her attention to the bowl. Pretending not to notice Jake's success in retrieving strawberries, she gave the batter a vigorous stir. Of course, the whip of her fork—she was using the pronged utensil because the green-eyed man had given her a scathing look when she'd tried to grab a spoon—drew as much attention as her stare would have done. More, probably. Jake's big frame sidled up beside her. He set down both a canister of whipped cream and the presliced strawberries, and his strong hand came to clasp her wrist, stilling her movements.

"I could swear I already told you at least twice that it's *supposed* to be lumpy," he said teasingly.

"And I already told *you* that I've made a pancake or two in my time," she replied, giving him a playful hip check.

He pretended to stumble. She grabbed his elbow and dragged him back again.

For the last ten minutes, they'd been doing the same

little dance. Putting on a show. One that would make them appear like a happy, utterly infatuated couple to anyone who happened to be watching. Anyone who was scrutinizing. Doubting the authenticity of their supposed relationship. And they were mainly doing it by making the enormous kitchen seem as tiny as possible.

They stood too close to each other at every turn. They bumped into one another accidentally on purpose. She giggled. He chuckled. And if one of them had to leave their shared space—as Jake had done a minute ago— they made certain to issue a light touch before doing so. His hand on the small of her back. Her fingers tracing a line down his bicep.

It was surprisingly easy to pretend. Norah didn't consider herself to be particularly flirtatious and she was sorely out of practice, too. But Jake was more than attractive enough to make it enjoyable. Even with his smile tightened by the devastating pressure he was under, the flash of his teeth was infectious. The rumbling bass of his voice drew Norah in, and his exaggerated chivalry was charming. It'd be a lie to have said it was unpleasant. But they weren't wasting time. The main focus was still on Desmond.

They'd set aside exactly thirty-five minutes for their romantic breakfast facade. And as they'd decided ahead of time, Jake was using the guise of sweet nothings as a means of whispering potentially useful information about his staff into Norah's ear. They finished the prep work with his breath tickling against her skin as he told her everyone's names, their length of employment, and any tiny detail that might stick out. Norah responded with questions she hoped would lead her to a hint at someone who might have nefarious intentions. But truthfully—disappointingly—there were no red flags. By the time they settled—side by side, with his ankle threaded between hers under the table—on the soft-backed bench seat in the corner of the kitchen, Norah had heard nothing that made her pause and ask for more.

Yes, the nondisclosure agreements were recent. Three months old, to coincide with Desmond's arrival. And yes, there were imperfections in the employees' lives. Like everyone's. But every one of them had been thoroughly vetted. With the exception of the nanny, each of them had worked for Jake before he had Desmond, and he'd handpicked them to stay on. And those marred pieces of their pasts seemed like the kind that every human being obtained over the course of a lifetime. From everything Norah could discern, a certain amount of trust was warranted. On top of that, none of them had an obvious motivation for taking Desmond. They were all well paid, they all received an annual bonus. And from what Jake said, they genuinely liked him.

Since she hadn't met them in person yet, Norah wasn't willing to completely write them off. There was still a modicum of hope that a threat of blackmail was still coming. But since no one had yet asked for money…she was starting to fear the worst. And with the fear came her self-doubt.

What if I can't help him? For real. What if I can't get Desmond back?

The genuine worry made their playacting seem suddenly hollow. And it stalled her. Literally. When Jake gave her elbow a little nudge, she realized she was sitting with the pancake-heavy fork raised halfway to her mouth.

"If you keep making that face," he said, his voice just above a whisper, "People are going to think you're here to kill me rather than marry me."

Norah knew she should've blushed or laughed, but she couldn't quite muster up the latter, and the former was unlikely with the coldness running through her right then. She forced a small smile, then set down her fork. She couldn't stand the thought of trying to swallow another bite, and she wasn't sure she'd be able to keep up their carefully crafted illusion if she sat still for any longer. And she was glad to see that Jake's plate was empty. It meant they could move on.

"I think I need the grand tour," she announced cheerfully.

"Oh yeah?"

"Definitely. Your future wife wants to check out her new digs."

She jumped up and held out her hand. Jacob didn't budge. But his expression was one of mild amusement rather than anything else. So why wasn't he moving?

"What's wrong?" Norah asked with more lightness than she felt. "Afraid I'll try to mess with your bachelor-chic decor?"

"No...it's not so much that..."

"What, then?"

"I'm just not sure whether I should be concerned about giving you the tour while you're wearing *that*." He winked like he was kidding, but something in the way his eyes ran over her as he spoke made Norah think maybe he was half-serious.

She glanced down, and she had to fight a self-conscious groan. And now her face *did* manage to warm a little. She'd momentarily forgotten that a part of their ruse included the morning-after look. She was still clad in nothing but one of Jake's dress shirts and her own underwear. When she'd grabbed the shirt and buttoned it into place, she'd been thankful that he was so tall. With her own figure as tall and full as it was, she'd never been one of those women who could toss on her boyfriend's clothes and get away with swimming in them. But Jake's shirt actually hung far enough past her rear end that she didn't feel too exposed. The dress she'd had on before was nearly as short, and it had definitely been hiked up even higher a few times over the last couple of hours.

"Well?" prodded Jake. "Are we going to go ahead and take this spectacle of debauchery to every room in the house?"

Norah lifted her face and gave him an arch look. "Guess you'll have to catch me if you want to stop me."

Flushing even more, she spun away the moment after she said it, then strode across the kitchen without waiting to see if Jake was following her.

For a couple of seconds after Norah turned, Jacob's eyes on her long, well-muscled legs watched as they carried her over the black-and-white tiles. It wasn't until she was actually out of sight that he realized she'd meant what she said about him having to catch her. Dropping a belated curse, Jacob slid out from the bench.

"Norah?" he called as he followed the path she'd taken. "The tour will be better with a guide, I promise."

When he reached the dining room, it was already empty. Frowning, he moved a bit faster past the long oak table that dominated the space. The two of them had agreed it was best for Norah to speak to the staff under as natural circumstances as possible. That didn't mean he exactly relished the idea of one of his security guards chatting up his fake fiancée at the first-given opportunity.

He reached the door to the hall, where he paused to look up one side of the corridor, then the other. Usually, he liked the vast-feeling layout of his home. He enjoyed the way each of the four main floor wings—though he felt a bit pretentious calling them that—seemed separate from the other. For the first time, it seemed like a negative.

"Which way…" Jacob muttered to himself.

After a second-long deliberation, he decided it didn't

really matter. The hallway where he now stood branched off in two directions and wrapped through the whole house, but the two pieces met up again between the office and guest suite on the other side. With a shrug, he turned left. His bare feet thumped against the hardwood as he glanced into the various rooms that lined the hall.

She wasn't in the two-piece bathroom. She wasn't in the oversize living room.

Jacob increased his pace.

"Norah?" he repeated, a little louder this time. "Trust me. I know where to find both the creaky boards *and* the best spots for kissing. So if you think that playing hide-and—"

He cut himself off with a sharp inhale as a muffled, masculine holler carried to his ears from up the hall. Fear for Norah's safety punched him in the gut, and without any further consideration, he dropped into a run. He raced over the floor. The hardwood burned against his feet, but Jacob was oblivious to the sting. He rounded the corner with his heart pounding, his head flipping through possible explanations, each one worse than the last. When he rounded the corner, though, he stopped short.

Norah stood just inside the south-facing sunroom, and she was clearly fine. Her hands were on her hips, a laugh was escaping her lips, and she was shaking her head in an amused way that made her soft blond locks bounce and catch the light filtering into the room through the glass panels. About two feet away from her was Pardeep, one of the security guards.

Well. That happened fast. Like you conjured it all up by just thinking about it.

Despite his relief, Jacob couldn't quite shake the kicked-in-the-gut feeling. He stayed in the hall, trying to rid himself of the unpleasant sensation. His attention remained glued to Norah. He couldn't help it. She was too stunning not to admire. His gaze ran over her, head to toe. Her smile was genuine, and it made her eyes shine. Her hands-on-hips pose pulled the borrowed shirt a little tighter, offering a hint of her curves. And her long, supple legs were temptation personified. They made Jacob's mind want to cease every proper thought. In fact, the sight of all of her exposed skin filled his head with some *im*proper thoughts. His hands ached to touch her.

Yeah, okay. Even if that was gonna happen...even if that was an okay thing to think about...would you be able to do it from here?

It wasn't until the uniformed man brought his fingers up to touch Norah's forearm—for no good reason that Jacob could think of—that sense kicked in. Or maybe sense wasn't the right word. Maybe it would be more accurate to say it was some kind of overblown machismo instinct. Either way, the need to step between Norah and Pardeep propelled Jacob forward.

In seven, quick steps—he counted them unconsciously—he made it through the sunroom door. In three more strides, he closed the gap between himself and the pair in front of him. Then in one not-so-subtle move, he slid a possessive arm to her waist. Pardeep had no choice but to let his hand drop.

Good. The childish thought came before Jacob could stop. Aloud, he did his best to keep the growl from his voice.

"Leaving me for another man so soon, babe?" he said, lifting an eyebrow in his security guard's direction.

Pardeep gave him a funny look and took a small step back, and Jacob realized he'd probably failed at sounding the slightest bit congenial. He usually went out of his way to be nice to the people he employed. Except he couldn't seem to muster up any kindness at that exact moment.

Norah clearly picked up on the unusual tension, too. She let out a laugh that managed to sound not *quite* forced.

"You'll have to excuse my new fiancé, Mr. Dhillon," she said, leaning into Jacob a little. "I think a lack of sleep is making him cranky."

Pardeep looked from her to Jacob, then back again before clearing his throat and inching away even more. "I was just telling Laura that she startled the you-know-what out of me. I was on my way to the house when I saw her through the window."

Norah let out a laugh that—to Jacob's ears, anyway—bordered on flirtatious. "He says *I* scared *him*, but it was really the other way around. I just about killed him with the vase. Might've done it, too, if I hadn't bumped my arm on the shelf."

She disentangled herself and stretched out the arm in question. An angry red mark glared up from her otherwise perfect skin. The soon-to-be-a-bruise spot was clearly what Pardeep had been examining, and even though the other man obviously had nothing to do with it, a surge of irritation hit Jacob. He bent his neck, then lifted her arm to his mouth and made a show of planting a slow, gentle kiss on top of the redness. Then he slung his arm around Norah once more, fighting a strong urge to lift her chin so he could put on even *more* of a show, and grinned toothily at his security guard.

"Like I always say…nothing scarier than a woman without pants, freely roaming the house," Jacob told the other man.

Norah tipped her head up and gave him an extra-sweet smile. "I *said* he thought I was stealing. Besides which…you're the one who told me it would be fine to look around."

His eyes followed the curve of her lips, and before he could think to stop himself, he reached his free hand toward them and pressed his thumb to the bottom one, tracing the line of it. "That was before I knew you were going to terrorize the staff."

"I'd picked up the crystal vase in the cabinet and I was having a look at the bottom of it," she said, her voice breathy.

"Is that right?" Jacob let his hand fall, but he couldn't pull his gaze from her mouth.

"I guess I look shadier than I think I do," she told him.

"Uh-huh." Jacob tipped his face toward hers.

And then Pardeep cleared his throat. "Um. Sorry. Boss?"

Jacob sucked in a resentful breath and tossed the other man a glance that *might* have been just this side of a glare. "What's up?"

Pardeep let out an awkward cough. "The reason I was on my way up to the house in the first place was to let you know that Philip's laid up something fierce with strep throat. He's been out of commission for about two days already and needs a bit more recovery time. So I'm bunking with Kyle. I'm gonna pull a few doubles to cover Phil's shifts for the week. If that's all right with you."

"I think you should say yes, Jake," Norah interjected. "I happen to know that Mr. Dhillon is *very* adept at sneaking up on people. He deserves some overtime."

Pardeep shifted on his feet, then offered a slight shrug. "Just doing my job. And I wouldn't be good at it if I clomped around like an elephant."

Jacob bit back an unreasonable urge to tell the man if he was really that good, he would've noticed in the first place that the so-called burglar was a woman without pants.

"Thanks for picking up the slack. Take all the overtime you need," he made himself say instead. "And I promise to call you if another beautiful woman is trying to rob me."

Pardeep gave him another uncertain look, then nodded. "You got it, boss. And congrats on the engagement." He turned to go, but only took a few steps toward the door before swinging back again. "Oh. Almost forgot. Kyle also wanted me to tell you that SafeGuard finally got their act together. Those cameras are up and running."

Jacob's thoughts about the other man's imaginary incompetency—he really *was* a great security guard—slid to the wayside, and nervous hope took their place. "Since when?"

"Earlier than expected, by about twelve hours. Came online last night." Pardeep paused and studied him for a second. "You all right, Mr. Pratt?"

"Fine," Jacob lied quickly. "Can I view the footage from Kyle's office?"

"Yeah. For sure. Or you can log into the SafeGuard server and get it from there. Something you want me to look for, boss?"

Jacob would love to have chosen option B, but there was no way he felt safe enough to chance perusing video footage on his computer. All the firewalls and anti-spy software in the world wouldn't convince him it hadn't somehow been hacked by the kidnappers.

He shook his head. "I'd rather see it firsthand. Just let Kyle know I'll probably be by a bit later to check out the new system. Maybe once I've grabbed my dearest *Laura* a pair of pants to wear."

"You got it, Mr. Pratt. And congratulations again. Let me know if you need anything else."

Chapter 11

The moment Pardeep was out of sight, Jacob slid his hand to Norah's palm, and started to pull her from the room. Her feet stayed planted.

"What's wrong?" he asked immediately.

"Come here," she replied, her tone full of exaggerated seduction.

Jacob stepped in, tugged her into an embrace, then swept side Norah's hair and dipped his head so he could speak into her ear. "We have to get you some pants, then take a look at that footage."

She pulled away and blinked up at him, momentarily—likely unintentionally—dropping the flirtatious facade. "You were serious about the pants?"

He started to say that he'd rarely been *more* serious, then paused as he realized how ridiculous he was being. Why did he care about whether or not she was fully clothed? It wasn't like she was indecent. Even if she *had* been, that wasn't really Jacob's business. He had no claim on her, no right to tell her what to wear. Truthfully, he wasn't even the type of man who would try to control a woman's wardrobe to start out with. He didn't think it was *any* man's place. So why was the maddening need rearing up now?

"Jake?" Norah prodded.

He gave himself a mental headshake. Pants—and whether she was wearing any—should be the furthest thing from his mind.

He bent to her ear once more, changing the subject without addressing her concern. "We have to see if the new security system recorded anything."

Thankfully, Norah was willing to accept the redirection in conversation. She put her hands onto his shoulders, then pushed to her tiptoes.

"I know it feels like we should run out of here and do that," she whispered. "But there's a chance that whoever has your son is listening to us. Which is the whole point of this."

It was his turn to pull back, but he only moved enough to be able to lean in and press his forehead to hers, lowering his voice even more. "I'm aware of all of that. But I *have* to find a way to see it. What's on there will tell us whether someone came onto the property, or whether they were already here. It's not even a choice, Norah."

Without warning, his voice grew hoarse at the end, and he closed his eyes as a vision of his son's face flooded his mind. He thought he'd been doing a damn good job of holding it together so far. His exterior projection of himself sure as hell didn't reflect the mess he was on the inside. Really, even his head and heart were as calm as he could keep them under the current conditions. How could he do any better? What more could he possibly do?

He didn't realize he'd made the speech aloud until Norah's head came to rest on his shoulder and she spoke softly right under his ear, her breath tickling on his neck. "You *can't* do any better, Jake. You're doing a fantastic job. I just don't think there's a subtle way of running to sift through hours of security footage. It's going to draw the exact kind of attention you don't want."

She was right. Again.

A renewed ache grew in his throat, and Jacob impulsively buried his face in Norah's hair. He couldn't deny the truth in her words, no matter how badly he wanted to. They didn't know exactly how closely the kidnappers were watching, and there was no way to be sure they hadn't heard Pardeep's little revelation about the surveillance cameras. They could've been listening to every word. They'd made it clear that they were waiting for one wrong move. Those uncertainties were the exact reason he and Norah had agreed not to discuss anything about Desmond's missing status aloud. And if there was one thing that Jacob *was* almost certain of, it was that the kidnappers would be less than pleased if they thought he was willfully trying to track them down. The consequences might be deadly.

"What are our options, Norah?" he said, not bothering to disguise his fear. "Because God knows I'm gonna need one."

"First off, we take a minute. Or three."

Norah's reply was muffled by the fact that she was now locked against his chest, but she made no move to pull away. Her arms were still on top of his shoulders, but they were folded around his neck now. Jacob had unconsciously slid his hands to her back. One rested in the center, while the other rubbed in a circle just above her waistline. The pose was utterly, undeniably intimate. It didn't feel like a part of the ruse, either. If anything, it felt natural—even though completely at odds with the conversation. Which Jacob knew was a good indicator that he should adjust their stance. That didn't mean he could make himself attempt to do it.

"Using up more time is the last thing I want to do," he told her.

"I know. But if we go rushing off anywhere, we might as well wave a big, giant sign saying that we're looking for Desmond."

"So what should we do in the meantime?"

As soon as the question was out, Jacob realized just how laden with innuendo it sounded. Especially considering their current pose. Norah obviously heard it, too, because she leaned back and arched an eyebrow.

"I *was* going to suggest that we find a different way to watch it," she said. "But it sure sounds like you have something else in mind."

Despite everything, a chuckle escaped from Jacob's lips. The wild urge to kiss her came back with a vengeance, too. Her lips were already so close that he could feel their heat, and he bent his mouth back to her ear before temptation got the better of him.

"I'll defer to your expertise. Any ideas on how we might be able to have a look without drawing that unwanted attention?" he asked, tightening his hold on her just a little.

Her answer surprised him.

"Actually," she murmured into his chest, "I did have a thought. I want to call my brother."

"Your brother?"

"Yes."

"Why?" asked Jacob. "Is he a tech guy?"

"No," replied Norah.

"Illegal hacker?"

"Also no."

Jacob's hand stopped its seemingly involuntary movements. "Why do I get the feeling that you don't *want* to tell me what he does?"

She exhaled a sigh that sent a puff of warmth through his T-shirt to his skin, then answered so softly that he could barely hear her. "Do you think your housekeeper is done with your bathroom?"

"Probably. Why?"

"Can we talk about it in your room?"

Jacob's attention flicked toward the glass panels that led to the yard. It wasn't visible from here, but on the far side were the outbuildings where the live-in staff were housed. Kyle's office was adjacent to the small, tidy row of homes. Which of course meant the video was, too.

Just out of sight. Just out of reach.

Jacob had to really work to keep from insisting that they forgo common sense. He threaded his fingers through Norah's, then led her silently through the hall. He couldn't quite muster up the playfulness required for the role of infatuated fiancé. Worry was tightening like a noose around his heart. The extra few hundred feet between them and the video footage felt like a few hundred miles instead.

When they reached the stairs, it took even more effort not to ask again—maybe to plead in the most unmanly manner—to forgo conversation in favor of action. Jacob actually stalled at the bottom, making Norah stop, too, one step up. She spun to face him, making them eye-to-eye. And he knew his expression had to be reflective of his feelings, because her face flooded with sympathy, and she freed her hand from his in order to cup his cheek.

Jacob leaned into the touch, and Norah's thumb slid pleasantly along his jaw. Jabs of sharp emotion slid through him. He wanted Desmond back so desperately. It felt like a millennium since he'd tucked the blanket around the little boy and whispered for him to have sweet dreams. It seemed impossible that it had only been the previous night. Even crazier was the fact that it wasn't even noon yet. How much longer could this insanity last? Yet, mixed with those thick strings of debilitating fear was a new thread. A warmth that seemed to stem directly from the woman standing in front of him now.

No, he corrected silently. *It doesn't just* seem *to. It does.*

He didn't know why—not yet—but there was some intangible draw. One that gave him a different reason for needing to get his son back.

"Come on," he said gruffly. "Let's get upstairs."

She gave his jaw a gentle squeeze, then nodded, and turned to head up. Jacob paused for an extra moment. And as he watched her take the steps, one at a time, his brain finally clued in to the reason why her pants-free state bothered him. It wasn't because she was his, and he thought he ought to have some kind of overblown, jealous claim on her…it was because she *wasn't* his. And he kind of wished she could be.

Norah was eager to get back to Jake's room, though not for the eyebrow-raising reason that his housekeeper clearly assumed as she passed them in the upstairs hall on the way to the master suite. Yes, the look on Judy's face as she told them she'd be back from the grocery soon— but not *too* soon—made Norah's cheeks warm. And no, Norah wasn't trying to deny that each time Jake put his hands on her, a new surge of attraction—a little stronger each time—hit her again. She couldn't even come close to pretending that his embraces, made under the pretense of their so-called engagement, didn't make her want them to be real. But none of that was what made her step quickly. What did it was the fact that felt like she might actually be able to follow through on some of the help she'd promised. And she wanted—very badly—to be able to do that.

All you have to do is convince Jake that this is the way to go, she thought as she stepped into the bedroom, then waited for him to shut the door behind them.

She just wasn't sure how amenable he was going to be to her idea. And his immediate, arms-crossed look told Norah he was already on the defensive. For all the right reasons.

But still.

"I can tell from your face that I'm not going to like this," he said. "But tell me anyway."

Norah didn't see a point in stepping lightly. "My brother is a cop."

Jake's body visibly stiffened. "I'm assuming you're talking about a different brother than the one you just told me you wanted to call."

"I only have one brother. Noah."

"Then no."

"Just hear me out," she said, moving to one of the chairs, then gesturing for Jake to join her.

He shook his head. "I can hear you fine from here."

Norah didn't let herself be fazed by his words or his abruptly cool tone. She completely understood his hesitation. She knew it had nothing to do with her and everything to do with Desmond. Her job was literally built on helping people who didn't want to involve police. But this was different. And she persisted.

"Noah's reasonably new to the RCMP, and he's being fast-tracked," she explained. "But his status as a cop isn't why I think he can help. Before he chose this career, he was a bounty hunter. He's got connections who don't mind bending the law a bit here and there to get stuff done."

"But he *is* a cop, and they have a professional obligation to report this kind of thing."

"You don't know my brother."

"I barely know *you*," he pointed out.

She didn't let that statement bother her, either. "But you trust me."

"Yes. I really do," he admitted. "But as much as I'd like to say that trusting you extends to trusting everyone that you trust, it'd be a lie. He might be your brother, Norah, but you're asking me to take a pretty big leap."

"You've already done it once."

"What do you mean?"

"You trusted Lockley not to report it, and she's a cop, too. A detective, even."

He gave his head a small shake. "I wouldn't trust her if I didn't know that she feels like she owes me because of her role in my sister's death."

"Then you have even more reason to believe me. Because even if my brother didn't owe me anything—which I promise you, he does—he'd still help us out. He's a good man. If I ask him to, he'll keep this between us. I know my brother."

"Norah."

Her name sounded like it hurt him to say, and it made her heart ache. She pushed up to her feet and took both of his hands in hers. For a second, she thought he might resist. But after a heartbeat, he pulled her in instead, holding her as close as he had in the sunroom. Only this time, it wasn't for show. Which made Norah ache in a different way. What was it about this man that made her feel like this? She wished there was some logical explanation for it.

"I know you believe all of that stuff you just told me," he said after a few moments, his voice rumbling just above her ear. "Because I'm really sure you wouldn't suggest anything that you thought would harm Desmond."

"I wouldn't," she agreed.

One of his hands came up to run over the back of her head and down the length of her hair. "The problem is that you're thinking of your brother *as* a brother. But about your brother as a cop? What makes you so sure he isn't going to feel an obligation to follow the law? What if something happens and he thinks that's what's best? Will he still be the good man you say he is, or will he be a good police officer instead?"

Norah leaned away enough to be able to gaze up at him. "I'd trust my brother with my life, no matter the circumstances."

"What about with my son's life? Would you trust him in the same way with that?" He asked the two questions in a gentle enough voice that there was no accusation attached to his words.

And Norah was thankful that she could meet his eyes, and answer with complete conviction. "There's nothing Noah values more than a child's life."

Jake took a small breath, then exhaled it slowly. "I can tell that there's a story behind that, and a big part of me wants to ask you what it is. But a bigger part knows that this argument is just wasting time we don't have." He let her go, reached into his pocket and pulled out the older-model phone that Norah had seen earlier, then held it toward her. "Go ahead."

Relief spurred a moment of spontaneity, and as Norah took the electronic device from his hands, she also pushed to her tiptoes to press her lips against Jake's cheek. The moment her mouth brushed against his skin, she realized what she was doing. But it was too late to subtly retract her movements. And—of course—thinking about it made her slow down instead of speed up, so the kiss became awkwardly protracted. With a silent, self-directed order to stop—*right now*—Norah finally managed to sink back down and took an embarrassed step away. To make matters even more embarrassing, Jake brought his hand up to touch the scene of the crime. Norah was sure her own face had to be flaming.

"Sorry!" she said, her eyes on the spot where his fingers met his skin.

Jake's hand dropped, and his mouth quirked up on one side. "Really?"

Feeling flustered, Norah started to smooth down her clothes. Belatedly, she remembered that her outfit currently consisted of *his* clothes, and she dropped her hands to her sides and balled them into fists.

"No," she said. "*Yes,* I mean. That was unprofessional."

His green eyes filled with amusement. "You don't kiss all of your clients?"

"I don't kiss *any* of my clients," she replied quickly.

"I'm glad to hear it."

There was more than one way to take his statement, and Norah had to fight with herself not to ask what he meant. Was he glad to hear she wasn't normally unprofessional? Or pleased that it was just him?

"I'll call my brother," she said, glad to have a valid excuse to stop the conversation before she could drive herself farther into a big hole of awkwardness.

Turning away because she thought it might be easier to breathe if she wasn't looking right at Jake, Norah quickly punched in Noah's number. Thankfully, he picked up on the first ring.

"This is Loblaw," he announced in crisp voice.

"What a coincidence. So is this," Norah replied.

There was a small pause, and she could picture him pulling back the phone to look at the call display.

"Norah?" he asked after a second.

"Unless you have another twin sister."

"Ever the comedian," her brother said. "Whose phone are you on? Where's yours?"

It felt good to hear her brother's voice, and Norah rolled her shoulders, tension easing away.

"I lost it somewhere along the line. But don't worry your pretty little head. I've got a stellar replacement plan, courtesy of my provider," she told him. "And you'll be delighted to hear that this phone belongs to a *client*."

"Not gonna lie, sis… I *am* delighted. Did you happen to get hit over the head to acquire the new job?"

"You don't want to know. But you'll be equally pleased to know that I'm calling you for your expertise."

"Guess there's a first time for everything," Noah teased. "What do you need?"

"I need a way to secretly access some digital footage on a security system."

"Wow. When you call in a favor, you *really* call in a favor, huh?"

She ignored the good-natured mocking, and instead said, "Can it be done?"

"Yeah, in all likelihood. My dear old friend Spud is the absolute best at what he does," her brother said, his voice turning serious as he added, "You wanna tell me what you've gotten yourself into?"

Norah couldn't help but flick a glance in Jake's direction. He'd moved across the room to sit on the bed. His eyes were on her, and his hands were wrapped tightly on the baby blanket she'd spied earlier. Her lungs compressed with painful sympathy.

"Are you still there?" said Noah.

She cleared her throat and brought her attention back to the phone. "I'm here. And you know my cases are confidential, so I'm going to need your word that this stays that way. Especially with this one."

She could picture the concern on her brother's face

as he answered, "I respect that. You know I do. But I'm going to need a little info if you want me to get my guy to illegally tamper with someone's security footage."

"Technically, it's probably not illegal, since the person who owns the footage is the same person who wants it hacked."

"That doesn't make me feel any more secure," Noah said, sighing again. "But I'm assuming you want this done quickly, so give me the bare minimum. A name and an address. Knowing which security company it is would be helpful, too."

Norah let out a relieved breath. "The company is Safe-Guard, and the client's name is Jake Pratt. Give me a sec, and I'll ask him his—"

Her brother cut her off. "Hang on. Did you say Jake *Pratt*?"

"Yes. Why?"

"Is that why this case needs more than usual discretion?" he asked.

"No." Norah could hear her own puzzlement in the single word.

"Okay, listen. Is he a tall dude?"

"What?"

"Taller than I am," her brother replied. "Sandy brown hair. Stupidly green eyes."

Norah looked over to Jake again, who was frowning a little, the very same green eyes locked on her face.

"Not the exact words I would use, but yes," she stated. "Why?"

This time, when the extra moment of silence came, Norah inwardly cringed. She knew Noah was doing the twin-sense thing, and right then, she didn't like the idea much at all. And sure enough, when her brother spoke up again, it was with that uncanny ability to know more about what was in her head than she knew herself.

"You like this guy," he stated.

Norah directed her face toward the wall so that Jake wouldn't see her flush as she answered Noah in as neutral a tone as she could manage. "Sure. Why wouldn't I?"

"No," her brother said. "I mean you *like* him. In the same way you liked Robbie Simmons in third grade."

"How do you even remember that?"

"I'm your brother. I have perfect recall for every detail of your life that might possibly embarrass you."

Norah rolled her eyes. "Of course you do. But that other bit of what you said is irrelevant."

"So irrelevant that you can't even say it aloud because Jacob Pratt—aka, Jakey P., the main attraction from *Zero to Hero*—might hear you?" Noah laughed.

Jakey P. It was what Steve had called him, too. But Norah didn't really get a chance to process that fact, because her brother's next words zapped a chill through her blood.

"Only you, my dearest sister, would be on work hiatus for a year, then throw yourself back into it by a heartthrob who got fired for being too…heartthrobby," he said. "Wait. Is this case related to that somehow?"

"What do you mean?"

"You clearly need to watch more reality TV. *Zero to Hero, Chef Edition*. They built up the whole season of the show around Jakey P. Guy grew up dirt-poor, won some cooking scholarship and dragged himself out of it all. The producers suddenly canceled his highlight and sent him home, and the rumor was that it happened because Mr. Pratt came loaded with a personal stalker."

The chill became an ice storm so thick that it took most of Norah's efforts to concentrate on the rest of her brother's words.

"I can't believe he has a kid, and it wasn't splashed all over the papers," Noah was saying. "Assuming it's *his* kid. I can't picture it. Who—no, never mind. We can talk about it—and I promise you we *will* talk about it—later. Right now, I'm gonna give Spud a call and have him see what he can do for you." He muttered something else about celebrity gossip, then cleared his throat. "Norah?"

"I'm here."

"Okay. Can I call you back on this number? I'll be as quick as I can. I'll aim for thirty minutes, but it could be a bit longer, depending on Spud. That okay with you, big sister?"

"Yes, that should be fine. Thank you, Noah."

"Always got your back."

With stiff-feeling fingers, she clicked off the phone and slowly turned to face Jake. He was on his feet again, and already moving toward her.

"What did your brother say?" he asked. "Can he—"

"You should've told me about your TV show and how it got canceled!" The words burst from her lips without warning, and the all-over chill became fiery heat.

Chapter 12

Norah could tell that her sudden outburst caught Jake off guard from the way he stopped and blinked at her.

"I *did* tell you I was on TV," he said. "Right before we came into the house."

"No, I asked you if you were, and you said, 'Something like that,' as if it were no big deal."

"It *isn't* a big deal," he replied. "It was barely a blink in my life, and to be honest, I've spent the last three years trying to pretend it never happened."

"Right. A blink. Is that why you forgot to mention that you had a stalker? Because that opens up a whole world of other suspects, Jake!" She bit her lip as she realized she was practically yelling, then took a breath and tried to adopt a calmer tone. "Famous people attract all kinds of crazy. It changes things. Maybe it changes *every*thing. We should've been making a list of people who might have something against you because of that."

"Norah, if I thought there was even a chance that—"

"It's not *your* job to decide what matters and what doesn't. That's *my* job. You have no idea what kind of line people can cross to get to someone they want. The violence that's out there... I told you not to hold anything back or this wouldn't work."

For the first time since their unconventional meeting, Jake seemed to let his emotions get the better of him. He grabbed the hem of his T-shirt and yanked it up hard. Norah's eyes dropped to his suddenly bared chest, and she sucked in a breath. A long, jagged scar covered his abdomen. It started at his belly button, then angled over his well-defined abs. From there, it ran up his rib cage and curved sharply under his left pec.

"I *do* know what kind of line people can cross," he spoke with more than an edge of bitterness. "Someone gave me *this* because I wouldn't hand over my boots. I was fifteen. The guy who did it was my foster brother. Someone I thought I could trust."

Still holding the shirt up, he spun so that his back was to her, exposing a puckered mark—about a half inch in diameter—just above his waistline.

"This one came from a buddy's dad," he stated. "He was showing off for his drunk friends, trying to force us two kids—we were seventeen—to do tequila shots. I refused, so he made an example of me with his cigar."

He dropped the shirt, then swung Norah's way again, his expression intense.

"Those are just the physical scars. The emotional ones..." He shook his head. "The first eighteen years of my life were a lesson in what it means to exist in the hardest of hard-luck spaces. My dad took off before my sister learned to walk. My mom split her time between getting blindingly drunk and doing her damnedest to stick with a twelve-step program. Scarlett and I bounced around like two ping-pong balls." He ran a rough hand over his chin. "I don't want Desmond to come close to anything like any of that. I don't want him to even brush up against it. That's why I need the nondisclosures. Eventually, I'll tell him everything. But I want to do it on *my* terms and on my time."

Norah's throat ached with the pain of his revelations. "I'm sorry you went through all that, Jake."

Without warning, he was at her side, his hand on her shoulder. And it was his touch that alerted Norah to the fact that she was crying. Embarrassed, she shook off his hand. But he just brought his fingers up again, this time to swipe his thumb over her damp cheek.

"Hey," he said gently, cupping her cheek as he spoke. "I'm sorry. I wasn't trying to make things worse. I was just trying to explain why I wouldn't have left out anything important."

"No. It's not you." Norah paused, then corrected herself. "I shouldn't say that. It *is* you. I'm scared for you. I want to help you more than I can explain."

"So don't explain. Just tell me what you think we should be doing. Do you want me to call and verify Pardeep's story? See if Philip really is sick? Or maybe find an excuse to get my accountant on the phone so you can see if she knows anything?"

"No. We should really wait until after we've seen what's on the footage. It'll save us the hassle of pursuing the wrong angle, and it'll also help keep our search a bit more secretive. But what I do want to know is why you wouldn't think it was *more* than important to tell me you had a stalker."

"Because I *didn't* have a stalker." He sighed and shook his head again, this time with a regretful look sliding across his face. "It was just Scarlett, like usual. She showed up at the studio where we were doing some prerecording interviews. She was high, and she was disruptive. Actually, that's putting it mildly. She crashed the set, destroyed a camera, demanded money from me, and had to be escorted off the premises by both the security guards *and* the police."

He let his hand fall away from her cheek, then moved back to the bed and sank down onto the edge. Norah followed him, and she sat down, too, sliding her hand over to take his. Jake gave her fingers a squeeze.

"After that," he said, "The producers decided I wasn't worth the potentially bad publicity, and they bought me out. The amount they gave me—courtesy of my very effective lawyer—was pretty damn close to the prize money that was up for grabs at the end of the show, and that was just fine with me. The settlement let me invest. I made a great move. It's how I could afford the apartment building, this house and my whole life."

Norah saw where the story was going. "Then someone got a hold of what happened with your sister, and they misinterpreted it."

"Yep. And the 'someone' in question was really *two* someones."

"That couple out front?"

"The very same. They pushed and pushed. Hounded me. And I guess they won a little, because the stalker stuff kind of took on a life of its own. It brought the extra media coverage. Which was ironic, since the buyout was meant to avoid that. It was also kind of hell, actually. Any time I left my place, someone would demand the story. They wanted to know who stalked me. If it was someone I knew. If I was scared for my life." He shrugged. "The worst part was figuring out that I'd never be able to have both privacy and open my own restaurant, which was the whole reason I entered to be on *Zero to Hero* in the first place."

"So why not correct them?" she asked.

"I'd love to lie and say that it had everything to do with the nondisclosure I signed. But if I'm being honest, it was just easier to let people think what they wanted about me being stalked by a fan than it was to expose my sister's problems in a public way." Jake looked down at their clasped hands. "Sounds pretty selfish when I say it aloud."

Norah almost laughed. "You gave up your lifelong dream to stop your sister from having to face a media poop storm. Right after she destroyed your shot at winning a reality TV contest that would've completely altered your existence. And then you still kept helping her. Jake. The absolute last thing you are is selfish."

"Desmond is my second chance. And I know that probably sounds a little off. But it's true. I was too young to help my sister early enough in her own life to make a difference. I didn't have the resources I needed to care for her."

"It's never wrong to want to make a difference in a child's life, Jake," Norah said.

"It's hard to tell myself that and believe it. And I guess I'm still ashamed of the whole thing. Especially the way I walked away from Scarlett like that. If I wasn't embarrassed, I would've explained it to you from the beginning, wouldn't I?"

"I think you can be forgiven for not telling a stranger all of those details right away."

"I've never told anyone those things before." He admitted, bringing his eyes up to hers, his stare intense.

"Can I ask you something?"

The look in his eyes made her pulse quicken. "Of course you can."

"*Are* we?"

In her mind, she was sure she knew what he meant,

but her mouth insisted on playing dumb anyway. "Are we what?"

"Strangers."

"We did just meet this morning," she reminded him.

His thumb slid back and forth over the back of her hand, and his mouth tipped up just the slightest bit. "I know. I was there."

"So I think that qualifies as making us strangers."

"Maybe." He tipped his head and studied her face. "Do you know what the first thought I had when I saw you was?"

"Aside from wondering how you'd just become involved in a felony?"

His lips curved up even more. "Yes. Aside from that."

"What?"

"That you were a very beautiful woman. Is that too predictable?"

"No." The word came out breathless, and she tried again. "How could that be too predictable? What woman doesn't want to hear that she's beautiful?"

Jake's eyes continued to hold her. "Okay, then. Want to hear the second thought?"

"If you want to tell me."

"I do."

"All right."

"It was that you were the *most* beautiful woman I'd ever seen."

His thumb stopped moving just long enough for his hand to slide down to her wrist. There, it resumed its motion, the slightly roughened texture of his skin creating a pleasant ripple of heat that cascaded up her forearm.

"My third thought was a little less complimentary," he added. "But don't worry. It was directed at myself. I wondered how I could possibly be noticing the way you looked when there was so much at stake right then. I asked myself if I was going crazy."

The warmth crawled higher. It was all the way up Norah's shoulder, and it was making its way toward her chest. She did her best to keep her breathing from trying to catch up with the pace of her heart.

"So I've been trying *not* to think about it," Jake admitted. "But it just keeps coming back. The more I look at you, the more beautiful you get." He let out a cough. "That is hands down the cheesiest thing I've ever said. Just so you know."

The heat had fully bloomed outward now, and it was almost making Norah feel light-headed. In a good way. With an anticipation that was an ache.

"Jake…" she said.

"Hang on," he replied without force. "I'm not quite done." He shifted a bit so that he was facing her on the bed, one knee bent and pressed against the outside of her thigh. "Thinking you're attractive physically is one thing. It's the bit that gets me here." He tapped on his chest, then settled his palm gently around her elbow. "I *know* we're strangers. But every minute that passes, I feel more and more like we're not supposed to be." His fingers slid up her arm, pleasantly taking ownership of her skin. "This isn't a thing I do, and it scares the hell out of me. So if you don't feel that same pull, Norah, please tell me now."

"I can't tell you that," she whispered. "Because it'd be a lie."

"Then tell me something else." He brought his finger to her lips and lightly traced their outline.

"Like what?"

"Your middle name."

She frowned. "It's Leigh. Why?"

His mouth quirked up even more. "Bear with me. Mine's Bill."

"Bill?" Norah echoed. "Not William?"

"Nope. Plain old Bill."

"Okay."

"Birthday?"

"September 20," she said. "And before you ask... I'm twenty-eight."

"Mine's August 4, and I've got two years on you," he replied. "Pie or cake?"

"Cheesecake. Or doughnuts. I really like doughnuts."

"Me, too. And cookies. Possibly some pastries, if I can get my hands on them."

"So...not much of a sweet tooth, then?"

"Why do you think I need such an elaborate home gym?"

Norah couldn't help but laugh. "This is probably the part where I have to tell you I hate working out. I take three really short runs a week on the treadmill, and I *force* myself into a Pilates class every week."

He shifted on the bed again, this time to take both her hands. "See?"

"See what, exactly?"

"We're not total strangers anymore."

"Ah. Very clever."

Jake moved yet again, making the small gap between them even smaller.

"Now it doesn't seem too crazy that I've told you all my secrets," he said. "And I don't feel so weird when I tell you that I think I like you, Norah."

"I think I like you, too, Jake."

"I think I could like you even *more*, given the chance."

"How? By telling you my favorite kind of bread?" Norah teased.

"That," he agreed, his voice growing husky. "And maybe a few other things. I can think of one, specifically, actually. You know how you said you don't usually kiss your clients?"

Her reply was a breathy whisper. "Yes."

"What if I asked you nicely to make an exception? Just this once?"

"I might be willing to do that."

He leaned away, just an inch. And it was *far* too far away.

"I have to have more than 'might,'" he told her softly. "I need to know that it's what you want, too."

"It is." There was more than a hint of eagerness in her voice, but Norah didn't care.

His hands dropped to her waist, and he eased forward. His lips touched hers, just a light brush at first. A tiny exploration. A testing of the waters. And as quickly as their mouths met, Jake pulled back. But he immediately came in again. This time his kiss was surer, and little longer. But still too light and too fast for Norah's liking. So when he dipped his mouth to hers a third time, she brought a hand to the back of his neck to stop him from moving away again. It seemed to be the signal he was waiting for. Because just like that, the contact went from a three to a ten.

His arms engulfed her.

His hands gripped her.

His tongue danced through her mouth.

And Norah's desire skyrocketed along with it all. She didn't know if the kiss lasted thirty seconds or three minutes. Time seemed all but nonexistent. All she was sure of was that she'd never—not in all twenty-eight years of her life—experienced such a fervent, need-drenched moment. When it tapered, she was gasping for breath.

And after a few more moments, Jake leaned back, and Norah didn't protest the halt.

He dropped his hands to her waist, drawing attention

to the fact that she was quite wantonly straddling him now. This almost stranger. Jacob plain-old-Bill Pratt. A man who'd hired her to save his son. A professional acquaintance, at best. And it felt normal. And so, so right.

"I wish I had some clue as to how I can barely know you but feel this way about you anyway," he murmured.

And his words held true wonder. True marvel. Like he really couldn't fathom the feeling, but that he loved it at the same time. Norah knew exactly what he was experiencing. It was the same for her. Except for one, small thing. She was pretty sure she knew just where the unspoken, unseen connection was coming from. And she really had to tell him.

As Jacob regained control of his senses, he immediately noted a change in Norah's demeanor. One second she was gazing into his eyes, her want reflecting back up at him. The next, she was easing back, her stare dropping guiltily to her lap.

"I need to tell you something," she said softly.

Worry pricked at Jacob, and he brought his hand to Norah's chin, then gently tipped up her face. "So tell me. I can take it." He offered her a slightly crooked smile as he let her chin go. "As long as you're not about to tell me you're in love with someone else."

He meant it as a joke, but as soon as the words were out, his mind filled with the terrible idea that it might be true. Just because he knew her middle name didn't mean he knew anything else. She could have a boyfriend. A husband. Kids of her own. Everything except the very last bit filled Jacob with an unreasonable amount of tension. The thought that her heart might belong elsewhere was enough to make his gut churn. Thankfully, Norah shook her head right away.

"No," she said. "God, no. I wouldn't have kissed you like that if there was someone else in my life."

Jacob's relief was so overwhelming that it was almost laughable. Or it would've been, if Norah's expression hadn't remained so utterly serious.

He took her hands and squeezed. "Then go ahead. Hit me with your worst."

She took a deep breath and then spoke in a rush. "I know exactly how it feels to be responsible for a sister's death. Because I've always believed I should've saved my own." Norah swallowed "Greta was three years old when she was taken."

For a second, Jacob thought she was using the last word as a euphemism for the little girl's death. He quickly realized she meant it literally. Her sister had been kidnapped, just like his own son. The revelation was unexpected, and it left Jacob speechless. He didn't know what he'd been anticipating, but it wasn't that. His silence gave Norah enough time to elaborate.

"My brother and I—we're twins—were already eleven by the time she was born. I think the pregnancy was a bit of a shock for my parents. They were pretty involved in their careers, and Noah and I were occupied with our own stuff. But there she was. Thrown into our orderly lives with her own brand of chaos." Her eyes closed, and her plump, kissable lips turned up as she went on. "My brother always tried to pretend he was indifferent to her. He wanted everyone to think that he was too cool for a little baby. But he'd sneak into her room at night and tell her how perfect she was all the time."

Jacob's throat grew scratchy. He knew the feeling well. The awe of staring down at a cherubic face, and the absolute adoration that went along with it. He was also sure of what was coming next, and as much as he wished differently, he understood the pain that went along with it.

"I was more open about it, but we both loved her so much," Norah said. "I never minded when we had to do things for Greta. Noah told me after that he *did* resent the time it took away from doing what he wanted to do, and that he always felt guilty about it after."

She paused then, and opened her eyes. She inhaled another breath, this one visibly ragged. Her chest rose and fell like it hurt, and Jacob could feel the burn himself. Especially as she went on.

She told him about a sunny afternoon at the park, describing in vivid detail how cool and bright the day was, and how the leaves were just starting to turn. She explained how their parents were away, and how Greta's nanny was sick, so she and her slightly resentful twin brother agreed to take their sister out for a few hours. As she recalled aloud the purple outfit the little girl had been wearing, Jacob knew she was stalling. And he didn't blame her in the slightest. When she got to the hard bit— the terrible bit—the love and sadness in Norah's voice just about broke Jacob's heart.

"There was this slide…" she whispered. "Greta always wanted to go up, and I always said no. But that day, Noah said she could. He told me I was too overprotective, and I was. But it got my back up. We fought. And Greta never made it down that slide."

As she made the statement, Jacob's heart lurched. The thread between them solidified. The pull he felt toward her made so much more sense in light of her past. He might not be a huge believer in fate or cosmic intervention, but he was sure that this kind of grief left an indelible mark. The kind that a person couldn't help but project out to the world, even unconsciously.

Jacob smoothed his hand over her hair and kissed the top of her head. "It's not your fault."

She exhaled a small breath, but she didn't answer him.

He knew why. All he had to do was look inward. The feeling of being at fault wasn't logical. It was instinctual. Unstoppable. The need to protect a family member—and the failure to do so—overrode sense. For months after Scarlett's death, Jacob had poured over the minute details of their intersecting lives, asking the same question again and again. *Could I have done something—anything at all—differently?* He'd wondered if each tiny decision had rippled out to the one where she died. He'd had crazy moments where he'd sincerely believed that the cereal that he'd chosen—on some morning back when he was ten, and Scarlett was eight—had brought the devastating present to fruition.

He knew that he wasn't responsible for Scarlett and her mixed-up life. Their upbringing had impacted her decisions, and her bad choices had compounded them. Jacob had done everything in his power to help her beat her destructive tendencies. Yet when she'd died, he'd blamed himself. He was sure that Norah's experience was the same. Magnified, probably, because her sister wasn't much more than a baby.

Like Desmond.

Yes, the guilt there was overwhelming, too. His son had been taken right out from under his nose. Why hadn't he woken up when it happened? Why hadn't he chosen that night—like so many—to pile up the pillows and leave Desmond nestled safely beside him in the king-size bed? No, Jacob hadn't done a single thing wrong. That didn't mean his heart didn't insist that he'd failed, no matter how illogical his head told him it was.

Like she was reading his mind, Norah at last broke the extended silence. "Fault is sometimes a feeling rather than a fact, isn't it?"

Jacob trailed a finger over her arm, and his reply was

thickened by emotional agreement. "Yes. That's completely true."

"It's funny…" she said. "I don't like telling people how Greta died. But I actually do it all the time. You're the first client who didn't hear this story before you hired me. I mean, I know our circumstances have kind of broken every mold out there, but I usually use it as a starting point."

"I get it. It helps you connect with the parents," Jacob replied.

She started to nod, then seemed to change her mind and shook her head instead. "It helps *them* connect to *me*. It shows them why I'm so desperately devoted to getting their kids back. It's the reason I do what I do. My parents were given a ransom demand, and they were advised not to pay it."

"That's what the police suggested, I'm guessing?"

"Yes. And don't get me wrong… I understand that their goal is still to get the kids back. And to get the perp at the same time. But what about the parents who just want the former? Or just care more about that part than the other?" Her voice cracked a little at the end, and it made Jacob want to hold her even closer.

He kissed her head again. "Your work is invaluable. I'm sure all those parents agree."

"Not all." Her whole body shuddered with the two-word sentence, and Jacob immediately realized that everything she'd just revealed about herself had only been a preamble to something else.

Chapter 13

For the first time in the thirteen months since it had happened, Norah let herself turn her mind toward the tragedy instead of away from it. She knew it was unhealthy to keep it in. After Greta's abduction and the horrifying loss of her life, Norah had been the first to jump onto the therapy wagon. Her brother had fought against it. Her parents had understandably fallen apart, and both rejected the idea of seeking any kind of closure. Which Norah believed was a falsity anyway. But that hadn't stopped her from doing everything she could—even at that young age—to fight her way back to normalcy. To salvage her life and do something good with it. To act. To thrive. To help create a world where no one would ever have to share the same grief-riddled experience that had torn apart her own family.

"I thought I was succeeding," she told Jake. "And then I met the Morrisons."

The second she spoke the name, she was tossed back to

the moment she'd walked into their house. And the more she talked, the more vivid the memory became.

It was a sprawling rancher on a stunning acreage just outside of Mission, BC. The exterior had been tastefully manicured to look just right. From the grass to the stables to the riding circle to the figure-eight pool. Norah's feet had slowed while her eyes drank it all in. And the interior was no less impressive. Every inch of the place had been custom-decorated. Artwork worth millions hung on the walls in the foyer. Imported rugs sat under antique tables, and everything was shiny. Oak. Marble. Teak. Crystal. Even Norah—who'd grown up in a wealthy home in a sought-after neighborhood, who'd inherited her share of wise investments, and who lived without worrying about counting her pennies—had been all but blown away by the Morrisons' home.

The parents were equally impressive. The father wore a bespoke suit. The mother was decked out in diamonds that sparkled far more casually than their worth. Both were polite and soft-spoken, and Norah recalled thinking that the word "classy" had never been so apt. Despite their daughter's missing status, Mr. and Mrs. Morrison had remained quite calm, with the father being slightly more tearful than the mother. Their abducted girl was named Pearl, after her great-great-grandmother. Professional photographs showed her to be a dark-haired, bright-eyed beauty.

"I asked all the same questions I always do," Norah said. "The things that give me a baseline for the family and let me know that I can move forward. I always check that they haven't already contacted the authorities. I make sure they don't have a suspicion of who it might be, because that can backfire. I gather as much personal information as I can so that when I speak to the kidnapper, they associate me with the family and not the police."

It was easy to remember what the Morrisons had told her. In fact, all of the details were surprisingly clear, considering how much time Norah had spent avoiding thinking about it.

Pearl's mother had said she was currently missing one front tooth.

Her father had added that she'd fallen from her horse the previous week and that the small abrasion on her left forearm was still visible.

They'd agreed that Pearl had grown a couple of inches since that last photo was taken.

There had been a brief moment of discord over whether they'd last seen her at three o'clock in the afternoon, or at four, but they'd very quickly split the difference and settled on roughly 3:30 p.m.

Mrs. Morrison had encouraged her husband to disclose the fact that they didn't want to involve the police because some of the clients at his law firm were less than savory. At which point Mr. Morrison also readily and heartily said he had no enemies.

They thought it was really important that she know the wealth was Mrs. Morrison's family money, and they explained that Pearl was their last hope, conceived by in vitro fertilization—the first and only success in twelve years of trying.

Finally, they'd presented her with the note.

"It was like the kind you see in the old movies," Norah said. "Letters cut from a newspaper and pasted onto a lined sheet. There was a lock of Pearl's hair taped to it, and the demand was for a hundred thousand dollars."

"Does that seem excessively low?" Jake asked.

"Yes. It was an odd amount, considering the amount of risk involved in taking a child, and also knowing just how publicly wealthy the Morrisons were."

She told him that she'd subtly broached the subject

with the couple. But truthfully, Norah hadn't pushed it. She couldn't think of a truly logical explanation, other than that the person behind the abduction wasn't aware of just how much money the Morrisons had. In her head, she'd concluded that the kidnapper was a true amateur. She distinctly remembered thinking those exact words, because she'd felt guilty after. As though she'd somehow ranked the perpetrators of the heinous crimes and found one better or worse than the other. But she'd stowed the guilt, and she'd proceeded as usual.

"The note requested a blind drop," Norah said. "I don't usually like to agree to those. But it would've been hard to say no, considering it was the only communication we had with the suspect. That's actually a rarity. Most scenarios involve a phone negotiation. Which is where the trust building comes in. I want proof of life, obviously. And I always, always try and set things up so that I can see the child *before* I hand over the money."

"Hang on," Jake interrupted. "You take the money in yourself?"

She nodded. "Of course. There's no point in doing all the negotiating if I'm just going to chance losing the kid by sending someone else in with the cash."

"That means you're risking your *own* life, Norah." His arm tightened a little on her body, and Norah almost smiled at the retroactive protectiveness.

"It's worth it every time," she said.

Jake sighed. "I believe you. And I know it's none of my business, but that doesn't mean I hate the idea any less."

"*I* know it's none of your business, too," she replied. "But that doesn't mean I appreciate your concern any less, either."

"So long as we're on the same page."

Norah bit her lip to keep from pointing out that she would do the same for Desmond, given the opportunity.

Instead, she pushed on to the next part of her story, which set her stomach churning.

She explained how she had little choice but to do what the pasted-together note instructed. It was what the Morrisons wanted anyway, and the mother had easy access to that kind of cash through her trust. So they did as requested. They put together a duffel bag full of carefully counted hundred-dollar bills, and Norah took it to the drop site at the instructed time.

"And she wasn't there," Norah said. "There was just another note. Same style. More instructions on making another payment, twelve hours from then. For me, it was the biggest, hugest, reddest of all red flags. But they didn't want to hear it."

"What did you do?" Jake asked.

"Panicked," Norah admitted. "I couldn't fathom a reason for the second request. Progressive ransom isn't usually a thing. Once the kidnappers have the money they move on."

She explained how she was completely honest with the Morrisons about not having any precedent on which to base a decision or any suggestions on what course of action to take. She'd pushed for some other kind of action. But they just wanted to pay again anyway. The father wondered if the first drop was some kind of test. The mother grew noticeably less able to maintain control of her emotions. The twelve-hour window had ticked by in minuscule seconds. And when the wait time was finally over, the result was the same. Another note. Another demand. And then again. It happened a total of five times, over three days.

"Five hundred thousand dollars," Jake stated. "Why not just ask for that much at the beginning?"

Norah inhaled a slow breath, then exhaled it quickly. "It was Mrs. Morrison's limit. The way her parents had endowed her estate. She could take out a hundred thousand at any given time, no questions asked. The annual cap was five times that. Anything more, and the lawyers and the accountants would automatically become involved."

"Only someone close with the family would've been aware."

"Yes."

"Who?"

Tears pricked at Norah's eyes as she walked Jake through the next series of events.

At the final drop site, there hadn't been another note. Nothing to indicate where Pearl was being held, or what the little girl's kidnappers wanted. Norah had stuck around. She couldn't help herself. She'd circled the area—a relatively unoccupied playground on a dismal day—and found a place to park. Then she'd stealthily made her way back and searched out a good spot to watch.

"I broke into a run-down old minivan," she admitted, the memory making her face heat. "I jimmied the sliding door open, climbed in and waited."

Thankfully—because she still had no idea what she would've done if she'd been caught—it only took about five minutes for someone to show up to retrieve the money. And the someone it was had shocked Norah to the point that she'd actually believed she might be seeing things.

"It was Mrs. Morrison." The words burnt her throat.

"The mom?" Jake's surprise was evident.

She closed her eyes, remembering the slow-motion feel of the moment. "She walked up, dressed in plain old jeans and a hooded sweatshirt. She had her hair in a ponytail. If I hadn't just spent three days *living* at their house… sitting beside her, holding her hand, comforting her… I honestly would've thought the woman was just a doppelganger. But I was sure right then that it was actually her."

Norah had climbed from the car and walked over. Slowly. And Mrs. Morrison hadn't run off. She'd just stood there with the bag in her hands and a slightly blank look on her face. Then she'd handed over the money and said two words. *The barn.*

Norah hadn't been able to get back to the Morrison property fast enough. She'd raced there with little regard for personal safety. With little regard for anything. The streets had been a blur. By the time she hit the winding road that led to the house, her foot was practically to the floor. She vaguely recalled being thankful that the gate was open, or she might've simply rammed through it.

"I can't remember why or how..." she told Jake. "But I was holding onto that bag full of cash. It wasn't until I ran into the barn that I finally dropped it. And she was there. Pearl. She was in the trunk of this classic car, and—"

The words cut off in a sob, and Jake suddenly swept her into his lap.

"You don't have to say it," he murmured.

Wordlessly, Norah buried her head into his chest. In response, his hands ran soothingly over her body, every which way. Like he hoped that his touch might take away the never-ending ache. And she wished desperately it could. She leaned into his caresses, trying to absorb the comfort he offered.

"I should've seen something," she whispered. "But I was too late."

"How could you possibly have known?"

"There were signs that something was off. I saw Mrs. Morrison flinch every time her husband mentioned Pearl's bruises and the horse accident."

"Any normal person would pass that off as parental worry."

"But I'm not *supposed* to be normal, Jake. I failed that family. I failed that little girl. I should've noticed from the photo album they showed me that Pearl had broken her arm three times."

His hand found her cheek. "You are *not* a failure."

"How can you say that? I'm the expert. I've probably said those exact words to you at some point over the last few hours. Your friend Lockley believed it, and she's a *detective*." The tempo of Norah's words was rising, and there was nothing she could do to stop the flow. "No. You know what? You're right. I'm not a failure. I'm worse than that. I'm a fraud."

"Norah."

"For more than ten years, I've been walking around like I had the solution."

"Norah."

"I never had it. I was fooling myself. Walking into people's lives like I could save them from everything I went through. Everything my parents went through. But this whole time…this whole *entire* time, it was just because I was winning."

"Norah!"

She shook her head. "The moment I lost, everything fell apart. And I realized I've been living a lie. Only you know what else? Right this second is the first time I've been able to admit—"

Without warning, Jake's mouth smashed into hers. And for a moment, Norah's brain tried to protest. She'd wanted to finish talking. To keep ranting and raving and orally self-flagellating. But before she could even start to pull away, the need to go on with her story slipped away. Then it vanished completely. A hungry need replaced it. And even though the tears were still flowing, they took a back seat to the taste of Jake and to the feel of his hands and the press of his body against her. The kiss enveloped her. Not just physically. Emotionally, too. It sapped away the drained feeling that had been weighing Norah down, not just in the last few minutes, but for the last year.

Her fingers clutched at Jake's back. They tugged on his hair. She knew there was nothing pretty or gentle about their shared onslaught, but Norah didn't care. All she knew was that she didn't want it to stop. She wanted to drown in it. Live in it. In moments, her breathing became ragged. Her pulse was a torrential slam against her veins. And still she didn't pull away.

At some point—Norah wasn't sure when it happened— Jake became topless. She didn't know if she'd torn off his shirt, or if he yanked it up himself. Either way, she suddenly had full access to the hard ridges of his muscles. Her fingers ran over them, appreciative and wondrous.

Then the pace changed. It slowed. The hard, quick kisses morphed into long, slow ones. The touches were prolonged and exploratory instead of hurried and desperate.

Norah didn't know how long it took them both to get fully undressed. She only knew that she resented the minute it took for him through every drawer for a condom. But moments after that, she forgot the passage of minutes again. Never had she fit so perfectly with a man. Never had felt such a boundless need to let go. Arms. Legs. Skin and lips. As each part of them met, time ceased to exist. When at last it came to a rising crescendo—or maybe it would be fairer to say things were just getting started—Norah was sure the question of strangers versus not-strangers had been smashed to oblivion. It was physical. It was raw. Her lids were heavy, her heart thundered, and she was sure she'd left a small piece of herself behind with Jake, whose inhales and exhales were in perfect pace with her own. The man whom she'd just slept with. But more significantly…to whom she'd just poured out her heart. A confession that she'd never made to anyone. Not even to her brother, who knew almost everything about her.

I should feel bad about this, shouldn't I? Or at least a little strange?

But all Norah felt was the rightness.

"Tell me something…" murmured Jake after several silent moments. "And don't let your guilt answer for you. If you *had* noticed Pearl's broken arms, would you have assumed abuse?"

Norah wanted to say yes, but as she opened her mouth, she realized it would never have been her first assumption. The Morrisons hadn't shown even a hint of discord in their family dynamic. She swallowed against the thick lump in her throat and shook her head.

"No," she admitted softly. "Mrs. Morrison seemed like any other distraught parent. The Morrisons didn't tell me that not all of their in vitro attempts had failed. The wife had miscarried numerous times. And she'd miscarried again just a month earlier. She'd experienced some pretty bad postpartum psychosis over the years. And she probably had a sprinkling of PTSD, as well. Her husband just really had no idea how bad it was."

"In all the things that you did over the course of that case, was there anything you could've done differently? Anything that would've changed the outcome?"

"Probably not." Norah breathed out. "The police said that Pearl was…she might've been gone before I even got there."

"So based on what you knew…" Jake replied. "You did everything in your power to help that family."

"Yes. I really think I did."

"It's not your fault that they lied to you. It's not your fault that you didn't recognize Mrs. Morrison's mental health issues."

Unexpectedly, the heavy load on Norah's chest lifted. "I just wish—so, so much—that it hadn't ended like that."

Jake leaned in and brushed his lips over hers, then leaned away again. "Of course you do, sweetheart. But that doesn't mean you're responsible for what happened."

She stared at him, the words hitting home. She couldn't quite believe how they cut through the last year of self-doubt. How they sounded so reasonable.

"Where have you been for the last thirteen months of my life?" she asked.

His mouth turned up. "I was kind of aiming for a 'where have you been for my *whole* life' scenario, but I guess I'll take what I can get."

A vast ocean of emotion swept over Norah. She opened her mouth again. And then the old cell phone chimed with an incoming text, pulling them back to the all-important tasks at hand.

Chapter 14

Part of Jacob's heart protested as Norah jumped up and pounced on Scarlett's phone. He wanted her to stay where she was. He wanted to hear her express in words what he'd seen reflected in her eyes. At the same time, though, he was strangely unworried about having to wait. He'd known this woman for mere hours. Yet he was counting on having days, weeks and months—and beyond—to share more moments like the ones they'd just had. But right then his son needed him.

He swung his legs over the side of the bed and waited as Norah read the incoming text.

"Your brother?" he asked.

Norah nodded as she lifted her eyes from the phone. "He wants to know if we can view a computer somewhere private. He wants to send over a link to an encrypted site that his friend Spud created for us. It'll show us the video feed for your security system just as though we were watching it at the source."

A new flash of hope pricked at Jacob, but his worry about what the kidnappers might see still hovered thickly underneath it. "I ditched my laptop downstairs because I was afraid that they'd be able to hack it. But I can bring it back up here if he thinks it's necessary."

Norah read his tone perfectly. "He wouldn't tell us to do something unless he was sure there was no risk. I promise. But if it'll make you feel better, I'll double-check that there's a safeguard of some kind."

She quickly typed something, and a few moments later, the phone chimed again. She glanced down, reading for several seconds before looking back up at Jacob.

"Noah says Spud took care of everything, including the issue of potential hackers," she said. "As long as we've got the site up, no one will be able to see what *we're* seeing or access the webcam or the microphone, even if they're dialed into your computer. Spud also told him if we're feeling really paranoid, we can play a music video in the background, and that should make things extra distorted. Does that sound okay?"

Jacob nodded his agreement and grabbed his pants from the floor. "If you believe it's safe, I do, too."

"I'll tell him." Her fingers flew over the phone, and the reply was almost instantaneous.

"That it already?" Jake asked.

She looked up from the phone and nodded. "I assume so. It's basically a random series of numbers, followed by a dot-com."

"Good. I'll go grab the computer. Should be back in less than a minute." He paused with the shirt halfway to his face. "Unless you want to come?"

Her gaze flicked down, then over toward the medium-size mirror that hung on the back of the bathroom door. Her glance was quick, but Jacob knew she was analyzing her appearance. The oversize article of clothing that she'd borrowed from him was wrinkled beyond reason. Her skin was flushed and mottled, her hair a delightfully disheveled mess. Anyone who saw her would assume she'd been doing far more than kissing. Jacob *liked* it. Clearly, though, Norah was less enthusiastic.

She cleared her throat and met his eyes, her cheeks growing even pinker as she spoke. "I know we're pretending to be an infatuated couple, but that doesn't mean I can't still maintain *some* sense of decency. I think I'll be fine here."

A chuckle escaped Jacob's lips. "Okay. There's actually a brand-new, still-in-the-box hairbrush in the bathroom drawer in case you want it. I'll only be a few seconds."

As he finished getting dressed and moved toward the door, he realized something—if he'd ever had any doubts about his faith in Norah, he had absolutely none now. She'd revealed the hardest parts of her life to him. Her deepest self-doubt and her biggest so-called failure. Yet all it had done for Jacob was solidify his attraction to her. Deepen it, even.

The only thing he'd been surer of in as long as he could remember was his love for Desmond. It made his heart ache in the most pleasant way possible. Five steps into the hall, he turned around and strode back into the room. He pulled Norah into his arms and kissed her with all the overwhelming tenderness that was coursing through him.

"Just in case you were wondering…" he said gruffly as he pulled away. "There's nothing 'pretend' about my infatuation."

Then he let her go and slipped out of the bedroom again before she could answer, almost as eager to get back to her as he was to get to the next piece of evidence that would help him find his son.

* * *

As she watched Jake disappear through the door, Norah brought a hand to her lips, gently touching the rough spot left behind by the kiss. Her mouth felt pleasantly raw. And admittedly, so did her heart. Jake's parting words weren't exactly a declaration of undying love. But that would've been ridiculous, considering how short a time they'd known each other. It wouldn't even be fair to try and skirt around logic by declaring an instance of love at first sight. She'd been scared for her life the first moment she'd laid eyes on Jake. She was *still* afraid. And though her fear was now on behalf of Desmond and his father, it was no less consuming. Norah was certain that alone should be a buffer for her feelings. Not to mention the fact that she'd just confessed more to Jacob than she'd ever done to anyone else before. All of those things—from her distant past to her more recent one, and right up to the current moment—were pretty much the least romantic circumstances Norah could think of.

No caviar, no champagne, no rom-com–style meet-cute, she thought. *And yet here I am…staring at an empty doorway, wishing that Jake would reappear. Like…*really *wishing.*

Clearly, the infatuation was mutual.

Giving her head a small shake, she made herself turn away from the door. As she did, she caught another glimpse of herself in the mirror and winced as she spied the disastrous mess of her hair. She sighed and decided to take Jake's suggestion of using the brush he'd offered up. But she only managed to get the bristles through her hair about five times before the now-familiar chime of the older-model cell phone drew her attention back to the bedroom. Thinking it might be her brother again, Norah dropped the brush and hurried to grab the phone. But she didn't get there quite in time, and when she picked it up, she saw that it wasn't Noah after all. Instead, an alert for a missed call flashed across the screen. And the message included a preprogrammed name.

D.L. Lockley.

Then the phone dinged again, this time to announce an incoming text. And while Norah didn't want to accidentally intercept a private message intended for Jake, the words that scrolled across the screen held her attention. And they made her pulse thrum nervously.

Call me back. Immediately. We have a situation.

Nothing good could come of the statement. It was really just a question of how bad things were. Swallowing against the fear that jumped up in her throat, Norah sank down onto the bed. Did Lockley have bad news that related to Desmond? Or was this something else? Norah had a feeling that the other woman would only reach out if the circumstances were dire.

Please don't let it be the worst news. Anything else at all. But not that.

As she made the silent wish, her chin hit her chest, and her eyes sank shut. But her lashes barely brushed her cheeks before Jake's voice made her jerk her head up once more.

"Hey," he said. "Everything all right?"

He stood just a couple of feet away, the laptop in his hands and a concerned look on his face. And she knew her own expression had to be the source of his worry. She was biting her lower lip so hard that she had a tinny taste in her mouth, and her forehead ached from frowning. Wordlessly, she pushed to her feet, then held out the phone. In response, Jake set the laptop down on the desk, stepped forward and took the device from her hand. His eyes only hung on the screen for a second before he quickly jabbed at the keys. The sound of a line ringing on the other end immediately filled the room, and then Lockley's voice burst through.

"Jacob?" she said. "I hope to God it's you."

"Yeah, it's me," he replied. "And Norah Loblaw, as well. We have you on speaker."

"Probably just as well," Lockley told him. "Saves you the trouble of repeating what I'm about to say." She paused. "In the interest of dotting the *i*'s and crossing the *t*'s… I'm assuming neither of you called 911 about five minutes ago?"

Norah's heart dropped to her knees, and Jake's face paled.

"No," he said quickly. "Neither of us did."

"You still haven't told me what's going on, but I figured you weren't interested in involving the authorities on any kind of official basis. But either way, *someone* on your property did make that call." The detective's final statement had a grim edge.

"You're sure?" Jake shook his head as soon as he said it, then muttered, "Of course you're sure." He ran his free hand over his chin, visibly trying to contain his agitation. "I just can't imagine someone placing an emergency call without telling me about it. What was it regarding?"

"Don't know," said Lockley. "It was a hang-up."

"Well, that's good news, isn't it?" he replied.

It was Norah's turn to shake her head, and she spoke up, answering before the woman on the other end could. "No. It's not good at all. A hang-up means they send out an officer to investigate. Sometimes someone calls in and they *can't* talk."

For a second, Jake's face grew hopeful. "So I'll just call back. Tell them it was a misunderstanding, and—" He stopped abruptly, his expression drooping. "It won't matter if I do, will it? Because I could very well be the person causing the need for the 911 call in the first place."

"That about sums it up," said Lockley. "On top of which, dispatch already did their best to return the call, and all they got was a good, old-fashioned busy signal."

Jake met Norah's eyes, and she saw the mounting fear there.

"A busy signal?" he echoed.

"Yeah. 'Fraid so. It's got people a little worried. The only good news I have is that I told them I knew you and that I was close by, so I'd be happy do the follow-up myself. I'm halfway to your place already."

As if to emphasize the fact that she was on the road, a horn blared in the background.

Jake's reply was tight. "I need you to find a way to *not* do that, Lockley. Please."

"Wish it was that easy, Jake," the detective said. "Even if I wanted to, I can't falsify a report. The new system means they track my car with GPS. Not following through on this could cost me my job."

Norah swallowed an urge to ask where that concern was when Lockley was blindfolding her and tossing her into a car. There was no reason for the reminder—she was quite sure that whatever was motivating the detective, it had everything to do with personal gain and nothing to with the real difference between right and wrong. And a potential solution had suddenly popped to mind anyway.

"What if I suggest a compromise?" she asked, careful to keep her tone even rather than desperate.

"Are there compromises where the law is concerned, Ms. Loblaw?" Lockley replied.

"Every day," Norah said. "Otherwise, we wouldn't have confidential informants or offer plea bargains, would we?"

There was a pause, and another horn blared before the

other woman heaved a sigh that carried through, loud and clear. "There's compromise, and then there's *compromise.*"

The slight emphasis on the repeated word tickled at Norah's negotiating instincts.

Lockley's looking for some reassurance.

"What if the compromise in question let you come to the house without being seen?" Norah asked, tipping her eyes to Jake, silently asking for a bit of backup.

He frowned for a second, and then his face flooded with understanding. "She's right. There's definitely a way you could do that, Lockley."

"Better spit it out, then," said the detective.

"You could come all the way to my street, then cut off and park in the shed where I normally keep my old beater," Jake told her. "If you're going slowly, you'll see the gravel road about halfway to my driveway. It's definitely close enough that your GPS will be in proper range."

Another momentary pause reigned before Lockley answered. "Then what? I sit on my butt while you do whatever you want? That's not how cop-life works. It was one thing when whatever this is just involved you. When it was a favor. Now that there's an official record…"

As the detective trailed off, Jake's hand found his chin again, then swept to the back of his neck, which he clutched tightly. Norah couldn't help but step over to him. She threw her arm around his waist and squeezed. He sagged against her. She knew that this new dimension of risk only added more tension to the already ever-tightening vise.

"Just give us a small window and a little bit of leeway," Norah said to Lockley. "Text us when you get to the garage, and we'll tell you what else we've found. If you don't like what we say, we can make a new decision then."

There was a light, repetitive tap, and Norah imagined the other woman strumming her fingers impatiently on the dashboard.

"You do both realize that I'd be more inclined to cut you some slack if you'd give me a hint as to what's going on, right?" Lockley asked.

"I really can't. I'm sorry," Jake replied, his eyes sinking shut. "Please don't ask me to."

For several long moments, the only sounds in the room were the slightly fuzzy connection, the light hum of cars behind it, and Jake's even breaths. Then the woman on the other end muttered something and at last relented.

"I'm about fifteen or twenty minutes away," she declared. "When I get there, I'll give you another fifteen minutes. If I'm not convinced that everything on your end is copacetic, I'm going to drive my car straight through your fancy gate."

The line went dead right after she said it, and Norah turned and tossed the cell phone to the bed. As it hit the duvet with a dull thump, she spun back to Jake, threw her arms over his shoulders and pressed her lips to his with entirely more gusto than suited the moment. But she needed the contact. She was unreasonably glad to be done with the conversation with the detective, and she wanted to rid herself of it even more thoroughly.

"That was pretty impressive," Jake said against her mouth when she finally pulled away a little.

"What?" she replied teasingly. "My kissing skills?"

He chuckled. "That, too. But I meant the way you handled Lockley."

"Literally my job," she replied. "You should see me with an actual bad guy."

The second the words slipped out, Norah wished she could take them back. They hung in the air, a reminder that so far, this was the closest she'd come to actually being given a chance to do any negotiating.

"I'm sorry, Jake," she said softly. "I wish I *was* using my skill the way it's intended to be used."

He dipped his head down and stole another quick kiss. "Me, too. But to tell you the truth, I'm just glad you're here."

Norah's heart fluttered. "Then I guess I'd better get to work, earning my keep."

She pushed to her tiptoes, kissed him again, then wriggled free and moved to the bed. She quickly grabbed the phone and stepped over to the desk where the laptop waited. After she'd plugged the computer into its previously discarded cord, she seated herself in the chair, then lifted the lid of the computer and waited for the screen to come to life.

"The first thing I want to do is to make sure your paparazzi friends are gone," she said.

"Damn," Jake swore. "I'd almost completely forgotten about them."

"Don't worry. This is where my brain works best— creative solutions to impossible problems. If they're still here, we can see if your body double guy can draw them away."

The computer prompted a password input, and Norah angled it to him. He leaned over her shoulder and pressed his fingers to the keyboard, speaking as he did.

"The password is Scarlett. Two *t*'s, no *e*. Just in case you ever need it."

A smile played at the corners of Norah's mouth, both because of the sweetness of the nod to Jake's sister and because of the show of trust. She wondered if it was possible to like someone more by the second.

All the more reason to keep this moving and get Desmond back as fast as possible.

"I'm assuming the security system has a view of the front of the house?" she asked, typing in the link her brother had shared via text.

"Yes," said Jake. "There's a wide-angle camera at the gate. It's the main feed, and it runs in real time on the main screen in Kyle's office."

As if on cue, the website loaded, and a panoramic shot popped up. It was black-and-white, but remarkably clear. The driveway and the surrounding area were sharply defined, and even the flutter of a bird in a nearby tree was detectable. But one thing that couldn't be seen was the husband-and-wife duo with their personal news van.

Jake let out an audible breath. "They're gone."

Norah nodded. "That's good. At least we don't have to worry about Detective Lockley getting spotted."

"So what now? How do we figure out who the hell called 911? And why?"

"We can't. Not subtly, anyway. I think we should stick with the original plan and see what the security footage shows us from last night." She pointed at the digital panel underneath the video. "I'm assuming you know how to use these?"

He nodded. "Yeah, I got the lowdown from the installation guy."

She slid out of the chair and gestured for him to take over. "Show me."

Obligingly, he took her place and started to clack away on the keyboard. In seconds, he had a three-hour timeframe selected—presumably the space between when he'd last checked on Desmond and when he'd been awakened by the kidnapper's ruse—and the recorded footage loaded up. A few more clicks, and the computer screen split into six different viewpoints.

"These are all the main entry points," Jake explained, pointing at each once as he named them off. "Here's the front, which you saw before. This is the rear gate, which is more of a service entrance. Or it would be, if I needed one. There's the *old* gate, too—the one where I crashed the car—just because it's technically still a viable entrance. Each of these ones is a view of a side yard opening. And this last one is the separate driveway for the outbuildings."

He went on for a few more seconds, explaining that there were additional cameras positioned at the front door, at the pool house, and one that pointed inward to the backyard from the rear of the house. One panned across the outbuildings where the on-site staff lived, and there was also a camera over the door outside the live-in nanny's suite.

"There are really only a few spots on the property that can't be seen from *some* angle," Jake told Norah. "Deeper into the surrounding woods, obviously. And that row of bushes where we came in."

"It seems like a pretty comprehensive system," Norah replied.

"Go big or go home. That's what they say, right? I think SafeGuard probably had me marked from the moment I asked for the upgrade." Jake shook his head, his expression regretful. "But apparently it still wasn't big enough."

She gave his shoulder a reassuring squeeze. "Hit Play. With any luck, we'll see something."

"Here's hoping."

He slid over and patted the minuscule space beside him on the chair, and once Norah had squeezed in, he gave the keyboard another tap. All six windows came to life. An icon on the screen showed that the footage was moving at twelve times the normal speed, which was just slow enough to still allow them to catch any anomalies. The dark night faded away and gave in to dawn. The gardener made an appearance in the early morning. After that, there were a few instances when the blur of a person would streak through. Each time, Jake would pause it. And it was always someone who belonged there. Pardeep or Kyle. Beverly or Judy. But no one else came or went.

Viewing the whole window of time only took a few minutes. Despite that, it was exhausting. And the futility left Norah feeling like they were in a worse place than when they'd started.

"This is bad news, isn't it?" said Jake, his voice etched with a disappointment that equaled her own. "You have no idea how badly I was hoping that there'd be some hint that whoever has Desmond doesn't live and work here."

"It still could be a stranger," Norah replied. "If someone wanted to get in here badly enough, they could've spent time surveying the property. They could've figured out exactly where to *not* be seen."

"Maybe." He didn't sound like he believed it in the slightest.

She twisted to face him, and she opened her mouth to tell him that she wouldn't have offered up the theory if she didn't truly think it was plausible, but the words died before they made it out. Because her movement sent her elbow into the computer's keyboard, inadvertently changing the camera view. The split screen disappeared. In its place was a new panoramic—one that showed the outbuildings. The fresh image drew Norah's attention for just long enough for them to see a shadowy figure— hooded, dressed in dark clothing, and seemingly aware of the camera angles—darting across the lawn. She felt Jake go very, very still, watching as the covered-up person flashed in and out of sight.

"Is that live?" Norah whispered.

"Sure as hell is," he said grimly.

The words hung in the air for a long moment. Then he shot to his feet. And before Norah could issue a protest, he bolted from the room.

Chapter 15

Ten steps out of the room, common sense did its best to rear up in Jacob's head. He should've been proceeding with caution, and he knew that his impulsivity and lack of care might cost him his life. Or worse. It might result in harm to Desmond. At the very least, he could've waited for Norah. Either to ask her opinion or bow to her expertise so she could lead the way. Really, he should've been approaching the situation in any way but tearing through his house toward an unknown fate. Yet he still felt compelled to continue on the current course. If the person in the hooded shirt had his son or knew who did…

It's not even a choice, he told himself.

So he kept on running.

Up the rest of the hall.

Down the stairs, two at a thump-thumping time.

Across the expansive front entryway.

Past the library and the powder room.

Then straight out the side exit.

He leaped from the cement stoop to the ground below, where his bare feet crunched noisily on the small, decorative rocks that spread from the bottom step. Vaguely, Jacob was aware of the sting as the rough edges jabbed into his soles. He was sure he'd pay for the disregard later. He ignored it anyway. The rocks quickly gave way to an old cobblestone path, and he tore over the uneven ground.

It wasn't until he reached the arbor that marked the split in the path that he managed to stop. Even then, it wasn't that his brain won out over his body. It was indecision. Which way had the hooded figure gone? The fork in the cobblestones started at the top of the slope, widening as it went down the hill. Between the two sections was a large chunk of well-manicured lawn. At the bottom, where the two pieces of path ended, were two sets of outbuildings.

Jacob swung his attention back and forth.

On his right sat a duo of square, flat-roofed structures. The smaller of the two was a communal laundry. The larger was home to both Kyle's office and a lounge that the security guards used as a place to relax between their rounds.

On Jacob's left was the cluster of cozy residences where his staff lived. They were arranged at nearly even intervals in a horseshoe, each one with its front door facing a shared yard. The larger two backed onto the curved tree line while the smaller two had back porches One of the two bigger units was used by Judy. The second was home to Kyle. The third and fourth were vacant, though not in disrepair. Both were nicely maintained for the unlikely possibility that Jacob wanted to invite some longterm guests.

He shifted from foot to foot for another second. A wrong move could turn the already ill-advised run into a complete failure. What was the intruder's intention?

That was the question. Had the guy in the hood somehow found out they were looking at the security footage? If so, he'd have headed straight to Kyle's office to try and cut it off. If he was simply looking for a place to hide out, though, he'd undoubtedly seek the empty cottages. Either way, the person's presence likely meant that Jacob and Norah hadn't been covert enough in their operations.

A renewed wave of fear for his son swept over him, making him grit his teeth. To make matters worse, the ever-increasing worry was accompanied by a new concern—a healthy dose of guilt at his recent abandonment of Norah. Jacob had to force himself not to look back in the direction from which he'd just come. He didn't want to think about a pair of hurt, frightened, and—in all likelihood angry—hazel eyes. Maybe she was even trying to follow him, albeit with more caution than he'd exercised himself. What he needed to do right then was focus on considering the options.

He did another sweep of the area and decided that if the hooded figure was going to bust in on his head of security or Pardeep, the well-trained men would be able to take care of themselves. If they couldn't, they'd make it known. Loudly. The two empty residences, on the other hand, were as unprotected as they were uninhabited.

Choice made, Jacob turned to the left and jogged down. Up until then, his movements hadn't exactly been subtle, but his mind had now cleared enough that he at last thought to add some caution to his movements. He approached in a wide circle, then slipped in behind Judy's building. He pressed his back to the exterior wall, and he held still, listening. Unsurprisingly, there was no obvious indication that anyone was nearby. Judy was still out, and Kyle preferred the recliner in his office to any space in his house. And the intruder sure as hell wouldn't be belting out an aria.

Jacob mentally counted to ten. The trees behind the house pressed in on him, making his breaths shallow. When nothing more happened, he shook off the invisible weight and kept going, slinking along until her reached the other corner of the house. There, he paused again. When there was still no noise, he turned and moved slowly along the side wall toward the front. At the next corner, he did another quick count, then leaned out ever so slightly. No one was in sight. He scanned the yard between the buildings in search of a hidden clue.

Nothing.

Doubt crept in. Worry compounded. Jacob was sure there ought to have been some indication of the hooded person's presence, even if just in the form of trampled grass. Except everything looked pristine. The smaller houses were idle, their steps silent. Not even a breeze ruffled the decorative trees that dotted the space.

Had he made a mistake?

Jacob's eyes flicked in the direction of the security office. He couldn't actually see the structure from where he stood, but if something was amiss, he would've heard it by now.

He switched his attention back to the buildings within the immediate vicinity. Did he chance walking up to the uninhabited cottages to try and steal a look inside? Would he succeed without being caught?

Once again, Jacob started to weigh his options. But as he stared at the small houses, a thought occurred to him.

What if Desmond is inside?

The possibility made his breath catch. His heart slapped hard against his rib cage. Even when he tried to dismiss it as wishful thinking, he had to acknowledge that it wasn't an entirely implausible idea. Hiding his son under his nose would be almost ingenious.

But would they really take that kind of risk?

"Maybe," he whispered before he could stop himself.

Desperate hope surged up, and Jacob scanned the yard again, searching for any evidence of life that he might've missed. Then he saw it. The tiniest flick of a curtain from inside one of the unoccupied homes—as though someone had peeked out before quickly drawing out of sight.

Jacob fought the need for another bout of impulsive charging, and instead made himself seek out an alternative. He spied it almost right away—another window, just in view on the side of the house. It was smaller than the curtained one around the front, and it was frosted rather than covered. The important thing about it, though, was the fact that it was cracked open. All he needed to do was approach, find a way to boost himself up, then get through the window. In silence, of course.

"Piece of cake," he muttered.

He eyed the frosted pane for a moment longer, then decided that he at least had to try. Hurriedly, he reversed his path along the small house. When he reached the other end—the spot that backed onto the trees—he darted directly into the foliage. Using the greenery as cover, he picked his way over to the rear side of Kyle's residence. When he reached it, Jacob didn't pause or move with slow caution like he he'd done with his housekeeper's place. Instead, he crouched low and set forward as fast as the awkward stance would allow.

For the entire ten seconds of the run, he half expected to battle a rain of bullets. But he reached his new target without issue, and when he came to a panting halt under the frosted window, luck went his way a second time. A large bucket, probably two feet in diameter and three feet tall, sat on the ground right beside his feet.

Tossing a thank-you heavenward, Jacob grabbed the container, positioned it directly under the window, then tested its stability. When he found it strong enough, he stepped on top. From there, he pushed one hand to the wall to steady himself and used the other to reach for the window. Carefully, he gave the pane a nudge. He held his breath, bracing for a screech. His worry was unfounded. The window not only moved without a sound, it also slid completely open as well, not even making a tap as it stopped on the other side.

Jacob exhaled. He didn't waste time looking around to see if anyone was watching. He grabbed a hold of the frame and hoisted himself up. His entrance wasn't pretty. His legs and arms battled for supremacy, and he didn't even know which body part won. The important thing was that he succeeded. One second he was outside, the next he was doing his best to make sure he didn't fall headlong into a toilet.

All right. His mental voice was as much of a whisper as the physical one would've been. *Let's see what I'm up against.*

He moved stealthily toward the bathroom door, then through it. He crept along the short corridor just outside, pausing at the bedroom to steal a glance inside. The bed was made, and the closet hung open and empty. An out-of-place, slightly floral scent filling the air made him draw in a breath, but aside from that oddity, nothing appeared amiss. There was nowhere for anyone to hide—no en suite bathroom, no space under the solid bedframe, and no dark or obscured corners. The only sounds were his own, muted breaths.

Satisfied that the room was empty, Jacob resumed his search. He kept his back to the wall and took quick, quiet steps through the rest of the hallway. At the end, where he had yet another choice to go left or right, he paused to listen once more. As he tried to discern a sound, he also attempted to recall the layout of the little bungalow. He was pretty sure that one side held a small kitchen and adjoining dining area, while the other branched into a living room and a second hallway, which attached to either another bedroom or a small office. One thing he *was* almost certain of was that the curtain twitch had come from the living room.

Doesn't matter, he told himself after a fruitless few moments. *The guy could've moved to any other part of the house anyway.*

Deciding that it would be easier to make a right since he was already pressed to that side of the wall, Jacob inched forward until he was close enough to sneak a look. The quick glance was enough for him to see that he was about to enter the living room. It was also enough for him to inventory the space. He saw the front door and the small, tiled area that acted as an entryway. He spied a plain brown couch, a glass-topped coffee table, cream-colored walls and a TV. Everything in the room was familiar—Jacob himself had dictated the neutral decor. But he could still smell that same floral scent, which again struck him as odd. He had no explanation for it. And the hooded figure was nowhere to be seen.

Where is he?

Frustrated, Jacob started to lean away again. Before he fully retracted his body, though, he at last heard something—the light taps of feet hitting the rug. For a single moment, the noise was promising. Then Jacob realized a problem. The footfalls came from behind him.

Jacob spun. He was a second too late. The hooded figure pounced. He gave Jacob a surprisingly light shove—just hard enough to make him stumble back into the wall—and then kept going, heading straight for the door.

Oh no, you don't.

Jacob pushed himself up to give chase. He darted after the intruder, but the guy in the hood kicked out a foot, sending the coffee table into Jacob's path. He stumbled again. His knee cracked against one corner of the glass, and he growled a curse. By the time he recovered, his assailant had made it to the door and was already turning the handle. Jacob shoved off the sting, then made a desperate move. He leaped *over* the table and threw himself toward the intruder, hoping to knock the guy to the ground. He was nearly successful. His fingers brushed the bottom edge of the other man's sweatshirt. Then slipped off. The intruder darted out, and Jacob slammed to the ground, his chin smashing to the tiles.

Groaning at the painful impact, he lifted his head and fixed his eyes on the other man's receding back. His window of opportunity to catch up was closing. There was no choice but to take a breath and get up. He pushed to his knees, grabbed a hold of the doorframe and pulled himself back to his feet. As he stood, a sharp stab shot through his head, and when he took a step, his vision blurred a little. The hood-wearing figure—who appeared to be moving at a puzzlingly light jog rather than a sprint—was not quite at the other end of the cluster of little houses.

Go! Jacob's mind hollered. *You can still get him!*

He fought against the dizziness. He made himself take a single, loping stride and was immediately rewarded with a wave of nausea. Two more steps, and the world bounced. Jacob couldn't stop, though. He didn't dare. Except when he'd pressed himself to go a little farther, he saw something that made him halt despite his resolve not to.

As the unknown invader made his way toward the slope that led up to Jacob's house, a second figure came darting out from behind one of the houses on the other side. For a moment, Jacob assumed that the newcomer was joining the hooded man. He barely had time to register the idea that his issues might be doubled before clueing in that it wasn't another intruder. It was Norah. And her appearance made him do a seconds-long double take. She'd scavenged a pair of pants from somewhere, and she'd found her shoes. She also now wore a borrowed T-shirt, which she'd cinched up somehow so that it rested at her waist. Her hair had been slicked into a small ponytail that stuck out in a way that would've been cute and amusing under other circumstances. As it was, Jacob only just managed to take everything in before he realized what was about to happen. She was going to accidentally go head-to-head with the hooded stranger.

Both the blurriness around Jacob's eyes and the roil of his gut disappeared. Protective instinct took their place. It surged through him and propelled him forward, pain and possible concussion forgotten. Thankfully, the need to keep Norah safe made Jacob fast as well as oblivious. He bolted at full speed toward the intruder, reaching him just seconds before Norah. His hands closed around a pair of jeans-clad legs, and they fell together to the ground. The tumble sent a wave of that floral aroma up Jake's nose, but he barely noted the strangeness before their fall turned into an awkward roll down the small hill. Thankfully, when they came to a bumping halt, Jacob was on top, pinning the uninvited guest to the grass. His triumph was only momentary. The tumble had knocked the hood free, revealing a face. A *female* face. One that Jacob knew quite well.

Chapter 16

For a split second, Norah couldn't do anything except stare. It wasn't just the way Jake had suddenly exploded out in front of her. It was the result. Because if she'd had to make a guess as to who'd be under the hoodie, she'd never have hazarded a supposition that it would be a woman who looked like a kindly grandmother. Yet there she was. Disheveled gray hair just touching her shoulders. Distinctly wrinkled face, thin eyebrows and a mouth that was creased into a permanent semi-smile.

Obviously, there was nothing to say someone's grandma *couldn't* be a kidnapper, but the woman on the ground was nowhere near the kind of person Norah would have expected to be sneaking around on Jake's property. The turn of events caught her off guard. And then her surprise compounded. Because as Jake eased off the older lady and spoke up, his single word was infused with as much confusion as Norah felt.

"Beverly?" he said.

It only took Norah a moment to figure out why she recognized the name, and she couldn't stop herself from addressing the other woman directly. "You're the retired nurse who looks after Jake's son?"

Beverly carefully pushed to a seated position, her nervousness obvious in the tremor of her voice. "I am." Her eyes flicked to Jake, and she added a question, sounding stronger. "Where *is* Desmond?"

Jake's face abruptly changed from puzzled to guarded. "Is that a real question?"

The grandmotherly woman blinked. "I... What?" Then her gaze slide back to Norah. "Who are you? What's going on?"

"I think we should be asking the questions." Jake's statement was almost a snap, and it prompted Norah to kneel down beside him so she could place a hand on his elbow as a quick warning. She needed him to take her lead. To be softer. And after the briefest hesitation, he slid back a bit. Still seated, he took a nonthreatening pose— knees bent, forearms resting on top of them.

"I think what Jake means is that you scared the heck out of us," Norah said, her tone kind. "We saw you running around with the hood, and he assumed the worst."

Beverly's shoulders dropped just a little, and she muttered, "This is so humiliating."

Norah let out a small laugh. "Is it worse than meeting your soon-to-be stepson's nanny for the first time while your soon-to-be husband tackles her to the ground?"

The woman's thin, almost-white eyebrows lifted. "You're getting *married*?"

Relieved that her bit of distraction had worked, Norah offered an enthusiastic nod. "I want to have the wedding near Christmas. I've always had this dream of snowflakes falling while I walk down the aisle. But Jake says with the Vancouver weather the way it is, I'd probably get sopping wet instead."

"He's not wrong." Beverly's lined face creased into a small smile.

Norah studied the woman for a moment. If she was feigning any of her reactions—from her embarrassment to her surprise to her amusement—then she ought to have been thinking about trading in her nanny status for a role in an award-winning movie.

"Okay," said Norah, smiling back. "He might be right about that one small thing. But I'm assuming that he *is* wrong about you being a knife-wielding maniac who's hell-bent on stealing his buried treasure."

Unexpectedly, an obvious blush crept up the older woman's cheeks. It filled the deepest of her wrinkles with crimson, and extended in a pink, lacy pattern all the way up to her hairline.

Why is she—oh! The explanation clicked for Norah. "You were meeting someone?"

Beverly's color deepened even more, and her attention tipped to Jake for a second before coming back to Norah, who was now wishing she could dismiss her "fiancé" for a minute or two. But she had a feeling he wouldn't budge, so she didn't bother asking.

"I'm not here to judge," she said instead, dropping a conspiratorial edge into her words. "In fact, I'm impressed. And happy for you. And I'm sure my dearest fiancé is, too, in spite of his general grumpiness."

The older woman made a bit of a face—clearly doubtful as to the veracity if Norah's claim—and her eyes once again turned to Jake. And her glance at last hung on him for more than a millisecond. Then she exhaled a heavy sigh and cleared her throat.

"I guess it's confession time," she said.

"I'm all ears," Jake replied dryly.

Norah gave him a nudge and focused on Beverly. "I'm a sucker for a good romance. Tell us."

The grandmotherly woman dusted a bit of grass off her pants, then spoke in a rush, sounding more like a guilty teenager than a woman with dozens of years of life experience. "It's Kyle. And I'm sorry for not saying something sooner, Mr. Pratt. At first, it was simply because it was a one-time thing. Then I guess it became a longer fling, but I knew it wasn't ever going to be long-term. He's fifteen years younger than I am. Not that that's a bad thing. Just…never mind that part. We've been meeting in that guesthouse." The color in her face went an impossible shade of crimson. "This sounds bad."

Norah put a reassuring hand on her forearm. "It's not bad at all. Look at Jake and me. We've barely met, and we decided to get married. We all do crazy things for love."

Beverly shook her head. "Kyle and I aren't getting married. In fact, we split up about two weeks ago." She sent an apologetic look Jake's way. "I really am sorry. And humiliated."

Jake smiled a smile that looked like it hurt. "It's fine, Beverly. I don't begrudge you a personal life. What kind of boss would I be if I did? But I don't understand. If you broke up…then why are you out here sneaking around right now?"

Beverly frowned. "This morning—out of the blue, really—Kyle texted me and asked me to meet him at our usual spot. It was kind of a cryptic message. A little unlike him. Initially, I told him no. He didn't respond. So I asked him why he wanted to meet, but he didn't answer that text, either. Then I called and got his voice mail. I started to worry, and I decided I'd better just come and see for myself what was going on. Except he wasn't there when I arrived. And, well…you know the rest."

Her words made Norah's instincts come to life. She

could feel every one of her hairs standing on end with nervous anticipation. She was glad her employment experience had trained her to keep a calm exterior under pressure-filled circumstances, because without it, she was sure she would've given something away. As it was, she was able to school her face into nothing more than a mildly curious expression.

"Is that weird?" she said. "Does he normally do things like that?"

The older woman shook her head again, this time emphatically. "No. He's compulsively on time and completely reliable. Mr. Pratt can vouch for that, I'm sure."

Jake nodded. "Kyle's an exemplary employee. Comes up with plenty of innovative things to make his security team operate more efficiently."

Norah's tingle of unease grew. Something was off. She was sure of it.

In an attempt to silently communicate her concern, she brought her eyes up to Jake's. "Maybe he caught Philip's flu."

"That's a possibility," Jake replied, his tight nod telling Norah that he understood she meant something more. "We'll find out for you, okay, Beverly?"

"I don't want him to think I went to you, trying to stir up any problems," Beverly said, sounding reluctant.

"I promise I won't let that happen," Norah assured her, pushing to her feet, then holding out her hand to help the other woman up. "Jake and I can go check on him. I wanted to meet him anyway."

"Are you sure?" Beverly asked.

"We're sure," Jake interjected. "I gave you the day off, remember?"

"You did." A frown creased the older woman's forehead. "Where did you say Desmond was?"

Norah's pulse tapped a nervous beat. It was the sec-

ond time the woman had asked. And it was understandable. Her job *was* to take care of Jake's son. So how easy
was she going to be to fool? But Jake was clearly thinking more quickly than Norah herself, because he spoke
up right away, his voice calm.

"Des is sleeping," he said. "Again. Think it must be
a growth spurt. But I got this new app on my phone that
works with the baby monitor to let me know if he wakes
up."

Beverly didn't look completely convinced, but she nodded just the same. "Technology never ceases to amaze
me." She stole a quick look back at the little cluster of
homes. "After you talk to Kyle, can you please let me
know that everything's all right?"

"Will do," Jake replied. "Go enjoy the rest of your day
off. We'll either pop by your suite or send you a text as
soon as we have any news. Sorry about tackling you."

"No worries. *I'm* sorry for not telling you about me
and Kyle." The grandmotherly woman blushed again, then
quickly turned and headed back toward the main house.

The moment Norah was sure the other woman was out
of earshot, she voiced her worry. "I don't like this, Jake.
Something feels off."

"Aside from the obvious, you mean?" His eyes hung
on Desmond's nanny, then shifted to the staff quarters,
then came back to Norah again. "Do you think Beverly
was lying? That she knows something?"

She shook her head. "No. She seemed genuinely confused."

"She left pretty easily."

"I think she was just really embarrassed."

"She also knew exactly how to avoid the cameras."

"She knew how to *almost* avoid them," Norah corrected.

"Maybe we shouldn't have let her go at all," he said,

his eyes seeking the now-empty spot where Beverly had disappeared.

"If I thought she could tell us anything, I would've asked her a few more questions," she replied.

She could tell Jake was growing antsier by the second. He ran an agitated hand over his hair, then scrubbed at his chin, and his jaw ticked.

"Well, Kyle called her here for *some* reason," he said.

"Jake."

He didn't appear to have heard her. "We need to go talk to him," he said. "Right now. More than right now. Five minutes ago." He spun and took three quick strides before noticing that Norah wasn't with him, and then he turned back, impatience and worry fighting for supremacy over his features. "Are you coming?"

"I am," she replied. "But we need to talk about something *else*, first."

"What?"

"Trust."

He gave her a blank stare.

"Do you trust me?" she asked.

His expression morphed in surprise. "I thought we established that already."

"So did I," she stated. "But then you ran off. Without any warning. Without any clue what you were headed into. And you did both of those things without *me*."

He took a few steps in her direction, but Norah inched back. The adrenaline that had been propelling her along was finally wearing off, and the ebb reminded her just how scared she'd been on Jake's behalf. How worried she'd been that he was about to screw up everything she'd been trying to help him do. Now that she was calmer, her mind went back to those moments after he'd left.

It had taken her a few seconds too long to clue in that he hadn't been about to come back. By the time she'd moved into the hall, he was gone. And she'd had to draw on all of her willpower to stop herself from simply dashing after him. There'd been a mental fight. Thankfully, caution had won out. She'd managed to collect herself so she could come up with a plan that would stop Jake from getting killed by the supposed intruder. A subtle approach. And yet here he was, trying again to take an uncalculated risk. It wasn't right or okay or anything close.

Suddenly, Jake's arms were around her, and Norah realized she'd said the last part aloud. And she was crying, too.

"I'm the damn expert," she said, punctuating the words with a moderately embarrassing sniffle.

Jake leaned away and looked down at her, guilt written all over his face. "I'm sorry. I know you're supposed to be the boss."

"Not just *supposed* to be."

"I know you *are* the boss," he amended without protest, swiping his thumb over her cheek to clear away her tears.

"All of this scared me, Jake."

"I'm sorry," he repeated. "I meant that. I just..."

"You're worried about Desmond. I understand. I do. I really do. But think about this...if you had waited just *two* seconds, I would've told you that I thought the lurker looked like a woman. I would've asked you if you recognized anything about her. Maybe her gait. Maybe her shoes. And maybe you would have, or maybe you wouldn't have, I don't know." Norah could hear her own voice rising, and she paused to draw a steadying breath, then went on. "But then think about *this*. What if it hadn't turned out to be Beverly? What if it had been person with a gun? Or the actual kidnapper? Do you honestly think you would've come out on the better side of things?"

Jake's shoulders dropped. "I don't know."

She shook her head. "The odds wouldn't have been in your favor. I think you can concede that no matter how big and strong you are, you're not bulletproof."

"So what do you want me to do? Take a back seat while you question Kyle? I trust you, Norah, and I do bow to your expertise. But the thought of *you* being at risk scares *me*."

She met his eyes. "I don't think we're going to find Kyle here."

"What do you mean?"

"If he was in his office, or even in his house, wouldn't he have come running out to see what the commotion was about? He's your head of security."

Understanding passed over Jake's features, then faded in undisguised concern. "It's him. He's the one who—" He stopped abruptly, like he was unable to say it aloud.

Norah placed a hand on his forearm. "We don't know that yet."

"But that's what you believe."

"I'm just trying to follow the evidence. And to me, the evidence says that Kyle either isn't here, or else he *is* here, and he doesn't want us to know. Either way, I think we should be extra cautious right now."

"What do you suggest?"

Truthfully, Norah just wished they had more time. She needed to regroup. To mentally sort through things. She wanted to think about why Kyle might've reached out to Beverly. And question if it was really Kyle at all, or if it was someone trying to make them *think* it was him. And what it all meant for Desmond was a whole other thing. All of that made her want to sit and sort through it. But she knew that if the security guard was watching, he might find it suspicious if they simply walked away.

She gave her head a slow shake. "No. You're right. We do need to check in."

Jake's relief was palpable. "Should we try the house, or his office?"

"We might as well start where we are," Norah replied. "If he *is* there, you lead the conversation. Keep it simple. Stay as close to the facts as possible. You saw someone on the property who you didn't recognize and when Kyle didn't come, you panicked."

"That's truer than I'd like it to be," he said.

She nodded. "And that's what makes it believable. Tell Kyle that when you realized your mistake, you got worried about him. Make a bigger deal about your concern for *him* than about anything else. When I say that I have a headache, that's our cue to leave, okay?"

"Got it." He slid his hand into hers, and they started moving down the hill toward the staff residences. "I'm actually *glad* you're the boss, by the way."

"You say that now…"

"Maybe I'm the kind of guy who likes a woman in charge."

"If you are, then you're in luck. My brother always says I have a real knack for telling people what to do."

"And as an added bonus, they probably don't even know you're doing it," Jake said.

"I'm not going to disagree with that," Norah replied.

He chuckled, but the moment of lightheartedness disappeared as they neared Kyle's home. The small house appeared to be still and—even in the sunlight—dark. And the closer they got, the more Norah's unease increased. When they reached the door, and Jake's firm but friendly knock sent it creaking open a bit, she wasn't surprised.

"I'm going to assume this is a bad sign," whispered Jake.

"It's definitely not good," Norah murmured back.

"What do we do? Go right in? Call out and see if he answers?"

Before she could even think about which option would fit best, a thick breeze kicked up from behind them, sending the door the rest of the way in. Its handle banged the wall on the other side. But the sound faded into the background as the living room came into focus.

Norah's heart didn't just drop. It sped at a hundred miles an hour from her chest to her feet. Because sticking out from under the coffee table was a scrap of blue fabric, and there was no mistaking it for what it was—a baby blanket.

Chapter 17

To his credit, Jake kept his word to let Norah be in charge, and he didn't go rushing forward. Although, right then, she wouldn't have blamed him if he had. She would've forgiven him, too. But he just stood still, his eyes roving over the room. So Norah took an inventory, as well.

Everything was tidy, homey and minimalist. A pair of boots sat on a rubber mat. A plaid jacket hung on a hook. The couch had a dip in one cushion, and the other side held a small stack of crossword puzzle books. A shelf took up one corner, and on it were five books and a photo of a man holding an enormous fish. The nearest wall held a beautiful piece of Haida art. The farthest one was empty. And the only thing that didn't fit in was the baby blanket.

After a few silent moments, Jake cleared his throat and said her name in an emotion-rough voice. "Norah."

She squeezed his hand. "It's okay, Jake. I don't think Desmond is here."

She left everything else unsaid—any suppositions or suggestions on where he might be, or why the blanket was there—and pulled herself free so she could step through the doorframe. There were no sounds. No lights. But the scent of burnt coffee wafted from elsewhere in the house, making Norah move with caution. With Jake on her heels, she tiptoed from the living room to the hall, then made her way carefully into the kitchen. There, she found the source of the smell. The coffee machine had been left on—clearly for some time—and the last remnants of the liquid had become heat-sealed to the bottom of the pot.

Norah walked over and flicked it off. She exchanged a look with Jake, then spun in a circle, eyeing the small space. Nothing looked odd. There was a single mug, a single plate and a single knife in the sink. The garbage can was empty, the fridge devoid of magnets. A tear-away calendar rested on the counter beside a very old, rotary-style phone.

"He's talked about that phone," Jake said softly. "He keeps it in case the power ever went out for an extended period of time. No electricity and no charge required."

"Well-prepared," Norah replied, her voice equally low. "That's Kyle."

Together, they moved out of the kitchen. They paused for a brief look into the bathroom before carrying on in silence to the bedroom. Even though Norah was sure they'd find no one inside, she put up her arm just outside the door to ensure that they entered with extra caution. And she was right about the room being as empty as the rest of the house. Except for one anomalous thing. A metal container sat in the middle of the bed, its lid hanging open. For a second, Norah thought it was the kind used by small vendors to hold cash. But then Jake spoke, his words alerting her to the more dangerous truth of the box's purpose.

"Why the hell does Kyle have a gun safe?" he said.

"Your security team isn't armed?" Norah replied.

Jake shook his head. "Not with guns. They carry Tasers. And Kyle knows how I feel about keeping this type of weapon on the property." He laughed humorlessly. "Not that I—apparently—really understand anything about what motivates Kyle." He took a step closer to the bed, then turned back to her, his skin notably paler. "The gun isn't here."

And Norah didn't need any of her training to hear the question underneath the statement. *What does this have to do with Desmond?*

If Norah hadn't been standing in front of him right then, Jacob would've lost his mind. As it was, she was the only thing anchoring him. He felt like his world was crumbling. Worse than that. It was as though it had started to crumble before he was made aware, and he was only just catching up with that fact right now. Desmond was gone. His head of security was sleeping with his nanny and he'd had no clue. And somewhere in there, that same man—the one whom Jacob had picked to guard his home, life and son—was likely at the source of everything that had gone horribly wrong.

His eyes slid to the empty gun box.

He'd been so careful in getting to know his staff. He was so sure that they could be trusted. How could he have been so mistaken?

"Jake?" Norah's voice was soft and worried, and he knew it was because his ragged expression probably matched the ragged feeling in his heart.

"I don't know what to do," he admitted. "I have no idea why Kyle would take Desmond."

"We don't know that he did."

"What other explanation is there for all this? It fits. It explains why the kidnapper would have access to the cameras so that they could watch me. He didn't have to get onto the property because he *lives* on the property." He exhaled something that felt close to a growl. "I swear to you, when I find him…"

"Let's just take a minute, okay?"

She put a hand on his arm, guided him to the bed, then pressed him into a seated position a few feet from the gun safe. For a second, he thought he should keep protesting. The last thing he needed was to be inactive. It sure as hell wasn't the right time for stillness. Except when his rear end hit the mattress, Jacob realized that sitting down was exactly what he needed right then.

He started to fire a grateful look in Norah's direction but stopped, midlook, when he caught the expression on her face. She was frowning at the lockbox, her lower lip pulled in between her teeth.

"What?" he said right away. "Is something else wrong?"

"This is brand-new," she replied. "The sticker's still on it."

"Do you think it means something?"

"I don't know, but…"

"What?"

Her gaze left the empty case and came to him. "How long has Kyle been working here?"

"Three years," Jacob replied.

"And he's never said he wants a weapon? Or brought it up at all?"

"No. His younger brother was badly injured in a firearms accident when they were kids, so Kyle's never been a big fan of guns, either. Despite his job."

"No criminal record at all?" she asked.

"No. He disclosed to me that he had an expunged drunk and disorderly charge from his twentieth birthday, but aside from that, he's never had more than a parking ticket," Jacob said. "I had a full background check done when I first hired him, and I had it *re*done when I got custody of Desmond. All of my employees are as close to spotless as it comes. Are you thinking something was missed somehow?"

"I don't know. In my experience, records aren't all that easy to fake. Not if your background checker is thorough. Someone always misses a detail somewhere. But something just isn't sitting right."

As Jacob watched, Norah moved closer to the gun box, her lips pursing thoughtfully as she bent over to get a better look. He was curious, but he kept patiently quiet. After a couple of moments of staring, her eyes widened. Quickly, she straightened up again. Then she spun toward the nightstand, grabbed a tissue from the box there, and used it to pull a slip of paper out of the case.

"This is a receipt for the box *and* the gun," she said after studying it for a second. "Both bought this morning." She set the slip of paper down again, her pretty features settling into an even deeper frown. "I guess it could be explained away by the fact that he never needed a gun until right this second."

"But you don't believe it," Jacob stated, trying unsuccessfully to read the trajectory of her thoughts.

"It just makes me have even more questions. Like… why leave this box out here like this? Why leave the receipt *in* the box?"

"A big hurry and then an oversight?"

"I don't know, Jake. I might buy that idea if it weren't for everything else. There's been *far* too much attention to detail for me to believe that whoever did this just ran off in a careless rush."

He couldn't disagree. Whoever had taken Desmond had spent a great deal of time planning. As sick as that made him feel, Jacob had to acknowledge that someone so fastidious wouldn't simply forget about a gun case and a receipt.

"It's some kind of setup," he murmured.

"You can probably tell by now that I hate jumping to conclusions…." she said. "But that's where my mind is going, too."

"I just don't understand *why*. I've never had any beef with Kyle. We've never even had a disagreement. I let him run the property how he wants. I pay him well." He gave his chin a scratch and muttered, "I really just don't get it. At all."

"I wish I had an explanation for you." Norah sounded like she meant it with her whole heart. "All we can do on our end is to keep looking for clues until we find one that sticks."

"Even if that means letting ourselves fall for the setup?"

She sank down beside him and grasped his hand. "Yes. Because we have no other choice, and because it's the only way we're going to get your son back. And we're not really falling for it. We have an advantage in that we suspect it *is* a setup."

She was right. Logically, he knew it. Except he couldn't shake the underlying fear for his son.

"Norah…" He trailed off, uncertain he wanted to hear the answer to the question he was about to ask.

"Yes?"

"Do you think Kyle took Desmond with no intention of giving him back?"

Norah's pause was a second too long, and Jacob knew the truth of it before she even replied.

"I think that when you take away the money aspect,

there are only a few other, plausible explanations." Her tone was soft. "And none of them is very good, Jake."

The dread that had been layering on since the morning thickened to a crescendo. He didn't want to think about even *one* of those other reasons.

Jacob swallowed against the rawness in his throat, but he didn't bother to disguise the worry that carried through in his voice. "So I guess we have to go to the security office and see what else Kyle left behind."

"Yes. And I don't think we should wait very long," she told him. "Lockley will probably be calling any second, and if we don't have anything to update her with, we might be dealing with another problematic risk."

"Damn," he swore, pushing to his feet as he spoke. "I legitimately forgot she was on her way."

Norah stood, too, then reached into her pocket and pulled out Scarlett's phone. "I remembered for you. And speaking of phone calls…one other thing I can do is to call my brother again and see if he can dig up anything else on Kyle. His guy is good at finding the things other people don't want to see."

"I should probably take whatever help I can get, right?"

"He's the best. What's Kyle's last name?"

"Berguson."

"Okay. Give me thirty seconds."

Jacob stayed where he was as Norah quickly dialed her brother's number. He only half listened as she gave her latest request in the teasing, bickering way she and her brother seemed to share. Jacob's mind was too occupied with the current turn of events to pay much attention to the details she gave out, and he paced the room, trying to calm his nerves. Neither his head nor heart wanted to believe what was happening. It was hell enough to have had his son taken from him. The fact that it was someone so closely tied to his life made his gut churn. What did the security guard want with Desmond?

Norah's voice cut through the tumble of his thoughts. "Jake?" she said. "All done here. Noah will call us back as soon as Spud has anything, even if that anything is nothing."

He stopped walking and faced her, taking in her features, using them to soothe himself. He couldn't believe that he'd crawled out of bed this morning not knowing she existed. It didn't seem possible. Spurred by the deep seed of ever-growing emotion, Jacob reached out and tugged her in for a slow, hard kiss.

"I don't know how the hell I'd be coping if you weren't here," he said as he pulled away.

Her cheeks were pleasantly pink. "Just doing my job."

He knew she was saying it lightly, but he quite suddenly longed for something more serious, and he reached up to trace the line of her elegantly arched cheekbone. "I sincerely hope you think of me as more than a job."

"You have to know that I do."

"Maybe I just want to hear it."

Norah's hazel eyes held him. "How about this, then? When I got up today, I was facing another emotionally challenging day after another sleepless night. I've spent the last year waking up and going to bed like that. Questioning every choice that I've made over the course of my entire adulthood. But somehow, since meeting you this morning, I've felt a renewed sense of purpose."

"That helps."

"It *helps*?"

Despite his desire from moments earlier for solemnness, Jacob's lips curved. "I just want to know a little more."

"Like what?" she replied.

"Which part cinched the deal? Was it where I jumped

on you in that parking lot? Or the moment when you kicked me? Or how I begged for you help?"

"The part where you showed me the picture of Desmond," she replied, her voice soft and earnest. "When I saw his face, and then when I saw your expression… I could tell how much you love him. It reminded me why I do what I do. And it made me question why I *wasn't* doing it. So I made a choice. I took a chance and went with the man who I was pretty sure had just orchestrated my kidnapping. And that man turned out to be you. The only person I've been able to tell about any of the things that made me quit working in the first place."

"Any regrets about that?"

"Not one."

"Then can I make you an offer?"

"Yes."

Jacob's chest burned with a desire to say things he had no place saying to a woman he'd known for mere hours. He forced himself to stay within reasonable bounds.

"When this is done…when we have Desmond back… leap in with me," he said.

"Leap in?" Norah echoed.

"With two feet. Like the expression says. I don't want something short and sweet. I want the long haul. Or at least the hope for it."

"How could I possibly say no to that?"

He bent his neck and kissed her again, this time gently. "I promise to make it worth your while."

She slid her hand to his and clasped it tightly. "It already is."

He gave her fingers a squeeze, and in silent agreement, they made their way out of the bedroom. The slipped up the hall, then into the living room. Jacob refused to look at the familiar blue blanket tucked into the couch. No matter how badly he wanted to pick it up and see if he could catch a whiff of his son's baby-powder scent, he knew that no good would come of it. Eyes forward, brain focused on the feel of Norah's hand in his, he led the way out the door.

They stepped down the stairs, then across the lawn toward the other outbuildings. Jacob made sure to keep their pace slow and casual, but he also took note of their surrounding, searching for anything that seemed odd. Nothing did, but he had no illusions. Someone was definitely watching their every move. Probably doing their best to assess what he and Norah knew. Undoubtedly wondering if their scheme—whatever that was—had worked.

Once again, the air felt heavy all around. The weight of what they were about to walk into—the unknown of it—seemed to suck out the oxygen. The clouds that blotted out the sun didn't help, either. By the time they reached the office, Jacob could swear that he had ten pounds of lead bearing down on his extremities. He ached everywhere except for the hand that gripped Norah's palm. But even that anchor wasn't quite enough to help him fight a wave of cold fear for his son as they reached the walkway just outside the building.

Desmond is going to be okay, he told himself when they paused. *Whatever's in there isn't going to tell us the opposite.*

Drawing on the self-directed reassurance, he took another step forward. Norah, though, didn't budge, and he was forced to stop again and turn her way.

"It's open," she whispered, nodding at the building.

Jacob swung his gaze up, and he belatedly spotted the crack between the door and the hinges. He exhaled.

"I know you're still the boss," he murmured, "But I think for sheer practicality reasons, you should get behind me."

"Not that I want to argue with you when it's to my benefit…" she replied. "But where, exactly, is the practicality?"

"I know the layout of the building, for one. And even if that weren't true, there's also something else to consider."

"What?"

"Chivalry."

He didn't wait for Norah to respond—he had a feeling she'd try to fight the old-fashioned excuse—and instead freed his hand from hers and quickly stepped in front of her. On light, still-bare feet, he ascended the stairs and moved toward the door. Mentally, he counted down from five and prepared to lean forward. He was aware that by the time he silently hit two, Norah had joined him on the small porch. He didn't try to send her back. It wouldn't have done any good, anyway. Jacob was thankful, at least, that she didn't try to stop him from going first. He might've tossed out the word *chivalry* like he was half kidding, but the truth of the matter was that he felt compelled to keep her safe.

He drew in a small breath and started to peer past the door. He stopped, though, as a mildly acrid scent filled his nose. It was as out-of-place as the floral aroma had been back in the small guesthouse. The difference was that this particular smell made him want to grit his teeth and back away. Jacob made himself take another step forward instead.

What the hell is—

The thought jarred to a halt, because the pungent scent—and his reaction to it—quite suddenly made horrifying sense.

Chapter 18

Jake's abrupt spin and the stricken expression on his face filled Norah with dread. She grabbed a hold of his arm and prepared for the worst. She already felt cold all over. Her heart seemed to be beating too fast and too slow at the same time. And when Jake spoke, the world swam so badly that she almost missed what he said.

"We should go." His voice was rough and vehement at the same time.

"Go?" she replied, startled.

Her attention flicked over his shoulder, and he shifted as though to block her from spying anything inside the building.

"You don't want to see any of that. *I* didn't want to see it." There was sorrow in both statements, and Norah's heart lurched.

"Jake. Is it—"

"No." He breathed out. "It's not Desmond. But that

doesn't mean it's good. We can head back to the house and wait for Lockley to call. We'll find another way."

"Another way to do *what*?" Norah replied.

"All of this."

"Are you serious?"

"Utterly."

He grabbed her hand and moved as though to pull her away. But she stood her ground.

"Whatever's in there...we can't just walk away," she said firmly. "If we're going to find your son, then we have to do this."

Jake's face told her that he wanted to argue some more, and quite suddenly Norah was sure that while he'd been shaken by whatever he'd seen, this insistence on leaving was for her sake.

"I know you're trying to protect me," she said, "And you have no idea how much it matters to me that you care enough about me that you'd pause our investigation into Desmond's kidnapping just for my sake. But I won't let you do it. Even if I have to kick you in the shins one more time."

He didn't crack even a hint of a smile. But he did exhale again, and then issued a forced nod and stepped aside. His reluctance to let her pass was still clear. But it would have to do.

With a quick, self-directed order to maintain calm, Norah slid past Jake and into the building. For a second, all she noticed was the decorative details of her surroundings. It was a comfortable-looking space that seemed like more of a man cave than anything else. Four individual recliners dominated the room, and a TV with a gaming system sat in front of them. One corner housed a small fridge, and a few dented street signs—*Yield, Stop* and *No Exit*—hung from the rear wall. The carpet was Berber, the color scheme a pale shade of army green mixed with browns and black. Nothing extraordinary.

Then Norah's gaze panned out a little. And her throat closed. Because there was one, all-consuming thing that she should've seen first.

A compact, fiftyish man in a khaki uniform-style outfit was sprawled out on the floor. One of his arms rested at an awkward angle on a footstool while the other was stretched straight across the carpet. A thick pool of crimson surrounded his head, looking like a macabre, satiny pillow beneath his gray-speckled hair. His eyes were open but devoid of life. There was no doubt that the man was dead. There was also no doubt about the source of his demise. A blood-spattered hammer was lying just two feet away.

Wooziness hit Norah hard, and she didn't protest at all when Jake's hand came out to steady her.

"Is it Kyle?" she asked, her voice sounding unnaturally loud in the small space.

His reply was gruff. "Yes. That's him, unfortunately."

"I'm sorry."

"Not as sorry as I am." Jake stared down at the man, shook his head, then brought his eyes back to Norah, concern darkening his irises to a forest green. "How the hell did it get to this point? My son is missing, and I've got a murdered man—a man I *liked* until about ten minutes ago, dammit—on my property."

She leaned into him, offering what minimal comfort she could in a sideways hug, then started to add some words of solace. But she stopped as she spied something else on the floor.

"Jake," she said, pointing. "Look at that."

He shifted his attention to follow the direction of her finger. Together, they stared in silence at the other item near the hammer. It was a portable phone with a large, digital display. And there was no mistaking the three numbers that were emblazoned across it.

911.

Jake's sharp inhale snapped through the air. "Any chance this means he wasn't involved in Desmond's kidnapping?"

"I think we can assume he wouldn't phone the police on himself," Norah said.

"No. Sure as hell wouldn't make any sense. But it *does* make things worse, though, doesn't it?" he asked.

Norah wished she could deny it, but she wasn't going to lie. "It really doesn't help."

"I didn't want Kyle to be the one who had Desmond," Jake said, his gaze flicking to the dead man for another moment. "But this takes us back to zero, with no clue who has my son. And whoever *does* have him…they're willing to kill to keep the police out of it."

She nodded. "Not only that, but they're either on your property, or they were a very short time ago. Which also means they're either here because they're supposed to be, or they have a means of getting in and out undetected."

For several long seconds after Norah's statements, a pensive silence ruled.

Then Jake sighed. "For what little it's worth…at least now we know where the call that Lockley intercepted came from."

"That's true," Norah agreed.

Without focusing too much on the dead man—she had to compartmentalize it, or she might not be able to keep going—she surveyed that scene in search of further clues. She pictured Kyle, alive and seated on one of the recliners in the room. It was plausible that he'd been sitting there, playing a video game. The TV wasn't on, but there *was* a solitary gaming controller sitting on one of the armrests. And there was an empty bowl beside that.

Had Kyle heard a noise, shut off the system he was using, and stood up to investigate? Why had the man in charge of security decided to call emergency services instead of taking care of things himself? What could he possibly have seen that would spur him to override his own expertise? And what had made him reach for the landline rather than his cell? Norah stole a glance his way. She could see the personal electronic device sticking out of his shirt pocket.

Jake's mind was obviously following a similar path, trying to seek some answers. Because he suddenly blurted out two words.

"Desmond's blanket," he said.

Norah turned to face him, frowning. "The one stuck in Kyle's couch?"

"Yes."

"What about it?"

"The proof of life video. Desmond was lying on *that* blanket. It's the only thing I can think of that would make Kyle call the police."

"I'm not following."

His features tightened a little—like he was trying to rein in some kind of emotion. "If he saw someone taking Desmond."

Norah's pulse leaped, but she answered carefully. "Except Desmond was taken very early this morning."

"He was. But what if whoever took him didn't leave right away? What if they stuck around, and Kyle spotted them as they were going instead of while they were coming?" He paused, his voice both urgent and hopeful. "Think about it. Imagine that he saw someone with Desmond. His first instinct might not have been to panic. Maybe he just wanted ask Beverly if she knew what was going on."

Something still didn't sit quite right, but she could

see the scenario in her mind just the same. "It's not implausible. And if he then realized it *was* an emergency,
he might've called the police from the landline knowing
that they'd be able to trace it immediately."

"But who the hell could have Desmond—*and* have
access to the property—that would make Kyle call the
police?" Jake asked.

"I think we need to carefully go over your staff as potential suspects again. One thing we can probably do is
start by ruling out Beverly. Since her job is literally to
take care of Desmond, it wouldn't make any sense for
Kyle to be concerned if he saw them together. Or to text
her about it."

She frowned, mentally recalling every person she'd
met since stepping into the house, trying to decide if any
of them stood out in the slightest. No one did. And Jake
was quick to speak up on the entire staff's behalf, too.

"It feels wrong to even consider any of them. I know
that sounds ridiculous." His hand found the back of his
neck, and he gave it a seemingly unconscious squeeze,
then sighed. "But objectively speaking, if Kyle saw someone he knew—someone he interacts with every day—
carrying Desmond around on the property, would his
immediate move be to make a 911 call? Or even his secondary one? I can't see it."

Norah had to agree. Even if an employee had abducted
Jake's son, and even if that same staff member had been
acting suspiciously, it made little sense for the head of
security to not at least *attempt* something else. Her mind
churned, mulling over the details of the last few hours,
trying to extract something meaningful from the puzzle
pieces.

Jake went silent, too. And Norah could see from his
contemplative frown that he was also seeking a new answer. She watched him absently as she continued to rack

her own brain. She saw his eyes sweep slowly over the room, and she noted how his fingers balled up at his sides. His forehead creased even deeper—a look that Norah was sure matched hers. She followed his gaze all the way until it at last found the dead man. But unlike Jake—who jerked his attention away again immediately—Norah let her stare hang there. Not because she was any less affected by the tragedy of Kyle's murder than she had been when she'd first seen his body a couple of minutes earlier, but because she abruptly recalled what had prompted them to seek him out in the first place. And what they'd found in his bedroom just a few minutes earlier.

"Where's the gun, Jake?" she asked, swinging her eyes his way.

His demeanor immediately changed. Instead of continuing with his slow and steady visual perusal of the space, he physically strode though it, searching the space in quick, furious movements. He dug his hands into the recliner cushions and peered into the trash can. He flung open the fridge and pressed himself flat against the floor to look underneath everything that had even the slightest space between itself and the carpet. And when he didn't find anything nearby, he wordlessly made his way to the other side of the room, where he pushed open a door, then disappeared through it.

Norah hurried after him, following him into the office. In the three seconds it took to her catch up, Jake had already seated himself at the single chair in the room. He'd also started yanking open the desk drawers at double speed. He offered Norah's entrance a brief acknowledgement with an incline of his head, but she was more interested in taking her own look around.

The room was a decent size, but sparsely furnished. The desk where Jake sat was the only one in the office, and it was enormous. It spanned the entire width of the back wall, but save for five computer screens—presumably the surveillance monitors—it was empty. Not even a sheet of paper graced the hardwood surface.

An open-faced key rack hung on the wall beside the door, and the keys that hung inside of it had been organized according to size.

There was one window, and four flashlights—ranging from pen-style to something that probably emitted a sun-like ray—had been mounted to the wall next to the shuttered blinds. Above the window was a shallow shelf, which held a bright red bag emblazoned with the words *First Aid Kit*.

She understood why Jake was tearing through the drawers—it was the only place that someone could've stash the missing gun if they were in a hurry. But his search appeared to have come up fruitless anyway.

"It's not here," he said, the announcement sounding like a curse. "Kyle doesn't even have a damn stapler hidden in his desk, let alone a gun."

Feeling deflated, Norah started to suggest that they forget the search for the gun for now and move onto to something else instead. But before she could speak, the first aid kit caught her eye again. And a resounding tingle across her spine made her shiver.

"Up there," she said, dread making her voice small.

Jake met her gaze, and she could see a new lick of worry in their green hue. "Okay."

With steps that seemed far too quick to Norah, he moved over to the indented shelf. With a swift, sure motion, he dragged the red bag down, then carried it to the desk. For a moment, it just sat there, its oversize presence filling the room with a cloud of foreboding. Then Jake muttered something unintelligible and reached out to grab the zipper. For no good reason, the rip of it opening set Norah's teeth on edge, and she had to blow out a breath she hadn't even realized she'd been holding. And as the air expelled from her lungs, everything slowed down.

Jake pulled the bag open wide.

He stared down.

He pulled it wider still.

He brought a hand up.

He started to slide it into the bag.

And something in Norah's brain clicked.

Without any thought on where the need to do so came from, she sprang forward, her arm outstretched. She hit Jake's wrist just in time to stop him from reaching all the way in. He took a startled step back.

"What was that about?" he asked.

Norah's gaze flicked to the bag. With her heart in her throat, she moved toward it. Using her pinky finger, she very gently gave one side a tug, and she peered inside.

"Norah?" Jake prodded.

She felt his hand land on the small of her back, and she was deeply grateful for the bit of comfort. But her hand still shook as she pointed into the first aid kit at the deeply out-of-place item that sat on top of a box of bandages. It was a hammer. And it was identical to the one that was resting on the floor out near Jake's murdered security guard.

"I think that's the one that actually killed Kyle," she said softly.

"What do you mean?" Jake replied. "What about the one out there, covered in blood?"

"A decoy."

"Why?"

"I don't know," she admitted, turning to face him. "Not yet, anyway."

His eyebrows had knit together, and his jaw was tense. Norah could practically feel the turn of his mind. Something was tickling at hers, too.

"Is one of the hammers yours?" she asked. "Do you have one like that?"

"No." Jake's tone turned a bit rueful. "I'm not much of a handyman. Give me five ingredients and a frying pan, and you'll be eating the most delicious meal you've ever had. But a plugged toilet is my ultimate demise."

For a second, they both smiled. Then Jake's mouth drooped, and his eyes darkened.

"Sorry," he muttered, giving his chin a rough scratch. "I know there's nothing funny about any of this, and I shouldn't be making jokes."

Norah put a hand on his chest. "It's okay, Jake. Life is sad and heartbreaking. It's stressful, and so, so scary sometimes. But sometimes it's funny, too. Which is okay. Better than okay. I often remind my clients that it's necessary to find those fleeting moments of pleasure."

Jake stole the quickest look toward the door, and Norah knew his thoughts were with his fallen security guard. And his next words confirmed it.

"You believe that's true all the time? Even when things are like this?" he asked, his eyes finding her once more.

"Yes. Even when things are like this," she said firmly. "I wouldn't say it if I didn't mean it, Jake."

"I know you wouldn't. Really." He sighed, then leaned in and pressed his forehead to hers. "Have I even bothered to ask you what you charge for all this sage insight and calmness inside the insanity?"

She pressed to her tiptoes brushed her lips over his. "Nothing."

He pulled back a little. "Nothing, huh? I bet you say that to all the pretty boys."

"Pretty boys, huh?"

"I'm sadly sure that's how they billed me on my TV show."

She pretended to study his features. "Maybe I'd concede pretty."

He made a face. "Ditto."

She kissed him again, then turned serious. "We need to figure out what this means."

"And where the damn gun is, and why someone would do any do any of this." He paused, his features growing stormy once more. "I won't let Kyle be relegated to collateral damage, Norah. Especially not if he was killed because he was trying to protect my son."

"I wouldn't ask you to do that. In fact, my head and my heart are both screaming at me to do something about it right now."

"Any ideas on what that something might be?"

Before Norah could answer, the cell phone in her pocket zapped to life.

"That's probably Lockley," she said. "Do you want to answer it?"

Jake shook his head. "You do it. Tell her to give us a few minutes. Use those negotiation skills. And don't tell her about this. Not yet."

It went against Norah's better judgement to keep the murder from a police officer, but she nodded anyway, then quickly pulled the old-model phone from her pocket. But instead of Lockley's name flashing across the screen, it was her brother's familiar number. Her heart did a hopeful little jump.

"Hi, Noah," she said as she tapped the answer key and lifted the phone to her ear. "Tell me you found something useful."

"Am I on speaker?" he replied curtly.

"No. Why?"

"Good. I want to run this by you privately so you can decide what to do with the info."

"Okay. I'm listening."

"Your celebrity chef friend might not be as trustworthy as you think. He transferred a cool two million dollars into Kyle Berguson's bank account this morning."

Her brother's words were like a cold slap, and Norah's eyes flicked to Jake, new worry seeping in.

Chapter 19

"Norah? Are you still there?"

She blinked and brought her attention back to the conversation. "Can you say that last bit again?"

"You didn't hear me wrong the first time," her brother stated. "Spud couldn't find much of anything about the security guard aside from some juvenile record stuff that was a few decades old. So he went headlong into bank records and found the deposit. He said it looked like someone tried—very badly—to cover up the source. But he unraveled it. Your man is the source."

"Noah, hang on."

"I'm not quite done, sis. As a by-product of backtracking the money, Spud found something else. Mr. Green Eyes over there also recently—like *this* morning recently—purchased himself a very nice gun. In person. Using picture ID. The shop confirmed it. So whatever's going on, my advice is that you quickly and quietly get out. Do you even know he has a kid for sure?"

"Noah."

"What? I'm merely stating the facts."

"Most of that wasn't fact," she said.

"Facts. Plus offering a very mild version of just how badly I want you to get the hell out of there," he amended.

"Look. Turn off the brotherly protectiveness for just a second and listen, okay?"

There was a very brief pause. "Fine. But it'd better be good, and it'd better end with you still breathing."

"Someone is *framing* him." Saying it aloud made it seem even realer, and she shivered.

"Or that's what he wants you to believe," Noah replied.

Under other circumstances, Norah might've rolled her eyes. "I don't know anything about the money you're talking about, but we found the gun."

"You *found* it?"

"Actually. Technically, we didn't find *it*. We found the receipt. And a brand-new lockbox. Neither of which Jake bought."

"That you know of."

Now Norah *did* roll her eyes. "He's been with *me* all morning. Literally since before breakfast. There's no way he magically snuck away and bought a gun."

Jake let out a sputtering cough. "What?"

Norah waved off his concern and kept speaking to Noah. "Besides which, he'd have to be pretty dumb to buy a weapon using his own ID."

"So maybe he's a dummy. Or maybe he has a doppel-ganger," her brother suggested.

He said something else, but Norah missed it. She was too busy making a mental leap. And too busy gasping out a name, too.

"Steve!" she said.

Noah and Jake answered her at the same time, their

matching puzzlement echoing in both of her ears. "What?"

She answered her brother first. "Hang on, Noah. I might have another person for Spud to look into."

"You know that he charges per search, right?" he replied dryly.

She ignored him and addressed Jake instead. "What's Steve's full name?"

Jake's face had taken on that slightly pale look he seemed to get every time he was deeply concerned. "Steven Harris. Not sure of a middle name. But his home address is in West Van, if that helps."

Norah redirected her voice to her brother. "Did you catch that?"

"Writing it down now," Noah replied. "But Norah?"

"Yes?"

"I sure as hell *still* wish you'd get out of there."

"I can't leave. But I'll stay safe, Noah," she promised.

"Damn well better," he grumbled.

The line went dead, and Norah breathed out, then met Jake's eyes. Very quickly, she reiterated the details about the money transfer to Kyle's account and the weapon purchase by a lookalike.

"I really do think someone's trying to frame you, Jake," she said.

"For my own son's kidnapping?" he replied.

"For that. And for Kyle's murder. Think about the pieces and how they'd look to the cops." Her voice picked up speed as she outlined how things might be perceived. "First off is the fact that you didn't call the police to start out with. I know they forced you not to. But without ransom as a motivating factor, what would stop you from doing it? There's no proof that they threatened Desmond. Nothing but your word."

"Except the note and the other stuff in the nursery," he interjected.

"Is it still there?" she replied.

His head jerked to the side, and he stared at the wall as though he might somehow see through both it and the distance to figure out the right answer. "I don't know. I left it the way I found it. And I have the picture I took."

"The picture *you* took. Not exactly hard evidence." She shook her head. "Let's add some law enforcement to the equation. If they questioned your staff, would anyone say you were acting oddly since this morning?"

"I guess they might."

"And would they say they haven't seen Desmond since last night?"

"Yes."

"So then the cops are wondering exactly what's going on," Norah said. "And since they are who they are, and they're doing their job properly with due diligence, they'll start looking for real evidence. And they'll find it. The cash transfer to Kyle could be a payoff to him for doing the dirty work. The blanket in his house is circumstantial proof that Desmond was there. And Kyle's inside knowledge and involvement is motive for murder."

"But…*why*?" Jake said, his features darkening with a mix of frustration, confusion and anger. "Why would I fake my son's kidnapping? And why would someone want to make the cops think that I had?"

"That I don't know."

"But you *do* think that Steve could've orchestrated all of this?" He gave his jaw a rub, his expression doubtful. "Not to sound like a jerk—because Steve has been a lifesaver to me—but he just doesn't seem like the big scheme type. And I've never told him about my son."

"Someone else—someone who *does* know about Desmond—could be the brains," Norah persisted. "And the other pieces fit. He has access to the property. He knows exactly how to sneak in without being caught. He also looks enough like you that no one would blink if he handed over your ID while making a purchase. It's not even ridiculous to think that he could've swindled the bank into making the cash transfer. And if Kyle saw him out in the yard with Desmond, realized it wasn't you and assumed the worst…"

Jake's expression had lifted as he spoke, but only marginally. Like he was trying to keep his hope under wraps. But Norah's own brain was buzzing with less muted enthusiasm for the conspiracy scenario.

"And I'm sure we're missing things, too," she said. "Like maybe whoever's behind the rest of it alerted your old paparazzi pals to try to make things harder for you in some way. So now we need to figure out what comes next."

"We should probably come up with some reasonable excuse for keeping Lockley away—if she ever calls, that is—then check whether or not the stuff in Desmond's room really is gone," Jake said. "After that, maybe establish a timeline for every person on the property since late last night?"

"Good ideas," Norah agreed. "But I was talking about what's next for the frame job."

"What are *they* planning, you mean?"

"Yes. If we can unravel what's coming up on their agenda, then maybe we can get a step ahead of them. Instead of trying to figure out what's motivating them or even making a decision about Kyle…" She swallowed as sadness made her breath catch, then made herself go on. "Instead of that, we can look for a clue that'll lead us to the next part of whatever they're plotting."

The guarded hope in his eyes bloomed. "Which might help us find Desmond."

"Yes. But I do think you're right about checking the nursery first. If everything is gone, then we know we're on the right track."

"Okay. Let's do it."

They locked hands and started to move toward the lounge area of the office. Jake's grip was tight, and Norah knew he was probably dreading walking past his deceased security guard even more than she was. She gave his palm a squeeze. He shot an appreciative look her way. But they only got as far as the door before a holler—wordless but guttural—carried in from outside the building and made them both freeze.

The cry cut through Jacob like a serrated knife. Sharp. Jagged. Painful. The yell itself was more jarring than any other would've been, given the current circumstances. The teeth-grinding sensation was more specific. Easily pinpointable. It stemmed from the sudden fear that someone else might be about to be killed because of the unknown attacker's personal vendetta against Jacob.

He spun to face Norah and spoke in a tight voice that he knew betrayed his feelings. "Is now still a bad time to go running headlong into trouble?"

Her mouth opened. Maybe in protest, maybe to offer a compromise. Jacob didn't get to find out which, because a second holler made her mouth snap shut for a moment. When she spoke, he was sure she'd changed her mind about whatever utterance she'd originally been going to make.

"If you go out there, I'm coming with you," she said.

Jacob wanted to argue, but he knew he wouldn't win, so he just nodded. "And we're both going to be very careful."

Moving in silence, they stepped from the office back onto the murder scene. Bile rose up in the back of Jacob's throat as they eased in a wide circle around Kyle's body. Not because he had a weak stomach, but because the loss of life sickened him. He didn't lay the blame at his own feet, but he did feel a sense of responsibility for the death. It had happened on Jacob's property. On his watch. To a man he'd trusted for years. It was a waste. A tragedy. One that should never have happened.

It's also one you don't have time to mourn right now, he reminded himself.

As if to drive home the thought, a series of dull thumps rose up from somewhere just outside the spot where he and Norah now stood.

Vowing to make sure Kyle got the full justice the man deserved, Jacob turned his attention to whatever the hell was going on in his yard. He gave Norah a little tug, guiding her to the window. There, he released her hand, positioned himself just in front of her—whether she liked it or not, he'd be her shield—and pushed his shoulder to the wall. Slowly, he leaned forward. He lifted a finger to the blinds and drew down one of the slats just enough that he could sneak a look outside. His efforts earned him an eyeful.

Two figures were locked in a scuffle beside the small porch. Grass and dirt flew. Limbs hit the stairs, sending out more of the bangs he'd heard a few moments earlier. From the current angle, it was impossible to see anything specific. No defining characteristics. The twists and turns of the wrestling match masked gender and age.

Jacob continued to stare, willing them to pause long enough—or at least move in a way that would give him a better view—that he might be able to discern what was going on so they could decide what to do.

Then the figures *did* shift. Only not in the way he expected.

Both of the combatants managed to get to their feet.

There was just enough of a break in the fighting that Jacob caught a flash of both blond hair and a contrasting blur of black locks. A millisecond went by, and the fairer one took control, rushing into the darker one. The move sent the second person flying forward straight into the building, and as the man's head smacked sideways onto the exterior wall, Jacob at last recognized him. *Pardeep.* Eyes closed. Mouth set in a grimace. Neck tense with resistance.

But who the hell is he fighting with?

Less than a heartbeat later, Jacob got an answer.

A hand slammed onto Pardeep's face and held him in place. The fingers were delicate. Their bitten-down nails had been painted navy blue, and the polish was badly chipped. A silver ring sat just below the knuckle on the first digit. Every detail was familiar, and Jacob knew exactly who held his security guard against the wall.

"Lockley," he said under his breath.

"What?" Norah's voice was right in his ear.

"I don't know what the hell is going on, but Lockley's got Pardeep in a—" His cut himself off as the detective's raised voice carried through the wall.

Her words were muffled, but still understandable. "Come at me again, and I'll be reading you your rights!"

Jacob turned and met Norah's eyes. "Do we chance going out there?"

"I don't think we have much of a choice." Her attention strayed to Kyle's body. "God knows we don't want *her* to come *in*. Especially since it sounds like she's out there in some official capacity. Cops tend not to take well to unreported murders."

"Fair point," he replied, then quickly stepped to the door and pulled it open.

As he did, Lockley hollered again. "Tell me where Jake is! If you don't, I swear I'm going to—"

"Right here!" Jacob interrupted loudly. "What's going

on, Lockley? Did my man do something I should know about?"

Her cool gaze slid to him, but her grip on his security guard didn't ease. "What your watchdog did was get a little overzealous in his handling of your guest. He jumped me at the top of that hill there."

"I called out three times," Pardeep interjected, his voice coming out slightly garbled, courtesy of the hand pressed to his face. "She didn't answer me."

"Because she didn't *hear* you," Lockley replied. "And when you tackled me, I identified myself as a police officer."

"Thought it was a lie," Pardeep said.

"Maybe you should try a little less suspicion?" the detective suggested.

"It's literally what I pay him for," Jacob said with forced dryness.

He was relieved to hear that Pardeep hadn't been up to anything unusual, but he was also eager to move the discussion away from the security office and its disturbing contents. Not to mention the fact that the detective's presence in lieu of her promised phone call filled him with dread. He felt Norah stiffen a little beside him, too, and he reached out to take her hand in silent solidarity.

They needed to get Lockley alone and out of sight.

"You should probably either let him go or find some reason to arrest him," he added as casually as he could.

The detective made a face, then dropped her hand to her sides and stepped back. "Happy?"

Pardeep gave his shoulders a roll, then rubbed his jaw. "Sorry, boss. I genuinely didn't realize she was legit."

Jacob issued a dismissive wave. "I'm just appreciative of the fact that you're so committed to mine and Desmond's safety."

"And the future Mrs. Pratt's safety, too," replied the

other man with a genuine smile. "It's my job, boss. And my mom always said that if something was worth doing, it was worth doing well."

"True story." Jacob released what he hoped was a convincing chuckle. "But I'm sure this wasn't what she had in mind. Why don't you take a breather up at the main house? I made some of those cheese scones yesterday. I know you love them, and there's a bunch left over."

Pardeep looked like he was trying not to jump at the offer. "Are you sure you don't want me to do some stuff in the office? I can check in with Kyle and see if there's anything he needs done."

"I'm sure. We'll meet you up there shortly."

"All right. Since you're twisting my arm." Pardeep cast a quick, doubtful look at Lockley, then turned and started up the slope.

Unconsciously holding his breath, Jacob waited impatiently for the security guard to get a reasonable distance away, then rounded back to face the detective. But Norah was already addressing her.

"I thought you were going to call us when you got to the garage," she stated.

"I *did* call you," replied Lockley. "Repeatedly. I got a good, old-fashioned busy signal each time."

Jacob dropped a mental curse and exchanged a look with Norah. It hadn't occurred to him that his sister's old pay-as-you-go line might not be equipped with call waiting.

"Probably when we were talking to your brother," he said.

"Probably," Norah agreed, a small frown giving away the fact that she was more concerned than her easy tone let on.

And her worry was immediately proven to be warranted.

Lockley's eyes moved to the office door, hanging there for a second too long before coming back to the two of them. "I think it's time to tell me exactly what's going on here."

Jacob just barely managed to stop himself from angling his body between the detective and the building.

"It was a false alarm," he said, glad that the lie came out sounding natural. "Kyle thought he saw something on one of the cameras and he overreacted."

"Kyle?" Lockley's tone was rife with seasoned-law-enforcement disbelief.

"My head of security."

"And he panicked?"

"I said overreacted, not panicked."

"Still. I think I'd like to ask him about it myself."

Lockley cast another look up toward the office. When she took one small step forward, then another, Jacob *did* shift his position to block her progress. Norah was right beside him, too, her hand finding the crook of his arm so that their bodies formed a wall.

Lockley stopped and blinked. "What's really going on?"

"We should go up to the house and get some coffee," Norah replied, her voice easy.

The detective clearly didn't buy it. "I'm not in the mood for chitchat. What the hell are you hiding?"

"It's a personal matter, Lockley. I promise you that." This time—even though his words were closer to the truth—they just sounded close to desperate.

Lockley's hand twitched toward her waistband, undoubtedly readying herself to grab the gun hidden beneath her jacket, and she spoke in a low, serious voice. "You're going to need to give me a damn good explanation not to force my way through here, Jake. I think I've been pretty patient. Downright helpful, even. But what

I'm seeing doesn't look right. Between the hostage negotiator who's suddenly being called 'the future Mrs. Pratt'
by your staff to the 911 call, and now *this*… I'm at a loss
as to how I can justify not investigating."

He took a breath. He readied a confession. A dozen ex-
cuses, and a plea. He had no idea what Lockley would say
or do. What other choice did he have? How long would
they be able to keep Kyle's murder under wraps anyway?
Except once again, before Jacob could open his mouth,
Norah spoke up, her tone somehow managing to sound
deferent without dropping as far as a plea.

"Detective Lockley…" she said. "If you have *any* feelings left from what happened to Jake's sister…then please.
Don't go in there."

Jacob tensed even more. He was sure that the already
on-edge police officer wouldn't give in to the request.
Yet after a moment, Lockley's expression changed from
combative to considering. Her hand slid away from the
general vicinity of her weapon, too.

"He told you about Scarlett?" she asked.

Norah nodded. "He told me everything. More, I think,
than he's said to you."

Surprisingly, Lockley didn't seem offended by the hint
of one-upmanship. "It was a hard time for both of us."

"I know." Norah squeezed Jacob's arm in a comforting way that he was sure was intentionally obvious. "And
what's happening now…it's kind of an extension of that.
Which is why we're asking for just the tiniest bit more
time."

Lockley went silent for several very long moments.
Too *many* long moments. The air was thick with waiting. Finally, she sighed.

"My gut says you're working me." She put up a hand
in a clear directive not to argue. "I know that's what you

do, so don't insult me by pretending it isn't. But I'm going to give you one more shot anyway."

"We're listening," Norah replied calmly.

"Good. Because I'm going to tell you what's about to happen, *exactly* how it's going to happen." Lockley paused as if to let the words sink in, then went on, her explanation spoken in a careful, slow way. "What *I'm* going to do is head up to the house. I'm going to call in my report, and tell dispatch that I *think* everything is okay, but that I want to hang around for a bit, just in case. Then I'm going to help myself to one of those cheese scones you mentioned. I'll take my time. Have some coffee The whole thing might take forty minutes, but I'd only count on thirty if I were you. Because I'm not feeling all that patient."

She stopped speaking again, and Jacob was sure she was being deliberately dramatic. Waiting for a prod. He indulged her.

"And after that?" he asked.

"After that… I'm going into the building, whether you like it or not," said the detective.

Chapter 20

Lockley fixed each of them with a look, then pivoted on the heel of one of her short, black boots and took off toward the house.

"You really *are* the best at this, aren't you?" Jacob said as soon as he was sure Lockley couldn't hear him. "You handled her by letting her think she knew what you were doing. A manipulation disguised as a manipulation."

Norah shrugged. "Over a decade of dealing with scumbags. I've gotten good at reading what motivates people." Her mouth drooped a little. "But none of that matters if we can't come up with a way to keep her from finding Kyle."

Jacob glanced toward the office. "Even if it was practical, I think trying to move him to cover up the crime would be a very bad idea."

Norah's blond hair bounced in a vehement headshake. "No. God, no. The last thing we need is to add another reason for the cops—Lockley included—to lay this at your feet. I think we need to spend the next thirty minutes doing what we planned to do before she showed up."

"Check out Desmond's room?"

"Yes. We definitely need to verify that much of our theory before we move on to anything else."

He forced off a tickle of worry that things might not turn out ideally, and he gestured up the hill. "Come on. We'll go in around the side so no one sees us."

They only made it about ten steps, though, before he stalled, then halted. There was a question that had been trying to invade his mind since he first realized that Lockley was on the property. One he almost would've preferred not to acknowledge, let alone voice. He felt compelled to do it anyway. So his feet stayed planted until Norah—who'd made it a few feet farther than he had—turned around.

"Hey. What is it?" she said.

"Do you think the kidnappers know?" he asked.

He didn't have to explain what he meant; Norah understood without being told.

"I'm not sure," she admitted. "If they're watching closely, they'll have to have seen Lockley, at least from afar."

"Is it bad to say that I was really hoping you'd just say no?" he replied.

She closed the gap between them and clasped his hands. "Even if they know she's on the property, that doesn't mean they know she's a cop."

"But they do know her. And they know that I do. They said as much to me on the phone. Norah…" He swallowed.

"Look. She's in plainclothes, and her persona doesn't exactly scream law enforcement, right?"

"No."

"So they might not even recognize her. Maybe they'll

think she's an old friend here for an unexpected visit. And by the time they realize she's more than that, we'll be on our way to figuring out exactly where Desmond is."

"Do you really believe all of that."

"We have to, Jake."

"Half an hour." The statement came out flat.

"We can do this," Norah replied. "We *will* do this."

Not trusting his voice, Jacob just nodded, then started walking again. They picked their way along the edge of the property, then slipped easily into the house. They didn't encounter any problems—or even any staff members—as they quietly padded up the stairs. But none of that made a difference to the mounting trepidation in Jacob's heart. He didn't know what he expected to find in his son's room, or what he was hoping might be there. The worst had pretty much already happened when he'd walked in and found the empty crib. If Norah was right, and all of the evidence was gone, they'd know were on the right track. Which was a good thing. Except there was a small, insistent part of his brain that worried what it would mean for his son's fate. If the kidnappers weren't after money, and they wanted Jacob to take the fall for this, what *was* their motivation? Quite frankly, the idea of forming any kind of answer scared him.

"Jake?" Norah's voice alerted him to the fact that he'd actually stopped moving right outside his son's room. "We should go in."

He took a steadying breath, lifted his hand and closed his fingers around the knob. He gave it a light twist, then shoved the door open. Immediately, a stabbing pain pierced his heart. The soft baby-powder scent— the one that always hung around when Desmond was near—filled his nose. More than that. It enveloped him. It overwhelmed him. He had to grab the doorframe to stay completely upright, and he had to draw a few more breaths before he could move forward. Even then, his vision blurred a little. It was Norah's words that finally forced him to focus.

"We were right, Jake," she said. "Anything that was here that would've proven you weren't behind Desmond's kidnapping is gone."

Jacob trod across the carpet to the crib. The digital recorder was gone. So was the note. The bedding had also been made up, the blanket tucked in all around, the large bear propped up tidily in one corner.

Jacob's skin crawled. Anger bubbled under the surface. Someone had been in his house. Again. They'd been roaming freely in his private space. In his *son's* private space. He stared down at the too clean, too empty space, fury mingling with futility.

"But they always make a mistake, right?" He paced the floor. "They're not evil geniuses."

"They're human," Norah agreed. "And from everything I've heard over the years from the people I know who work on the police force, a big chunk of crime solving does come from human error. And from luck, too. Timing. All of those things need to line up *with* the skills and training. I'm sure Lockley would tell you the same."

Lockley.

Her name was a reminder of their ever-shortening deadline.

Jacob paused in his pacing and fixed his eyes on the blinds. He could physically feel the pressure. Not just of the detective's impatient presence downstairs, but of everything. Kyle's body was out there, needing answers and justice. Desmond was out there, too—somewhere— needing saving. So where was *their* much-needed luck and timing?

He didn't realize he'd spoken the question aloud until Norah answered him.

"I guess we're just going to have to create our own," she said.

Something in her tone made him turn away from the window so he could see her face. "You've got an idea?"

"A few seconds ago, when you said, 'They're not evil geniuses,' I thought of Steve. And I just realized why," Norah said, her words laced with barely contained excitement. "If he isn't the one orchestrating things, it might not have occurred to him to mask his cell phone's location. I'm pretty sure Noah will be able to help us track it. And if we can ping Steve's phone against the location of all of your employees' phones, maybe we can figure out who he's working alongside without even asking."

As she finished speaking, hope buoyed Jacob's heart. He pulled her in and kissed her, hard and quick.

"In case no one's ever told you before…your brain is truly a beautiful thing, Norah," he said.

Her face flushed. "I can honestly say that's the first time I've ever received that compliment. But don't thank me too exuberantly. Not until it works, anyway."

"Noted. Compliments being stowed until we have my son back."

She wriggled out of his embrace, dragged the phone from her pocket, and tapped out her brother's number. Jacob was close enough that he could hear both the solitary ring as it cut off halfway through, and Noah's quick, urgent-sounding greeting.

"I was literally about to call you," he said.

"I'm going to put you on speaker," Norah replied, shuffling the phone, then tapping it again. "Does this mean you've got news about Steve?"

"Yeah. And it's not good." Even as staticky as her brother's voice was, his grimness carried through. "A man named Steven Harris was admitted to Vancouver General about an hour ago. Drove his motorcycle into a pole. No witnesses. In a spot where there just *happens* to be no street cams. Normally, I'd say it was bad luck, but not today."

Jacob's simmering anger surged up. "Is he alive?"

"Barely," said Noah. "He's in surgery, and from what little I could glean, the fact that he's breathing at all is nothing less than a miracle."

Jacob dropped a curse.

"Do you think this means his partner was trying to tie Steve off as a loose end?" Norah asked.

"That's where the other bit of info might help," her brother replied. "If Steve is a part of this, he's a mastermind at keeping it under wraps. And by that, I mean he'd really have to be hiding in plain sight."

"Plain sight?" Norah repeated.

"His life is an open book to someone like Spud," Noah explained. "He tracked Steve's phone and remotely hacked into his computer. Nothing weird or even interesting. The guy runs a personal training business from his house, and he doesn't leave too often. Gets his groceries delivered. Bought three comedians' autobiographies this year. When there's a run of good weather, he rides his motorcycle out to the same Squamish area. I can go on."

Jacob gave his chin an impatient rub. "Don't bother. That's all stuff *I* could tell *you*."

Noah didn't seem fazed by the disgruntled tone. "My point exactly. Either Steve is running the best long con in the game, or he's legitimately this straightforward in his life."

Jacob went silent, and he met Norah's eyes. He was sure she was considering the same thing he was—whether it was worth the time and effort to do what she'd suggested and compare his staff's locations to Steve's whereabouts over the last little bit. It only took a second for him to shake his head. Too many minutes had already flown by. Then something else came to mind.

"What about the gun? Did he buy it?" he asked.

"He did," Noah confirmed. "But I think he believed he was doing it for *you*."

"How could he believe that?" Norah replied.

"Text message," her brother said. "Spud ran a program through everything Steve's sent and received over the last week, flagging certain words. He found what looked like an exchange between Steve and you, Jake. One where you requested that he do his 'usual' thing, pose as you and pick up the weapon. You offered him three times the usual payment if he never brought it up again."

Jacob expelled a growl. "I sure as hell didn't ask him to do any of that."

"No, you didn't," Noah agreed. "It was some kind of phone twinning app that did it. But here's the crappy part about that. Right after Spud found the messages, they disappeared. Fully wiped in a way that he couldn't recover."

"So still no proof," Jacob said through gritted teeth.

"Not unless—*until*—Steve wakes up," Norah added.

"On that subject…" said Noah. "I called in the smallest favor and had a friend on the VPD station himself at the hospital. He's going to keep a very subtle eye on Steve and make sure no one does anything to impede his recovery."

"Thank you," Norah replied.

"Anything else I can do?" her brother asked.

"We'll let you know," she stated.

There was a pause, and then the other man spoke up again. "Hey, Jake?"

"Yeah, man?"

"I'd *really* love to tell you to keep my sister safe, but I know she'd probably deck me if I did. So I won't actually say it."

"Understood."

Norah rolled her eyes. "Bye, Noah."

"Bye, sis."

She clicked off the phone and met Jacob's eyes. "We're not giving up."

"As long as Desmond isn't here where he belongs, I'll never give up," he told her. "But I hate this feeling. Every time I think we're getting closer, another step backward seems to be lurking around the corner. How many people are they going to kill—or try to kill—before this is over?" The question came out more sorrowful than bitter. "This just isn't right."

"Something will give," Norah said. "It has to, sooner or later."

"Sooner's the only option, though, isn't it?"

Jacob immediately regretted saying the words. They hung ominously in the air, weighted with the hopelessness that the last few hours had brought to his world. Yet he couldn't draw them back in. He was grateful when Norah slid her arm across his waist. He brought his hand up to her shoulder and pulled her even closer. He kissed the top of her head, then closed his eyes to let himself take a moment of solace from her presence. As his lids dropped, though, her voice forced them open again.

"Jake…what is that out there?" As she said it, she wriggled free and stepped toward the partially open blinds.

He stepped in behind her and peered through the slats. "Where?"

"I swear I just saw someone moving across the lawn, and then…"

"Where?"

"Look. Right there by that pile of lumber near the gazebo. What is that?"

Jacob pulled two of the blind slats a little wider apart. For a second, he didn't see anything. Then the sun came out overhead, shining a strong beam down on the yard.

And he spied what Norah was referring to. It was an out-of-place lump of…something. It almost looked like a pile of blankets. Except then Norah spoke up, her voice soft but filled with deep concern.

"I think it's a person," she said.

Jacob knew immediately that she was right. But who was it? And were they alive…or dead?

Lockley.

The police officer's name leaped to mind as Norah stared down at the crumpled form on the grass. Truthfully, she couldn't make out anything identifiable about the person's appearance. Not their clothes nor their hair. Not their complexion nor their age. The clouds had rolled in again, and everything about the figure just looked grayish and indistinct. But the detective's name continued to stick in Norah's head anyway. Maybe because whoever it was down there appeared small and somehow feminine. Or maybe it was just wild supposition. Either way, Norah's pulse surged. Because if someone was willing to assault or even a kill a cop…that ramped things up to a whole new level.

And Norah knew she wasn't hiding her worry well, because Jacob's hand came out and closed on her elbow.

"What?" he said. "What is it?"

She swallowed. "Do you think Lockley's still in the kitchen?"

His eyes slid from her to the window then back again. "Why? You believe that might be her?"

"I can't tell," she admitted. "But it was the first thing that came to mind."

"Well. There's only one way to find out," he said.

"Yes."

"We shouldn't assume anything, though, right? Let's sneak a look into the kitchen first. If Lockley's at the table, eating scones, we'll go straight outside and decide what to do from there."

"Sounds like a good plan."

Jacob held out his hand, and when Norah tucked her fingers into his, she remembered that hours earlier, it had struck her that it felt oddly normal to walk with him like this. Like they'd been doing it forever. And now it really would've felt stranger to have left the room without their palms pressed together. Maybe that should've been the most absurd thing of all—to truly believe it wasn't weird. To no longer even have a little voice in her head asking if she was insane. Instead, her hand tightened. Jacob squeezed back. And a warm, just-right sensation spread through her chest.

As they moved from the nursery to the hall, then padded silently toward the stairs, another new thought—a question that seemed to come as a direct result of the heated feeling—sprung up.

What would I do without him?

And that—at least—should've been a bizarre thing to wonder about. She barely knew him. She'd lived an entire life before meeting him. Except in her heart, she knew that the last few hours had changed her. And in spite of the terrible circumstance, the shift she felt was a positive one. A resurgence of hope for the future.

An overwhelming need to tell Jake made her feet slow, and she gave his hand a tug. He stopped walking—they were halfway up the hall now—and turned his head her way.

"Everything all right?" he whispered.

"I know the timing is off. But I just wanted to say thank-you."

"Definitely bad timing." His mouth curved. "But you're welcome. Even if I don't know what you're thanking me *for*."

"For helping me," she replied.

His forehead creased. "I think you've got it backward."

She blew out a small breath, slightly embarrassed at the amount of emotion running through her. "I've been trapped for the last thirteen months, Jake. Stuck in my own head, I think. As crazy as it is, I think being accosted by Lockley and being forced to decide what to do about you and Desmond freed me. So you might think I'm helping you, but I promise that the reverse is true, too." She pressed her palm to his cheek. "That stuff you said before about leaping in… I'm already there, Jake. I think I jumped before I even knew there was a cliff."

His green eyes were bright. "I don't know if I've ever heard a better thing, Norah."

"I just wanted you to know."

"Thank you." He bent his head down and brushed his mouth over hers.

Automatically, Norah pushed to her tiptoes. Her hands came up to grasp the back of Jacob's neck, infusing their touch with as much passion as the moment would allow. But the kiss didn't last long at all. It was cut off by a light bang and a loud, pain-filled moan, both of which emanated from up the hall, undoubtedly carrying out of the kitchen.

Norah pulled away, and she nodded as Jacob lifted his index finger to his lips. In unison, they moved to the wall. Shoulder to shoulder, they inched along until they reached the doorway that led to the impressive cooking space. Jacob was in front, so it made sense that he take the lead in peeking around the corner. But that didn't mean Norah wasn't worried about his safety, and as he leaned forward—ever so slowly—she couldn't stop herself from placing a protective hand on his arm. She could feel the tension in his body. Her own muscles were rigid with worry about what they'd find, and her heart did its best to clamber up her throat. She sent up a silent prayer. She wished she'd thought to grab something—anything—to use as a weapon. But when Jacob at last got his head out far enough to see around the corner, there was no immediate retaliation from the other side. And as he eased forward a little more, his initial reaction was nothing but a sharp inhale. Then, a heartbeat later, he softly called out an unexpected name.

"Pardeep?" he said.

There was no response. And after another second, he moved forward with palpable caution. Norah followed close behind, and the moment she stepped into the kitchen, she understood Jacob's indrawn breath.

The security guard was slumped over, his back pressed to a row of built-in drawers. A smear of blood marked the surface behind him. His eyes were wide open, which made Norah's heart sink from its current spot in her throat all the way down to her toes.

Chapter 21

Norah's full-out panic only lasted as long as it took to realize that Pardeep's stare wasn't the same, dead one that Kyle's had been. Instead, it was glassy. Notably confused. And when Jacob crouched down beside him and gently touched his arm, Norah saw only the barest recognition in his gaze. But the dazed security guard did manage to stutter out a greeting.

"H-h-h-hurt," he said through chattering teeth.

"I can see that, buddy," Jacob replied gently. "Do you know who hit you?"

The man on the ground started to shake his head, then groaned, the motion clearly paining him. The guard closed his eyes for a moment, then opened them again, his stare momentarily clearer.

"Where's the c-c-op?" he asked.

Jacob lifted his gaze to Norah as he spoke. "I was going to ask you the same thing."

"She ran," Pardeep told him, his eyes glazing over once more.

Norah nodded once at Jacob, her mind going to the figure out on the lawn. "One of has to go out there and see if that's her."

"*One* of us?" he replied.

"I don't think Pardeep should be left alone," she said.

As if to emphasize the words, the security guard mumbled something utterly incomprehensible, then slid sideways, his torso practically in Jake's lap. And Jake didn't try to move the other man away. He just brought his hand to his own chin and gave it a rough scratch.

"I don't disagree," he stated. "My friend here is going to need some serious medical attention, too. The second we can safely call someone. But right now, I have a strong hatred for the idea of separating. And I'm honestly not even sure how to decide who should be where. Which of us is will be more at risk—the one staying here like a sitting duck, or the one out there, skulking around?"

"Let's call it equal. And it'll only be for a minute."

"I don't know if you've noticed, but minutes seem to be more like hours today."

"Now *I* don't disagree," Norah said, doing her best to offer a small smile. "But since Pardeep seems to be helping us make the decision…" She nodded toward the man in question, who really *was* in Jake's lap now. "I'm going to offer to be the one to go outside anyway."

Jake looked like he wanted to argue, but he just shook his head. "I guess trying to order you to stay here would be the epitome of an overprotective, male-biased hero complex?"

"To put it one way…"

"Fine. Then grab a knife from inside that drawer over there under the coffeepot. If you're going to go, you'd better have a little bit of protection."

Norah dipped down to place a quick kiss on his cheek, then hurried over to the drawer in question. But when she opened it, she found an item that didn't belong there at all. Nestled in between two wicked-looking blades was a gun.

She swallowed. It had to be the one missing from the case back at Kyle's place. The one that Jake was supposed to have appeared to have purchased. Why was it hidden there? What had it been used for? Norah was tempted just to slam the drawer shut and pretend she'd never seen it. But what if that was the exact intention of the person who'd tucked it inside? What if they meant it to be found in this spot at a later hour or later date, or—

"Norah?"

At the sound of Jake's voice, she jerked her attention toward him.

"I thought we were in a rush here," he said. "Is there something wrong with the knives?"

She exhaled, reached into the drawer and lifted the gun out as she answered him. "We *are* in a hurry. But I think the knife is probably going to be less effective than *this*."

There was a split second of silence, and then Jake spoke, his voice hard with worry. "What are you doing? If that's the gun that Steve bought—and I'm assuming it is, because I don't normally keep weapons beside my utensils—then someone planted it there. You sure as hell shouldn't be touching it."

"I know," Norah replied, sliding down the clip to confirm that it was loaded. "But that doesn't change the fact that it might come in handy."

Jake's face might as well have been a storm. "Norah."

"It's safer for me to be far enough away to use this than it is for me to be close enough to use a knife."

"And if they're already that close?"

"Then they'd better pray that I don't panic and shoot them somewhere they'd rather not be shot."

"Is there somewhere they *would* rather be shot?" he countered.

Tucking the gun into the rear of her waistband, she stepped in and kissed him once more. "Foot is probably better than heart."

As she pulled away, he grabbed her wrist and tugged her close again, pressing his forehead to hers for a brief moment. "Come back to me."

His words were underlined with emotion—an unspoken declaration of more.

"I will," Norah replied a little breathlessly.

"Promise me."

"I promise, Jake."

Seemingly satisfied by the statement, he let her go, and Norah slipped silently out of the kitchen. But admittedly, for several seconds after her exit, she had to battle a powerful urge to just go running back to him right then. The plan might've been her own idea, but that didn't mean she liked the idea of being separated, either. She didn't know exactly what—or who—she was going to find outside. And she was scared. And not ashamed to acknowledge it. It'd have been more foolish to deny that the situation called for a renewed dose of fear.

You have the gun, she reminded herself.

But the weapon was a weight pressing to her back, not as reassuring as it ought to be. Her steps up the hallway were heavy. So was her heart. But when she reached the sunroom and the sliding glass doors that she planned on using to make her stealthy exit, she spied a tiny blue sock sitting on the floor beside one of the wicker chairs. And the scrap of blue—Desmond's, for sure—prompted her to put aside her fears and refocus on why she was doing what she was doing.

She paused at the door to pull the gun free before heading out. It felt as unnatural in Norah's hands as it had in her waistband, but the weight of it added a hint of power. That helped propel her forward, too.

She sneaked through the door without a sound. She crept along under the cover of the house for as far as she thought she could, then darted to a decorative bush. From there, she ran to a pile of wood near the gazebo construction site. Her next move would lead her straight to the fallen figure, but she took a moment to catch her breath and steel her resolve once more. She slowly counted to ten, then stepped out onto the lawn. She immediately felt exposed. Vulnerable. But the all-over tingle of nerves no sooner came than it quickly faded to the background as she realized something. The space in front of her was empty.

Startled, Norah swung her gaze back and forth, wondering if she'd miscalculated her position.

But she was 100 percent certain that she should've been able to see the person on the ground from where she currently stood. Or from anywhere within a ten-foot radius, for that matter.

Frowning—and wary—Norah gripped the gun a little tighter and took three more, cautious steps. And a little way away, she *did* spot a section of beaten down grass. One that was decidedly body-sized. But she wasn't sure if she was relieved about it or not. She turned in a slow circle. When she didn't see any evidence of anyone nearby, she moved closer to the flattened piece of lawn. And her unease exploded into dread. Because the trampled-on area was marked with a thick splotch of reddish brown.

Blood.

Norah didn't have to look any closer to know that it was true. There was no mistaking it. And to make things even more nerve-racking, a trail of smeared red led over crushed grass away from the spot.

Norah bit her lip and cast a glance back toward the

house. Her conscience told her it was wrong to follow the blood without telling Jake. But her gut told her that if she didn't go now, she might lose a crucial window of time.

She issued a silent apology, then took off at a speedy pace, alternating her gaze between the trickles of crimson and the space around her. Very quickly, she realized that the trail was leading toward some of the thick shrubs that lined the property. It wasn't the same spot where she and Jake had come through. That was on the other side of the yard. But when she got closer to the bushes, she realized that someone had definitely pushed their way through. The greenery was snapped and broken.

Now moving even more carefully, Norah stepped toward the hastily created escape route. Who had gone through it? Why run away from the house when they were injured?

She shoved down another pulse of fear and made herself ease into the foliage. She only got half a step in when the sound of someone clearing their throat carried in from the other side. The noise made Norah freeze. And she was glad it did, because a second later, she realized she could see through the branches. It took her a few moments more, though, to piece together what was going on.

The first thing she became sure of was that the person who'd let out the small cough-like noise was Detective Lockley. The platinum blonde woman was standing in the middle of what appeared to be a white gravel road. Her hands rested on her hips, and her attention was focused on the horizon. The sight of her made Norah blink in puzzlement. Not just because of her presence, but because she didn't look like she was hurt at all, let alone badly enough to have left behind so much blood. Lockley's posture was straight. Her movements were easy as she glanced down at the silvery watch on her wrist. The worst she seemed was impatient.

What's going on?

Norah very nearly stepped out and asked. But both her words and her motions failed her as her gaze dropped down for just a moment, giving her a new view—the source of the blood. A body. One Norah knew. *Beverly.* The older woman was curled into the fetal position. She was still clad in the gray hooded sweatshirt, but the fabric was darkened with blood and shredded all down one side. Then the nurse's body moved—just a little—and a coldness swept through Norah.

She's alive.

The realization was horrific. The idea that someone could be bleeding so much but still be holding onto the threads of life...

Norah swayed a little on her feet. But she barely had time to process any of the revelation before the world seemed to kick into fast forward.

First, the crunch of tires on gravel filled the air. The sound was followed by the source—a seen-better-days sedan in rust-flecked maroon paint. It pulled into the space in front of Lockley and Beverly and came to a grinding halt.

Next, a man climbed from the vehicle. He was tall—taller, even, than Jake—but rail-thin. His skin was sallow, and his hair was so fair that it made the detective's platinum locks seem dark. The clothes he wore hung on his body, and they were in poor repair. To say his appearance was unnerving would've been an understatement. But the expression on his face was worse. There was a cold fury there that made Norah want to cringe away from him, even from her hidden position. Then he spoke, and the anger in his voice redoubled the feeling all the more.

"What the hell is she doing here?" he demanded, jerking a thumb toward Beverly. "I thought you killed her."

"Yeah, I thought I did, too," Lockley replied. "Until I saw her crawling across the lawn."

"Crawling across the— Why am I even asking? Why the hell didn't you just shoot her again?"

"Don't you think I would've, if I could've? The first time only worked because the nanny suite is sound-proofed. The original homeowners had some kind of music studio down there. I couldn't exactly fire a shot out in the open."

For a moment, their voices faded. Norah's eyes dropped to the weapon in her hands, and a head-to-toe shiver racked her body. It was *this* gun. The one that had shot on Beverly. And it was Lockley who'd done it. The woman who supposedly felt responsible for Jake's sister's death. She was a murderer. *She* was framing Jake. She and the decidedly shady character out there.

A hundred thoughts fluttered inside Norah's mind. They all battled for supremacy. But none won. And then the two voices faded in again.

"Leave her here," said the man.

"Are you sure?" Lockley replied.

"Yeah. Everything will still line up. She'll bleed out. The cops'll have one more body to toss at Pratt, even if she's out here. And we'll be long gone."

Sickness slithered through Norah's gut, and before she could consider what the next step should be, the choice was taken away. Two car doors slammed, and the tires crunched again. The sedan pulled a U-turn and started up the road. And as the vehicle slipped away, Norah caught sight of the most chilling thing of all. In the back of the car, just visible above the lower edge of the rear wind-shield was the top rim of a car seat.

A need to act slammed into her.

She darted out from the shrubs, bent down to Beverly and spoke in her calmest voice.

"I don't know if you can hear me…" she said. "But in case you can… I'm sorry that I can't stay here with you. If I did, I might not be able to save Desmond. And I really think you'd understand that. But I promise you, I'm sending help right this very second."

Fighting guilt-tinged nausea, Norah stood up and pushed her way back through the bushes. She also made good on her word. Her instincts and her experience told her that there was no longer a need to keep law enforcement out of things. In fact, her gut was telling her that the threat had been nothing but a ruse to start out with. So she tugged the old cell phone from her pocket and dialed 911, and when the dispatcher picked up, she gave a very quick outline of the current need. Using as few words as possible, she mentioned Kyle's demise, described Beverly's precarious state and unusual location, and she told them about Pardeep. She left out only one major thing—Desmond.

It was obvious that the person on the other end of the phone wanted more details, but Norah cut her off by asking for multiple sets of police and paramedics. Then—despite knowing better—she hung up and switched from a jog to a run. She no longer made any effort to be quiet or subtle in her movements. She burst through the door and slammed her feet to the hardwood as she made her way to the kitchen.

Jake—who had managed to extricate himself from Pardeep—greeted her with a worried look. "Norah, what's—"

"Have you got another car?" she gasped.

"Yes, but—"

"Thank God."

"What about Par—"

"Let's go," Norah said. "If we wait much longer, we're going to have a lot of complicated explaining to do to the police, and there's no way they'll let us go after Desmond on our own."

"The police?" he said, surprise now mingling with concern on his face.

"I'll tell you everything as soon as we're on the road," she told him. "But trust me. It was safe to call them. And necessary. We need to hurry, Jake!"

Although his concerned look didn't change, he seemed to get that urgency had taken over her. He didn't push for any more of explanation. He just took her hand and pulled her back through the house, then out the front door, slipping his feet into a pair of boots as they exited. Without speaking, they headed up to the driveway, which curved around a bend and led to a looped piece of pavement and an oversize garage. There, he punched in a code on the electronic keypad.

The automatic door rolled open immediately, but it still seemed to take forever. The more seconds that ticked by, the more harried Norah felt. And relief still felt desperately out of reach.

Hurry, hurry, she willed to the universe at large.

Jake stepped into the garage, snagged a set of keys from a rack on the wall, then gestured to the quad cab truck that sat in the middle of the cement. Norah didn't hesitate. She all but sprinted to the passenger side and yanked the door open. By the time Jake reached his side, she'd already climbed in and buckled up.

"Do we have a destination?" he asked.

"Just away from here as fast as possible," Norah replied.

He nodded, then turned the key, and as soon as the engine hummed to life, he eased the truck out of the garage. The ride was smooth and easy—a direct contrast to the thunder of Norah's pulse. She gripped the front of the seat bottom with white-knuckled tightness, her eyes closed, her hearing focused on the slightest hint of a siren.

She grew tenser still when she heard the front gate slide open, because she worried that someone on the property would see them go and report their departure in a way that would somehow get them caught. Then she remembered that there *was* no one to watch them go. Judy was—thank God—still at the store. Pardeep was incapacitated. Kyle was dead. And Beverly was on the brink.

Remembering the last thing brought an image of the nurse to the front of Norah's mind, and she couldn't shake it. Her throat burned. Would the other woman live? If she didn't, was there more Norah could have done?

As the emotion washed through her—not so much guilt as human decency and sorrow—the need to keep listening for approaching emergency vehicles slipped to the wayside. So when a sudden onslaught of sirens cut through it all, she jerked her eyes open with surprise. Red, white and blue flashed by. She counted one ambulance, two patrol cars and a fire engine before realizing that their own truck wasn't moving. They'd reached the bottom of the hill that led up to Jake's street, and they'd pulled onto the shoulder of the road to allow the chaos to pass.

As the noise faded somewhat, Norah she made herself speak. "It's Lockley, Jake. She has Desmond."

She went on for a minute, explaining what she'd seen on the other side of the hedges. With each word, Jake's face grew paler and stonier. When she was done, she tensed for an outburst. But he didn't express any shock or anger. In fact, the silence was a thunderclap. And after a second, Jake just slammed the truck into Drive and swerved onto the road with furiously spinning tires.

Chapter 22

There were no words to express the thoughts going through Jacob's head. None. He wasn't angry. He wasn't stunned. He was…*what?* Indescribably outraged. Devastated. But more than that. So much more.

He hit the freeway hard. He was speeding. He shouldn't be. A lack of caution would get them caught. Except he couldn't seem to ease his foot up off the gas pedal. He passed a sports car and a motorcycle. He whipped by a caravan of soccer moms. When he cut onto an exit, he didn't signal, and that earned him a honk from some agitated motorist. He didn't care. Norah said his name gently a few times, but he didn't answer. Even after she gave up prodding him, it still took him several long minutes to work up the will to speak.

"Tell me again what the man looked like," he growled.

It clearly wasn't what Norah had been expecting to hear. "What?"

"Describe him."

"Okay." She sounded understandably puzzled. "He was tall. Skinny. Very, very fair hair. That white blond you see on toddlers more often than adults."

"You're sure?"

"Yes. I'm sure."

"And you said his skin made him look sickly?" Jacob asked. "Like maybe he hadn't seen the light of day for a while?"

"Those weren't my exact words," she replied. "But they fit. Jake...what's going on?"

His hands held the wheel so tightly that they hurt, and his answer came out stilted. "That man. The one you saw. That's Milo."

"Milo? You mean the man who went to prison for your sister's murder?"

"The same."

"How is that possible?"

"I don't know." Jacob's tone was as grim as his thoughts.

"He couldn't have escaped," said Norah. "There would've been news."

"You'd think." He shook his head. "And why is Lockley working *with* him? She's the one who put him behind bars. Her testimony was the lynchpin in the case. The whole reason they were able to get the conviction so damn quickly. Why would—" He stopped, realizing just how obvious the answer was.

"An affair," Norah filled in, her voice soft.

"Damn." He squeezed the steering wheel even harder than he had a few minutes earlier. *"Damn."*

He went quiet again, understanding for the first time what it truly meant to have a reeling mind. He racked his brain in search of clues that he might've missed. He wondered who—if anyone—knew. And he tried to come up with some reason as to—*why, dammit*—the two of them would've taken his son.

Flicking on his signal again, he pulled over, cut the engine and faced Norah.

"Can you call your brother for me one last time?" he asked.

"Sure," she replied quickly. "What do you want him to do? Look into Lockley?"

"No. I just need a number for Chief Larry Lawson."

As she tugged the phone out and dialed, Jacob's eyes lifted to the end of the block. As wild as his driving might've been, it hadn't been blind. The cul-de-sac was utterly familiar. So were the black-and-gray townhomes that curved with the road. This was Lockley's address. Jacob had been here about a half a dozen times right after Scarlett's death. Sympathetic tea. A discussion of the case. Now he felt sick about all of that.

Gritting his teeth, he zeroed in on her unit, noting that even from here, he could see that the driveway was empty. Everything about the place was still, actually. He knew that didn't mean no one was there.

Norah tapped his shoulder lightly and held out the phone. "Here. I typed in the chief's number. You just have to hit Call."

Loath to take his attention away from Lockley's place, Jacob took the proffered device and looked down only long enough to do as she'd said. The line rang twice, and then a booming voice—the kind accustomed to commanding entire rooms—filled his ear.

"This is Lawson," said the other man.

"Hello, Chief," Jacob replied. "This is Jacob Pratt."

"Jacob Pratt," echoed the chief, his tone growing abruptly more subdued and at least a little bit guarded. "Long time no talk. To what do I owe the pleasure?"

"Why don't *you* tell *me*?"

"Not sure what you mean, sir."

Jacob didn't feel like playing nice. "Tell me what's going on with Milo Knight."

The request was met with silence, and Jacob knew—even more than he had already—that something was very, very off. He just wasn't sure *what*.

"And Detective Lockley," he added, his voice soft.

The chief cleared his throat. "Really don't think it's in your best interest to bring her into this, Mr. Pratt. Probably just get you into trouble."

"Chief Lawson, I genuinely don't know what you mean."

"If you're trying to figure out where she's moving to, I'm not going to fill you in. The only reason her request for a court order to keep you out of her life was denied was the fact that *I* personally recommended against it. You've been through enough. I told her the recent antics were undoubtedly a direct result of the stress of finding out Milo had been released. That you were taking it out on her because she was your liaison, but that you'd get past it."

"What?" Jacob couldn't keep the shock out of his voice.

There was a pause. "Lockley came to me last month. She confessed to me what's been going on. The threatening notes. The unexpected visits. All of it."

"Back it up a sec," Jacob replied. "Why the hell was Milo *released*? When?"

This time, the pause was longer. "Are you telling me that Lockley didn't inform you of what was going on?"

"I haven't got even the remotest clue what you're talking about."

Jacob swung his gaze to Norah. She was clearly following along. Her expression perfectly matched the stunned feeling in his head and the mounting pressure in his chest.

"Please, Chief Lawson," he said. "I'm not asking you to disclose anything personal about Lockley. I just want to hear what she should've told me."

The senior police officer on the other end sighed, then launched into an explanation that left Jacob practically speechless. Three months earlier—right around the time he'd received custody of Desmond—Milo Knight had acquired a new lawyer. One who'd found a flaw in the murder investigation. Subsequently, that had led to Milo's release. For the sake of everyone involved, they'd done their best to keep it out of the papers. Lockley was assigned to keep Jacob in the loop, but about five weeks ago, she'd come to Chief Lawson with concerns about Jacob's reaction. She said she felt he blamed her. She was worried about Jacob's mental state.

The perfect beginning to the setup, Jacob thought as the other man tied off the story.

"But you're saying none of that happened?" Lawson asked.

"Not a lick of truth to any of it, Chief," Jacob replied.

"Bizarre. Any reason you can think of that she might lie about all that?"

Jacob felt his mouth twist into an unamused smile. "I wish I had some completely rational explanation. And I understand if you don't believe me. It'd be pretty unreasonable to expect you to take my word over that of a VPD employee."

"I don't *want* to not believe you," said Lawson. "I'm just puzzled. And more than a little concerned."

"I guess that makes two of us."

"You going to take this okay?"

"I've been hit with worse, and it hasn't broken me yet.

Thanks for the filling me in. I'm sure we'll be talking about it again soon."

"I'm very certain we will."

Jacob moved to end the call, but Lawson spoke up again, stopping him.

"Hang on a sec, Mr. Pratt," said the other man. "There's one thing that might ease your mind about Lockley."

"What's that?" Jacob asked.

"I probably shouldn't be volunteering this, but in the interest of giving you the benefit of the doubt until I sort out what's going on—and since it's really a matter of public record anyway—Lockley *isn't* a VPD employee anymore."

"Since when?"

"She gave her two weeks' notice. Today was her last day."

"Good to know, and I appreciate the trust. Thanks, Chief."

Jacob clicked off the call, then met Norah's eyes. He didn't know the big reason behind Lockley's entire scheme. But he had a damn good thought on why she'd done things the way she had.

"She's moving," Norah said, voicing his conclusion. "She's moving somewhere far away, and she's taking Desmond with her. This whole, elaborate thing—*killing* people, for God's sake—was her way of creating the distraction so she could keep him. Even if the police believed you eventually, she'd be long gone before that happened."

With a dry throat, Jacob nodded. But he didn't get a chance to speak his agreement aloud, because the cell phone rang again, and that number on the screen was labeled as blocked. He knew it was them.

Jacob stabbed at the keys, then answered in a snarl. "Hello, Milo."

The response was a digitally modified laugh, followed

by a robotic voice. "Ah. You figured it out. Nice to finally be recognized, Jakey P." There was another laugh. "Then again. You never really enjoyed the fame, did you?"

"Where's my son?"

"Haven't we been over this?"

"He is *legally* my son."

"But biologically, he should've been mine," Milo replied.

Jacob closed his eyes, feeling exhausted. "That doesn't even make sense. You and my sister split up a long time before Desmond was conceived."

"Just because you don't understand something, my friend…doesn't mean it's not true."

"We aren't friends, Milo. We never were."

"Tell him you should talk in person," Norah whispered suddenly, her hand finding his elbow. "I think that's what he wants to hear."

He opened his eyes and nodded at her. "Listen. If you really think that there's something I need to understand, then we should meet."

Milo went quiet for a moment, and Jacob had a feeling the other man was trying to give the impression that he was carefully considering the request. Then there was a click, and Milo spoke again, the robotic modification gone.

"I'm assuming you know where Lockley lives?" he asked.

Jacob had to pretend that hearing the other man's voice—the same once that had tried to deny culpability for Scarlett's death—didn't make his skin crawl. "I do."

"Good. Meet us there. And don't forget to bring that so-called fiancée of yours."

The line went dead, and it took some serious effort not to throw the phone out the window. Jacob settled for crushing his fingers hard around the device in his hand instead, but Norah reached out and closed her palm over-top of his tight knuckles.

"I know you don't want to see him," she said. "You wanted to throw away the key when he was locked up. But we have an advantage here, Jake."

"Are you handling me again, Norah?" The words—intended to be teasing—came out flat, and he exhaled. "Ignore that question. You know there's nothing I wouldn't do for Desmond, but if you'd asked me yesterday if I would rather be forced to look at Milo Knight or stab myself in the ear with a pencil…"

"I understand. But I think I've figured out what they want. Milo wants to best you, and he wants you to know exactly why and how he's doing it. And Lockley wants to make you suffer while it happens."

"Refreshing."

"Sorry, Jake."

"Are you sure they both don't just want to kill us?" he asked dryly.

"Oh, they definitely do," she replied. "But we're not going to let that happen."

He gave his chin a scratch. "Any idea if Desmond was just a convenient way to do all of that?"

"Is it better if I say no, or better if I say yes?"

"Equally bad. All I want is to have him back safely, Norah. I've had a lot of long days in my life, but this one has taken a year to pass, and it's not even over yet."

She squeezed his hand. "Then let's get going. How far away is Lockley's place?"

Jacob nodded toward the front windshield. "About a forty-second walk."

Norah's eyes widened. "Then I stand corrected. We have *two* advantages. Because there's no way they have any idea how close we are."

* * *

Norah was accustomed to thinking on her feet. Her job required her to act quickly, and to adapt even faster. And she was good with noticing details, too. So when she and Jake had finished sneaking around to the back of Lockley's house, then tucked themselves securely behind the free-standing shed that stood in one corner of the yard, she immediately looked for options. And with her mind in work mode, she spied a possibility right away.

"Jake…" she whispered. "What if we could get in, get Desmond, and get out again without getting caught?"

"Sounds like a dream," he replied, his voice equally low. "And I mean that in two senses—that I'd love it, and that I don't see how it would be possible."

She jerked a thumb toward the back of the house. "That latticework."

He followed her gesture with his eyes. "What about it?"

"It leads up to that second-floor window. And it's open."

"There's no way that will hold my weight."

"No. But it will hold mine."

"I thought we agreed that we were only getting closer to the house so we could use our surprise advantage," he said.

"This is better," she replied.

"Norah."

"Just hear me out. It'll take all of minute to scale that thing. Another few seconds to get inside. Lockley and Milo will be downstairs, watching the front."

"Or they'll assume we're going to try and sneak in," Jake countered.

Norah shook her head. "Even if they do, they'll also be assuming that it will take us a while to get here."

"And do what when you get inside?"

"I find out where Desmond is. When I do, I'll give you a signal. Then you create a distraction out here, and I'll grab him and run."

"There are too many variables," he argued. "What if someone sees you climbing up and calls the police?"

She swept her hand over the yard. "There's greenspace behind us. There's a big tree blocking the view from that side. And someone from this side would have to be both looking out and leaning in at the exact right moment."

"Luck hasn't been on our side."

"We're creating out own luck now, remember? If I don't think it can be done, I'll sneak back out the way I went in," she promised. "And we'll be right back here. But we have to *try*, Jake."

He growled something under his breath, and his attention flicked to the latticework, then back to Norah. "I don't like it."

"You don't have to like it. You just have to agree to it."

"You still have the gun, right?"

"Yes."

"Do *not* get hurt," he ordered gruffly. "I'm only just getting started with you. With *us*. Shoot them if you need to. And keep Desmond safe. Please."

There was a desperate edge to the last word, and it made Norah's heart ache. But she was afraid that if she acknowledged it, she might cry. So she kissed him very lightly and very quickly, then darted off before he could change his mind.

She forced herself to focus on what needed to be done rather than what she was feeling.

And she wasn't wrong about her time predictions.

She scaled the trellis with ease. Once she reached the top, she was able to steal a glance through the window. Thankfully, it was a darkened bedroom with a closed door.

Taking a deep breath, Norah tested the grip of her left hand. When she was sure she was secure, she reached up with her right hand and gave the window a push. It slid easily, so she adjusted herself again, then hoisted her body up and in. Bad luck did seem to strike when she flailed a little on entry, banging a box and knocking it over right before landing on the floor.

She sprung up and held her breath, ready to grab her weapon if the noise drew unwanted attention. But the room stayed still and quiet. She let out the breath, then started to move forward. Then stopped as a small sound caught her ear.

Spinning slowly, she realized she wasn't the only one in the room. In the corner sat a car seat. And in the car seat was a contentedly sleeping baby with his thumb jammed into his mouth.

Desmond.

Norah almost couldn't believe her own eyes. She blinked, half expecting the little guy to disappear. But he stayed just where he was, his chest rising and falling in perfect rhythm.

Norah's heart started to race. She looked from the baby to the door to the window. Could she carry him out? Could she chance it?

"I have to, don't I?" she murmured. "I promised your dad."

She took a step toward him. And that one move was all she was able to make before the door creaked open, and Lockley's startled gasp carried in.

Norah started to fumble for her gun, then realized it would be sheer folly to fire it anywhere near Jake's son. She opted for a direct attack instead, diving straight at the other woman. But Lockley had had just enough time to ready herself. She dodged out of reach. Norah stumbled. Then she tried again, lunging hard. Once more, Lockley threw herself sideways. This time, Norah went flying into the doorframe. She hit the ground hard. But Lockley didn't take advantage, and Norah realized that the former detective's objective was as much to get to Desmond as it was to overpower her. She couldn't let it happen.

More desperate now, she pushed to her feet. She reached for the gun. Too late, she clued in that the weapon had fallen free. She swung her gaze back and forth, but she didn't spy it anywhere. And now Lockley had her hand around the handle of the car seat.

Norah launched herself at the platinum blonde once again. And she was at last triumphant. The other woman went over backward, her head hitting the ground with a sickening thump.

Norah didn't wait. She grabbed a hold of the car seat and bolted for the bedroom door. She only got as far as the stairs, before she saw that she had another problem in the form of Milo Knight. He was loping up the steps, his too-long, too-skinny legs making the journey seem impossibly short. And a *thump-thump* from behind alerted Norah to the fact that Lockley had recovered, as well. As the two crooks barreled toward her, she could think of only one option. She had to take it.

She dug her heels in, holding still until both Lockley and Milo were almost on her. At the last second, she flattened her body against the wall, gripped Desmond's seat as hard as she could, and waited. And it worked. Although Lockley did bump into the plastic carrier, the impact was nothing more than a glance. But the other woman continued forward, her body slamming in Milo's and sending the two of them thudding together down the stairs. Milo let out a cry that was cut off in a sickening crunch.

The baby started to cry, and guilt and a need to comfort him surged through Norah at the same time.

"Shh, shh," she said as she started forward. "We're going to get to your daddy soon."

Counting on the fact that the fall had done as much damage as the noise indicated—but not prepared to take the chance that it hadn't—she spun toward the bedroom with the intention of going back out the way she'd come in. She'd call down to Jake and get him to spot her and Desmond, and then they'd get the hell out.

But she wasn't quite home free yet.

"Stop!" Lockley shrieked. "I've got a gun, and I *will* shoot."

Fearful for Jake's son, Norah turned back. The former detective's left arm hung at a bad angle, and blood streaked across her face. But she did, in fact, have a gun in her shaking right hand. And Norah realized the former detective really might fire it.

Think, she ordered herself. *Think and talk.*

Channeling every bit of inner calmness that she could muster, she very carefully set the car seat on the floor and stepped between Desmond and Lockley, a human shield.

"We can work this out," she said, starting with one of her classic openings.

Lockley laughed. "Work it out? Milo is *dead* down there. His neck is broken. And Jacob Pratt is trying to steal my baby. Again."

Norah kept a smooth tone. "Again?"

"God. You think he told you the whole truth, don't you? But then. He didn't really know, did he?"

"If he didn't tell me…maybe you should."

The other woman laughed again, and there was more hysteria in the noise than humor. "He was also so focused on Scarlett. On his junkie sister. Milo and I were in love before she ever came along. Did Jake tell you that?"

"No," Norah replied carefully. "He didn't. He did say you were undercover."

"What a joke that was. For all of five minutes, I kept my job a secret. Then I realized that Milo was the love of my life."

"Until Scarlett."

"She *stole* him." Lockley jabbed the weapon forward. "But he realized she wasn't right for him. She was selfish. And I got him back." She swayed a little. "He was mine again. He was. But I needed to be sure." He words were getting slurred, a clear sign of severe concussion. "I was pregnant. Ten weeks, when we set up that accident."

The accident that had killed Scarlett.

Now Norah infused her voice with sympathy. "But something went wrong?"

"It bounced."

"What bounced?"

"The truck. And I jumped out. I hit the pavement hard." Lockley blinked, tears mixing with blood. "I lost that baby. Milo's baby. And they said I could never have another. He went to jail for *me*. To protect *me*. That's love."

Understanding slipped in, and Norah nodded. "Then you found out about Desmond."

The former detective's head bobbed in affirmation. "That junkie had him. She *had* him. And she gave him to her selfish, self-centered brother."

"And when you found out…"

"I hired the lawyer to get Milo out so we could make a family like we were always supposed to."

"I get it," Norah said. "I really do. You love Desmond as much as you love Milo. You just want what's best for him."

Lockley's eyes gleamed. "I do. I'd be a good mother. I came up with a good plan. One that would teach Jacob Pratt a lesson."

"You did. But something—some *things*—have gone wrong again."

"What do you mean?"

"There are witnesses."

"I killed them." Confusion played over her macabre features. "And I made it Jake's fault."

Norah shook her head. "Beverly's alive. And we talked to Chief Lawson, Lockley. If you take Desmond now, you'll be living life on the run. Is that what you want?"

"It won't be that hard. I have two million dollars coming to me."

"No. You don't. We figured that out, too. The money will be going back to Jake."

"Impossible."

"True." Norah caught a flash of movement—familiarly tall and familiarly wide—over Lockley's shoulder, but she didn't acknowledge it. "Look at my face, and you'll know I'm not lying."

The other woman took a small step forward. But as she moved, her mouth opened in a silent cry. Her eyes rolled back, and her body fell forward. And from behind her, Jake dropped the silver vase from his hands and strode into the room.

Norah pointed to the car seat. "Him. Then me."

Jake nodded, then moved at double speed. He scooped his son out of the car seat, swept Norah into his arms, and clutched them both with ferocious warmth.

"I would've talked my way out of it," Norah said against his chest, her voice shaking.

"I know," he replied. "But you didn't have to. Because you've got me now. You know. Just in case words ever fail you in the future."

She laughed a tremulous laugh. But the truth was, right then, they *didn't* fail her. In fact, there were three very important ones that came to mind, and she knew she would be using them sooner rather than later.

* * * * *

Check out Norah's brother, Noah's romance in

High-Stakes Bounty Hunter

Available now wherever
Harlequin Romantic Suspense
books and ebooks are sold!

COMING NEXT MONTH FROM

⊕HARLEQUIN
ROMANTIC SUSPENSE

#2139 COLTON 911: GUARDIAN IN THE STORM
Colton 911: Chicago • by Carla Cassidy

FBI agent Brad Howard is trying to solve a double homicide—
possibly involving a serial killer. He never expected
Simone Colton, daughter of one of the victims, to get involved
and put herself in jeopardy to solve the case.

#2140 COLTON'S COVERT WITNESS
The Coltons of Grave Gulch • by Addison Fox

Troy Colton is a by-the-book detective protecting a gaslighted
attorney beginning to fear for her life. Can he keep
Evangeline Whittaker—and his heart—safe before her fears
become reality?

#2141 CLOSE QUARTERS WITH THE BODYGUARD
Bachelor Bodyguards • by Lisa Childs

Bodyguard Landon Myers doesn't trust Jocelyn Gerber, the
prosecutor he's been assigned to protect, but he's attracted
to the black-haired beauty. Jocelyn finds herself drawn to the
bodyguard who keeps saving her life, but who will save her
heart if she falls for him?

#2142 FALLING FOR HIS SUSPECT
Where Secrets are Safe • by Tara Taylor Quinn

Detective Greg Johnson expects to interview Jasmine Taylor
for five minutes. But he's quickly drawn to the enigmatic
woman, and the case surrounding her brother becomes
even murkier. With multiple lives—including that of Jasmine's
niece—in the balance, can they navigate the complicated
truths ahead of them?

Greg had been heading to his home gym when his phone
rang. Seeing his newly entered speed dial contact come up,
he picked it up. She'd seen his missed call.

Was calling back.

A good sign.

"Can you come over?" The words, alarming in
themselves, didn't grab him as much as the weak thread in
her voice.

"Of course," he said, heading from the bedroom turned
gym toward the master suite, where he'd traded his jeans for
basketball shorts. "What's up?"

"I…need you to come. I don't know if I should call the
police or not, but…can you hurry?"

Fumbling to get into a flannel shirt over his workout T-shirt, Greg was on full alert. "Are you hurt? Is Bella?" Had Josh been there?

"No, Bella's fine. Still asleep. And I'm…fine. Just…"

He'd button up in the car. Was working his way one-handed into his jeans.

"Is someone there?"

"Not anymore."

Her brother had shown her his true colors. And she'd called him. "You need to call the police, Jasmine." They couldn't quibble on that one. "He could come back."

"He?" For the first time since he'd picked up, he heard the fire of her strength in her voice. "Who?"

"Who was there?" She'd said *not anymore* when he'd asked if someone was there.

"Heidi."

Not at all the answer he'd been expecting.

Grabbing his keys and the gun he didn't always carry, he headed for the garage door and listened as she gave him a two-sentence brief of the meeting.

"Hang up and call the police and call me right back," he told her, pushing the button to open the garage door and starting his SUV at the same time.

He was almost half an hour away. The Santa Raquel police were five minutes away. Max.

Heidi could still be in the area.

Don't miss
Falling for His Suspect *by Tara Taylor Quinn,*
available July 2021 wherever
Harlequin Romantic Suspense
books and ebooks are sold.

Harlequin.com

Get 4 FREE REWARDS!

We'll send you 2 FREE Books
plus 2 FREE Mystery Gifts.

Harlequin Romantic Suspense books are heart-racing page-turners with unexpected plot twists and irresistible chemistry that will keep you guessing to the very end.

FREE
Value Over
$20